MW00749186

Endless Incarnation Sorrows

YOU LIVE AND DIE AND REPEAT.

Endless Incarnation Sorrows

A Spiritual Odyssey of
Mortal Imprints on Earth

Lucia Mann

Grassroots Publishing Group

GRASSROOTS PUBLISHING GROUP™
4560 Woodlands Village Dr.
Orlando, FL 32835

Copyright © 2020 by Lucia Mann
www.LuciaMann.com

All rights reserved. No part of this book may be reproduced or transmitted in any form or by any means, electronic or mechanical, including photocopying, recordings, or by any information storage and retrieval system, without written permission from the author, except for the inclusion of a brief quotation in a review.

All characters in this book are fictitious, and any resemblance to real persons, living or dead, is coincidental.

10 9 8 7 6 5 4 3 2
First Edition 2020

Printed in the United States of America

ISBN: 978-0-9975677-3-1
Library of Congress Control Number: 2019915370

Cover & book design by CenterPointe Media
www.CenterPointeMedia.com

DEDICATION

This book is dedicated to my ancestral
Jewish birth mothers, both good and bad.

ACKNOWLEDGMENTS

"When a person doesn't have gratitude,
something is missing from his or her humanity."
—ELI WIESEL

Sincere thanks to the Haida Gwaii shaman who educated me with spiritual knowledge that was initially beyond my natural comprehension. I thank my dear friend and editor, Nesta Aharoni, for coming out of retirement to be by my side on yet another storytelling journey, and Matthew and Joan Greenblatt of CenterPointe Media for putting up with my *fussy* printing and illustration requests!

My appreciation extends to the many friends and colleagues who have supported me on my literary journey, including Pam Isbell an ardent reader of my books, for catching errors; my *adopted* daughter, Caroline Fergusson, for her never-failing encouragement; Simon Wallis, B.Sc. Pharmacy, my best friend of forty-one years, for his scientific support and proof reviews; Home Hardware, Nakusp, for their ongoing support of all my book sales to date; Trish at What's Brewing on Broadway, for displaying and selling my books in her coffee shop.

Thanks are also due to Dr. Norman Lea for his professional dedication to my "special" medical needs.

Last, but certainly not least, heartfelt thanks to my beloved husband, Hector, aka Hassam el-Din, for his unflagging moral support and for preparing many meals when my fingers were glued to the keyboard.

TABLE OF CONTENTS

"The hippocampus is where short-term memories are turned into long-term memories."

Déjà vu

Déjà vu, also called *paramnesia,* is a French term describing the feeling that the present moment, the here-and-now, has previously occurred, that one has already lived through a situation and feels familiar with it as if having experienced it in the past through memories (accumulated data) stored in the brain. According to neurologists, these memories are the source of our thoughts, emotions, perceptions, actions, and memories. How this process works, however, remains a mystery.

Hippocampus

The *hippocampus* (Greek words *hippo*, meaning horse, and *kampo*, meaning monster) is in the medial temporal lobe of the brain, the place where short-term memories are converted to long-term memories. The hippocampus plays a role in the workings of the mind and how knowledge is obtained. It has been described as the heart of the brain.

Episodic memories are formed by and retrieved from the hippocampus portion of the brain.

Amygdala

In the nineteenth century, Burdach discovered an almond-shaped mass of gray matter in the anterior portion of the mammalian temporal lobe (in front of the hippocampus), which he called the *amygdala* (ancient Greek for almond). Amygdalae (clusters of neurons) are essential to our ability to feel a vast number of emotions ranging from joy to sadness, disgust to excitement, and regret to satisfaction. It is also associated with fear and the physical changes caused by fear, and with the perception of emotions in other people. The amygdala modulates critical reactions to events that are vital to our survival. Do these brain functions hold the key to reincarnation? Are they the *spirit* of force that leaves the body at or after death? Defining a *soul–spirit–entity* departing a mortal vessel is not as straightforward as it may seem.

Epigenetics

Epigenetics (the demise of biological determinism) is the doctrine or belief that everything, including every human act, is caused by something and that free will does not exist. It is the study of physiological and psychological mechanisms that silence or activate human genes—markers. I believe lifestyle choices impact risk factors for disease that operate through mechanisms of epigenetics. In addition, traumatic experiences are transmitted from past generations to future generations via epigenetic memories, establishing a way to inform progeny of salient information necessary for survival. In other words, transmitted ancestral memories, ripples through the proverbial sands of time, are passed onto ensure survivability.

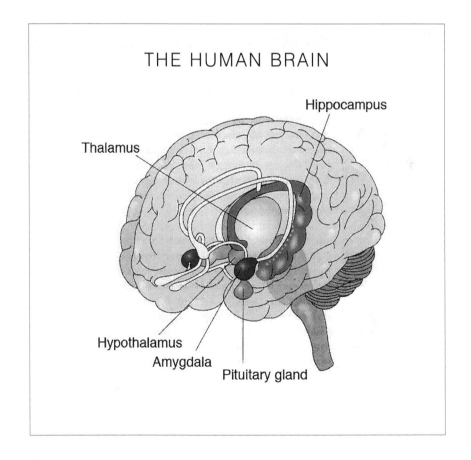

THE HUMAN BRAIN

Hippocampus

Thalamus

Hypothalamus
Amygdala
Pituitary gland

INTRODUCTION

"I believe present-day traits, illnesses, and the maladies
and those of past lives *are* connected."
—Lucia Mann

I t is remarkable what you can discover from a bit of saliva.

According to forensic geneticists, DNA reflects how we got here—our rebirths over millions of years. North Africa is where my human story begins.

DNA test results traced my first *mutation* K1a genome marker back to ancient Israel before and during the period of Ramesses II (1303 BCE, Before Common Era). My first footprint (birth certificate) began in the North African desert. I'm a 72 percent Ashkenazi diaspora descendent, the result of ancient ancestral human migration. That leaves 28 percent divided: Roman, Spanish, Irish, Polish,

Sicilian, South African, and Scandinavian. Yikes! What a funky genetic signature, with *Viking* blood to boot! But it hasn't been ruled out that I'm not a hybrid Neanderthal or a hybrid Alien! I like the idea of the latter.

I have gleaned through mitochondrial genetic material passed exclusively from mother to child that I could share the same haplogroup, K1a, genome with an ancient Israelite named Amminadab, Queen Ingrid Ragnvaldsdotter of Norway, Queen Isabella of Spain, Pablo Picasso, Katie Couric, and Meryl Streep. So it begs the question, have we lived before?

The sins of the father being visited upon the children is a biblical principle (*Genesis*), so should one of the sayings from the *King James Bible*—"Our fathers have sinned, and are not; and we have borne their iniquities"—have also embodied the sins of the *mothers*?

What is this author's view on this incriminatory supposition?

Well, I'll tell you.

When I sat down at my keyboard, fingers ready to pounce, to begin writing *Endless Incarnation Sorrows*, I had misgivings. Who should this story speak to? Should I write it solely for *my* release of imprinted memories settled in the overloaded hippocampus of my brain, or should I gear it toward readers around the world who profess to have open minds? As I reveal my discoveries on the pages of this book, it is not my intention to convert anyone to my way of thinking. However, if, you are not comfortable with hypothetical theories, then this work might direct you to the philosophical concept that an aspect of a living being starts a new life in a different physical body or form after each incarnation—until the last death.

How did *my* acceptance of reincarnation evolve? After being resuscitated three times following major surgeries (in my current life), I began experiencing intimate cognition of people and places from historical periods I had no understanding of. The flashbacks of apparent past lives began surfacing from deep within my subconscious, a process I couldn't control.

After my first hospital resuscitation, my sleep was routinely disturbed by nightmares, dreams of previous incarnations that emphasized people and places unfamiliar to me in my waking hours. Many nights my husband cradled me in his protective arms when I awoke screaming, paralyzed with fear of the terrifying events I had been *shown* the probable premise of rebirth. I do not believe this phenomenon is self-delusion because, in conscious and rational awareness, I'm stimulated by a supernatural sense that déjà vu does *open* the portal to past lives. Subsequently, my hippocampus (associated with episodic memory) assaulted me relentlessly after I suffered a rare spinal-cord infarction in 2005. This malady—leaving me with spasticity paralysis, weak muscles, and torso imbalance from the waist down—is, I believe, consistent with past-life ailments.

In one of my reoccurring, unconscious dream states, I found myself an onlooker at a scene being played out in fifteenth-century Spain. A five-foot-five-inches tall young girl with fair hair and amber-brown eyes was bound hand and foot and paraded in front of a jeering crowd. She was identified as an undesirable, a heretic. I checked her features intensely. I recognized her face instantly. We *shared* a physical similarity, the birth defect I have today—a large oval facial blot. Not the typical red salmon or café-au-lait birthmark, but a roasted coffee bean birthmark that darkens in intense sun. We shared the same hair color and the same height. I witnessed her handwriting, a trait as distinct as a fingerprint, which had been scrawled on an *Admission of Guilt* document during her persecution in an Inquisition trial. It was virtually identical to my calligraphic writing of today. In my vivid dream, I felt her charismatic vibrancy, her outspokenness. I sensed her high intelligence, which, although it had served as her most useful survival tool, wasn't a match for religious fanatics. She was fluent in many languages, as am I. She was handicapped. I, too, have a disabled body. I believe present-day traits, illnesses, and the maladies and those of past lives *are* connected.

The morning after *seeing* myself in medieval Spain, I awoke to a fetid odor mixed with a tinge of sickening sweetness. I sensed that bacteria were clinging to the hairs in my nostrils. It smelled nauseating. Imagine a piece of rotting meat with a few drops of cheap perfume. That is my description of what a burning human being smells like. I recall tasting the death odor in the back of my throat and then fleeing my bedroom in search of clean air.

Now, as I reach my final years as a mortal, I firmly believe in past lives and the existence of more than one universe. When I met my husband, I knew very soon that I was going to spend the rest of my twenty-first-century life with him. Initially, I struggled to make sense of it, but a different reoccurring dream—one I had been experiencing for many years before I met him—helped me make sense of my mysteriously intense feelings. Finally, I knew. I *had* known this person in a past life. I chronicled this experience in my book *Addicted to Hate*. The relationship of Lela (pronounced Lala), daughter of Rebekah bas Sora, and Hassam, son of Mohammed el-Din, was fated. Past lives are forever entwined in a sacred pathway of the human brain as it flees its prison of flesh.

The following life stories—the many incarnations of Lala and the tragedy of being born a Jew—is compiled to the best of my photographic recall. It reflects my dreams and my lives before this century. This book begs the question, does the Law of Karma play a role in rebirth? Is it a real, cold-hearted fact? In my case, yes!

Ancient Tibetan writings teach us that karma provides the soul (*entity*) with opportunities for physical, mental, and spiritual growth—the opportunity to find the *self,* the real *us*.

I believe each entity that re-enters the Earth plane as a mortal human being has subconscious access to the characteristics, mental capacities, and skills it has accumulated in previous lives. However, each new entity must also combat the influence of experiences in which such negative emotions as hate, envy, fear, jealousy, cruelty, and greed delayed its progress. The entity's task as a mortal must make use of successive rebirths to balance positive and negative karmic demands. One of the consequences is the general logical question asking the why and wherefore of apparently needless suffering. This spiritual law of cause and effect states that our thoughts and behaviors in one life determine how and when we will be reborn in the next. I believe that escaping this rebirth cycle involves attaining a state of perfect wisdom.

In other words, those who cease to reincarnate do so only when Earthly desires and karma have been worked out on the *etheric planes*. However, science *has* proven that some people do have a biological predisposition to possess the weak—meaning they were born *evil* by a chain of repeated reincarnations.

Are some humans simply born to suffer? Absolutely!

I believe mortals must suffer to reach the realm of enlighten-ment—immortality. As a result of my higher neurospirituality, the result of spiritual progress, I feel I have done just that—worked out my bequeathed hereditary karma of suffering. However, an obvious question remains. Can science support rebirth in the same way it claims to with biological predisposition? The battle between mind control and scientific belief in previous existences vie to claim a resurrection that I believe *is* possible. But, naturally, I question … are my multiple rebirth wanderings over? Yes, I trust they are. My twenty-first-century end of life (a shaman prophesied that I would survive to the ripe old age of 94) will finally close the chapters of my current life and those I lived before.

Then, the hereditary debt, the punishment dished out by *Yah-weh* (God), will be paid, right? Everlasting *peace* for all eternity!

Do pigs fly?

PROLOGUE

"With a free and open mind, I listen attentively to the Indian doctrine of rebirth and look around the world of my own experience to see whether somewhere or somehow some authentic signs are pointing to reincarnation."
—C.J. JUNG

It does not matter whether individuals believe in reincarnation or not. Recollecting incidents and facts seemingly beyond human recall, events people have no control over, is personal. There is limited modern-day research to disprove that previous existences resurfacing deep within the subconscious, beyond the reach of our rational senses, are the acquisition of knowledge from past lives. In ancient Israel Josephus plainly said that of the three main sects of Israel, both the Essenes and the Pharisees taught reincarnation.

Rebirth is also an Inner Doctrine of the *Kabbalah* of the Hebrews.

Ancient Greek philosophy maintains that every soul coming into this world is strengthened by the victories and/or weakened by the defects of its previous lives.

The *Koran* states that God generates beings and sends them back repeatedly until they return to Him.

The Russian mystic Helena Petrovna Blavatsky wrote on reincarnation, "There isn't an accident in our lives, not a misshapen day, or a misfortune, that could not be traced back to our own doing in this or another life."

Are these philosophical writings simply products of unwitting fantasies, of delusional or fraudulent or insane minds?

Do the memories of our ancestors determine the color of our hair, physical features, phobias, and illnesses? Do they give us our most important trait, *Instinct*?

Are our micro-recorded genomes–genetic patterns–imprinted at each rebirth?

I have fallen into deep, regular sleep, then into a realm of *before*, encountering universal forces beyond my mortal control. I will now journey with you into my own uncharted waters of previous life histories, where my subconscious memory banks neither consist of nor depend on a shell of human flesh.

Can unresolved social transgressions, sinful acts, and negative aspects of past lives continue into future lives, demanding that we pay our ultimate inherited penalties? *Yes!* I believe that the effect of sin is naturally passed down from one generation to the next.

I invite you to take this incredible journey with me, as I travel back 35,000 years to my first imprint on Earth as a mortal being, and beyond.

You will discover much food for thought: Will a twenty-first-century reincarnation provide entry to the invisible kingdom, never to be reborn again? Have the *sorrow lessons* of 35,000 years, mapped out for a pipeline the hapless souls, finally be rewarded higher powers?

Maybe!

Probably not!

CHAPTER ONE

- 609 BCE -

The Judean Desert

"Cursed be everyone who does not abide by all things written in the Book of the Law."
—GALATIANS 3:10

Through cloudless summer skies, the scorching 45-degree-Celsius, sulfur-yellow sun grilled everything in sight. For the sweat-sodden women walking single file on desert sand, the extreme temperature felt like being trapped in hot milk. They worried, realizing they were being tailed by a haboob (sandstorm). Sculptures of dryland were carving patterns of dunes in their wake.

As the Hebrew travelers continued onward through unfamiliar territory, the haboob began to swirl like a sidewinder on a hunt, stalking the women. There was no immediate shelter for the migrants. As far as their eyes could see, the parched wilderness featured an endless landscape of red-yellow sand and dead grasses. The only thing that broke up the emptiness was an odd, brittle bush. Trying to avoid the possibility of being choked by sand specks, they covered their faces and picked up their pace. Thankfully, the wall of dust disintegrated, covering the travelers in a coating of fine sand.

Sighs of relief echoed through the desert.

The advancing group included three wild goats—sources of fresh milk—meat, clothing, and tools. When the goat milk was shaken vigorously in a goatskin bag, it yielded soft cheese and *leban*, a yogurt derived from soured milk. The goats' skins and silky hair provided clothing and leather flasks to hold water. Neither man, beast, nor any other signs of life had been evident for three days.

In the lead was pregnant fifty-year-old Rebekah bas Sora. Close on her heels were sixty-four-year-old Tikva, her mother, who was followed by two young, female paternal cousins, Abriyah, fourteen, and Yokova, fifteen. The two younger girls replaced pack animals. Their job was to lug a portable tent, goat hair sleeping mats, cushions, cooking pots, and food supplies, such as dates, sycamore figs, barley, salt, and parched grain. Grinding stones used to crush grain provided the women with flour to make bread, an integral part of every meal. Could the women adapt, as had the Bedouin tribes that were known to exist in these parts since the beginning of time? Or was this a hostile environment that conspired against human life?

No. The birth of civilization, the earliest stages of human evolution dating back 7 million years, is believed to have originated in the arid lands of North Africa.

⌁

As the group's long and exhausting day began to wane, a multi-hued sunset unleashed dark camel-shaped shadows. Rebekah was concerned. Increasing wind speeds were preparing to thrash their faces. Her head pivoted to address her companions in their primal Hebrew tongue. "Hurry!" she urged. "We must quickly set up camp before this sandstorm buries us in its path," she called tensely, trying not to let her panic grow.

The youngest girl, Abriyah, knitted her brows. "But where shall we set up camp, *Doda* (aunt) Rebekah? I see no big rocks. No trees. There is nothing to stop the winds from blowing the tent away."

All four veiled heads rotated from side to side like metronomes. Dry and weary eyes scoured the landscape seeking a suitable place to rest in a land where breezes, known to reach hurricane levels, could whip up the sand and plug people's mouths and nostrils to the point of suffocation. While her anxious heart raced, Rebekah lowered the protective head shawl wrapped around her face to get a better view. Instantaneously, her large brown eyes became transfixed. But a shimmering airstream quickly distorted her view. Was it an optical illusion? Did she really see a bright green patch of vegetation ahead, on this oven-baked landscape? Could it be an oasis, a source of badly needed drinking water? She focused on the possibility. Upon entering the desert, Rebekah had prayed that this venture into the unknown would provide refuge. She heard a voice speaking in her head: *Do not fear the desert. Seek and you shall find.*

Rebekah's long, black hair freed itself from her headdress and danced to the rhythm of her footsteps. The plain leather hide and cords that formed her sandals threatened to break loose. Her five-foot-six-inch body dashed toward the splash of color she thought she saw amidst the sand. Her hands supported her swollen belly. As Rebekah's headdress soared upward like a kite, her baggy blue mantle (the outer garment she wore at night) flapped at her ankles, and her dangling pendant and bracelets jingled. As she hastened forward, followed by her family, her sandals carved a deep path in the sand. The goats, straining their rope halters, trailed their masters.

The women stumbled across a small subterranean natural spring. This remarkable find, a fertile area of lush greenness—ground-hugging shrubs, short woody trees, and date palms—was a welcome sight to the dehydrated travelers. As they charged toward the sanctuary, their nostrils twitched with the distinct odor of camels, the ships of the desert. The smell of fresh dung was ripe in the air. Camel-herding nomads were known to move on quickly and frequently to prevent exhausting an area of its resources. Had a group spied the foreign travelers and left abruptly?

The women lowered their bodies into the water, gulping refreshing mouthfuls. When Rebekah released the goats from their restraints, momma goat and her kids, also needing hydration, charged down the oasis bank, their hooves kicking up sand. When the goats plunged into the water, they frolicked and drank happily. After Rebekah's thirst was quenched and her clothing was dripping with water, she cheerfully announced, "We have found the perfect spot. We will go no farther."

For the displaced Hebrews, this was now home.

To make the blustery desert night less frightening, Rebekah lit a fire with dry palm leaves and dried dung she had collected along the way. Her cousins set about erecting their large tent between the date palms. The tent allowed air to circulate within, keeping them fresh during the day. To keep them warm at night, goat hair was used as insulation.

Tikva, with her bottom resting on her heels, sat on the oasis embankment under the restless skies. She gazed heavenward and gave thanks. "Yahweh, God of infinite mercy, you have led us to this source of life. But, please, send me a sign that you have forgiven my daughter's weakness of the flesh." The older woman humbly bowed her head. A gush of tears flowed past her sand-dusted eyelashes and onto her chapped and flaking lips. Her earlier self would never have questioned God's divine potentials. But now, a troubling question surfaced. *Is this life-saving water a sign from Him that all is well?*

Now isolated from her previous life, Tikva's mind raced with horrific memories. Could she have prevented the dreadful event that had resulted in this diaspora? Should she have turned her back on her only daughter? Should she have cast Rebekah out of the family home? Should she have thrown the first stone? By their laws, punishment for this wrongdoing, if proven, was death by stoning.

Tikva quickly covered her eyes, but she couldn't erase the memory from her mind. Her aging orbs filled with tears. She loved her daughter and had forgiven her, but had the heavenly powers absolved her? Was another punishment yet to be meted out? Tikva sighed heavily. Echoes of recall rang in her mind. She and the others were not fleeing from the Egyptian conquerors who had taken the menfolk, including her own son, from the village, but, instead, from an eyewitness who had attested to the violation of a restrictive Hebrew law. Rebekah's crime merited capital punishment. The penalty would have been execution. Had they stayed, Rebekah would have been forced to a hilltop and stoned to death. A mother's heart couldn't allow that, even if she felt disgusted by Rebekah's unholy sin. The thought of ending Rebekah's life herself had fleetingly crossed Tikva's mind before she acknowledged the public law of stoning.

The skies sprinkled stardust on Tikva as she slumped onto the embankment and watched an earlier life rewind.

CHAPTER TWO

- THE YEAR BEFORE -

A Settlement on the Outskirts of Jerusalem

"The weaknesses of the flesh are the forever scars on the soul ..."
—ANONYMOUS

I n the wake of Egyptian conquerors laying siege to Jerusalem—imprisoning men both young and old, terrifying women who thought they would be next—residents fled the settlement carrying whatever they could to help support life elsewhere. The twice-widowed and now aging Tikva bas Sora was not afraid to remain behind. Though she realized it wasn't going to be easy, she was steadfast in her decision. With Ephron, her only son, gone, she would have to depend on her daughter, Rebekah, for sustenance.

Tikva's life since birth had been centered around this hilltop residence. Her baked clay and straw abode was adjacent to a local spring that sustained life and growth. Other homes bordered hers and were grouped together. Overgrowth—thick pine groves and bushy clusters of terebinth trees—draped the rugged hills, but they had not been thick enough to hide the inhabitants from foreign invaders. At the rear of her property was a fenced courtyard for her livestock. Near the enclosure was a well-maintained garden, her source of food. Beans, lentils, grapes, pomegranates, and olives grew in abundance. Despite her fear of capture should the invaders return, the widow resolved to remain and live off the land. On this distressing day, believing her only son gone forever, Tikva covered her eyes, glassed over with age, and returned to her youth.

She wished she could erase these personal ruminations!

At age ten—as hormones surged from her pituitary gland, hair erupted in unfamiliar places, menstruation flowed, and breasts developed—Tikva transformed from child to young adult. Being a vivacious only daughter, sister to five brothers, her *growing pains* were quickly noticed by her mother, who promptly informed her husband that the *time* had come. As was the custom, her father immediately arranged a match. "You have chosen well," his wife declared. Tikva's paternal uncle was privileged, having made his fortune selling spices. The delighted mother was sure the customary dowry—*mohar*, gift of cash—would bring about welcome changes to their impoverished state. They were barely making ends meet on a herdsman's income—selling goat's milk and meat at the marketplace. And Tikva's family would have one less mouth to feed during this tough time. They were experiencing an extreme food shortage due to crop failure.

In this ancient period, Tikva was not recognized as a woman, but, instead, as chattel to be bought in a marriage negotiation. A bride-to-be does not question established customs and beliefs that are viewed as precedents. The ten-and-a-half-year-old obedient child married her paternal uncle, Saul, twenty years older than she, without question.

Was this transgression of Jewish law, which forbade marriage with a blood descendant, blatantly overlooked or naively ignored? Were moral teachings merely misunderstood?

Tikva's father insisted that the newlywed couple occupy the flat roof of his house. He reasoned that this would be the best arrangement for his daughter because his younger brother, Tikva's husband, traveled for extended periods selling spices, and Tikva would require help when her birthing time came.

Five months into her pregnancy with her first child, Tikva's husband developed a fever that expressed itself with angry red boils over most of his body. Dysentery further weakened him and ended his life a month later. Was Saul's illness the result of drinking polluted water? Or had God's laws been disobeyed?

"... *Any other than kin* ..." the law decreed. (A moral message in Leviticus 18 includes a detailed list of banned sexual relations.)

For the old soul inhabiting the young mother-to-be, the prohibition spoke volumes.

The day after Saul's death, his corpse was wrapped in linen cloth and laid horizontally and face up on a bier. He was placed in a natural cave that had been cut into soft rock near their water source. The grieving widow tore her upper garment as a symbol of mourning, paid her last respects, and returned home. There she vowed in her mother's presence, "Life must go on without him. Shortly, I'll have another precious life to take care of."

Tikva gave birth to a son and named him Ephron, after her father, who had succumbed to Saul's same malady two weeks before the delivery of his grandson. But all was not well with this listless, scrawny newborn whose pasty pallor, blotchy skin, inconsolable crying, and refusal to breastfeed spoke of a weak disposition. At three months old, the habitually ailing baby had his first seizure. His blank stare, gurgling and choking, and rhythmic jerking sent his young mother into a panic. She bundled him up and rushed to her neighbor's home, clinging tightly to her writhing child. (Epilepsy, a transient abnormality in brain activity, was unheard of, undiagnosed, in this ancient era. Today, though, it is genetically recognized that some types of epilepsy are due to an abnormality in a specific inherited gene.)

"... Any other than kin ..."

The aroma of sweet medicinal herbs assailed Tikva's nostrils as she entered the home. Stricken with fear, she begged, "Help me, Healer, my baby is dying."

The ancient healer woman, thought to be over 100 years old,

took the writhing child from Tikva's arms and laid him on his side on a flat surface, allowing his saliva to flow from his mouth. Loosening the tight garment encircling the baby's neck, she placed her hands on his hot body and announced to Tikva, whose face was drained of color, "Hush, young mother. Your child is not dying. He has a sickness of the brain."

Bewildered and distraught, Tikva queried, "What is this brain-sickness? Can it be cured?"

The healer shook her head side to side. "I'm sorry, but I know no cure for this condition. Nor do I know whether your child will live with it for the rest of his natural life. But I suspect he will."

Overcome by the prognosis, Tikva wept. The healer embraced the distraught young mother. "Your tears show weakness," she chided. "You must be strong, for there will be troubling times ahead. I will make you a remedy to give him every morning before sunrise to lessen the fits."

Tikva wiped away her tears with her garment sleeve and nodded. What had been disclosed was beyond her mind's reach. However, from that day forward, she unfailingly administered the healer's *magic* powder. She never questioned whether the herbs would help or not.

Time passed, and Tikva was overjoyed that Ephron's sickness lessened as he grew older. As an adult, his handsomeness shone through his inherited, infantile illness. He was of medium height, with sun-baked skin and deep brown eyes that could melt a girl's heart. About one thing, Ephron was adamant. "It's *my* choice. I don't wish to marry. With grandfather and father deceased and no other man in the house, I choose to take care of you."

Tikva did not protest, for nothing she could have said would have altered her son's stubborn thinking.

When Ephron was one year old, Tikva remarried. Her arranged marriage was to a fifteen-year-old village boy. Tikva's mother received a dowry of 150 shekels.

The newlyweds had grown up together, and thirteen-year-old Tikva was pleased with this decision. As before, their married life was centered on the flat rooftop. Tikva's newfound contentment was evident in her smile, laughter, and dancing around the eating table. Then, as if she were destined for ill fortune, fate once more crushed her joyful heart. Her loving, kind, and companionable husband died of neurological complications, paralysis, and acute renal failure eight weeks into their marriage. He had carelessly picked up a rock near their familiar water source and had awoken a venomous sand-horned viper deep into its winter hibernation. Sharp fangs struck the young husband without mercy. This very snake was known to cause the deaths of village livestock and herdsmen. Tikva's husband was merely its next victim.

After his burial, the matriarch of the settlement, an ancient healer, took the grieving Tikva aside under a darkening night sky. "Look up, child."

"What am I supposed to see?" Tikva asked.

"Do you see millions of shining stars?"

"Yes."

"Then know, Tikva, that these heavenly orbits house our loved ones. They twinkle brightly to signal us that the people who are dearest to us are in a place where there is no suffering, no tears, and no illnesses."

"Will I join them one day?"

"If you have not broken any of Gods' laws, then, yes, you will have your own star home."

"And what if I do break His laws?"

"Then your soul will be reborn and suffer *endless incarnation sorrows.*"

That profound forewarning flew over the inexperienced young woman's head.

Tikva, now pregnant with her second child, followed her late husband's corpse in the fading light of evening. He was interned in the cave next to Saul. The *al-ma-nah* (widow) grieved over his loss for a brief period. She then cleared her mind's sorrows by seeking and finding harmony within her lively spirit. She vowed to help others and to learn to heal the body of ailments, such as the ones that had stolen two husbands and two parents from her short life. Tikva gathered information on herbal remedies from the healing woman and set about growing the life-saving herbs in her garden.

Some months later, Tikva gave birth to a healthy baby girl. She named her Rebekah, after her mother, who had joined her father in death. It was rumored that, after the death of her beloved husband, Tikva's mother had died of a broken heart. Others argued that knowing she had broken a Torah law by handing her daughter over to sin, she had deliberately stuck her hand in a venomous snake's nest.

Ephron now had a baby sister. They were inseparable. He absolutely adored her. When, at age ten, her *growing* pains became evident, Ephron, as head of the family, began looking for a suitable spouse for her. But his sister had acquired some of his character traits—stubbornness, negativity, and rebelliousness—which complicated his task.

Rebekah snubbed the traditional *joining* with the opposite sex. She yearned to be someone more significant than a kept woman whose religion tells her: *Your desire shall be for your husband, and he shall rule over you.* Living for the sole purpose of child-bearing was not Rebekah's cup of tea. For most other females, marrying and raising children was their ultimate goal, their most important achievement, and they devoted the bulk of their days to child rearing, housecleaning, cooking, and teaching the laws of their faith. But not for a hard-wired Hebrew girl who wanted the freedom to express her inner feelings.

On the day her brother was captured by Egyptians, Rebekah vowed to take care of her mother. She became the *man* of the house. All of that changed when Ephron suddenly reappeared forty years later.

He was unrecognizable. He might as well have been a stranger. His white hair was scanty, his shoulders bowed, and his features drawn and wrinkled. His once mesmeric dark eyes were now glassed over and watering, his mouth twisted to one side. Wasted arms and bulging veins left little doubt that he had aged well beyond his years, and with suffering. Tikva's previously crushed heart now swelled with gladness. Having both offspring home with her was as close to shamayim (heaven) as she could get.

In the days that followed, Tikva set about healing her son. Within months he was a new person. He gained weight feeding on lamb fat, and high-protein meals served to him by his doting mother and sister. The former sickly Ephron reclaimed his life. He chopped wood, repaired their home, tended the gardens, and shared with his sister the herding of the livestock to pasture. He also eked out a modest income as a leatherworker, making sandals for the market located adjacent to the walls of their settlement.

In Tikva's society, children of both genders were loved equally, but males were preferred for the simple reason that females left home when they married. Sons, however, were permanent assets. Aware of this, Rebekah imagined Ephron to be more favored than she. Outwardly she hid her emotions, but inwardly she was jealous. For many years Rebekah had loyally remained by her mother's side. But now, she made a point of distancing herself while Tikva doted on her son.

Months passed. One day at dusk, when the sun began to sink below the treetops, a chorus of chirping birds welcomed the evening. Tikva sat on the beaten clay floor grinding barley between two flat stones. When the dough had been kneaded into pita-like-rounded shapes, she headed outside. She opened the door to an oven heated by twigs and placed the barley mixture on hot stones to bake. The bread, dipped in olive oil, would accompany their evening meal: vegetables, beans, lentils, and a roast pigeon snared by Ephron earlier that day. Homemade red wine would complement the food.

Tikva busied herself with the meal preparations. Her children, always hungry, were due back home any moment. Rebekah was the first to arrive, and Tikva, ever nurturing, knew instinctively that something wasn't right. Rebekah's disheveled appearance raised her mother's hoary eyebrows sharply and lifted her sagging facial folds. Tikva assailed her daughter with questions. "My child, what has happened to you? You are covered in sand from head to foot, and there are more leaves in your hair than on a bush! And why are you wearing the back of your robe on the front of your body?"

Rebekah's moorings became unglued as she rushed past her mother, heading for the flat rooftop. Tikva raised her voice in urgency. "Come back. Something is terribly wrong. I feel it strongly." She paused to glance toward the entranceway. "And where is your brother?" she pleaded.

With a deep frown creasing her wrinkled forehead, a mystified Tikva stepped outside. Ephron was nowhere in sight. When Tikva noticed the shadows of two sisters herding sheep into a neighbor's courtyard, she called out. "Have you seen my son, Ephron? Does he follow you?"

"No," a shaky voice returned. In a flash, the girls disappeared.

The mystery of Rebekah's strange behavior and Ephron's absence left Tikva sorely troubled. He had never, not once, been late for the most important meal of the day.

Tikva climbed the steps to the rooftop, where she was greeted by intense sobbing. Dashing to her daughter's side, she said. "I have not heard you wail like this since you were a child when your pet goat died. Rebekah, please, tell me what is tormenting you."

Obscured by her head shawl, Rebekah's nervous face was slick with perspiration. Her tale was shocking, and she would be the sole person accountable for the telling. Should she tell the truth? Being honest would require courage. If she was, would her life afterward flow more naturally? An unconscionable thought moved from the fringe of her morality to center stage: *Live your own truth.*

Rebekah embraced the weight of her guilt as she softly said, "Don't hate me, Mother."

"Why do you say such a thing? Your *ima* (mother) could never hate you?" Tikva leaned forward and removed the shawl that covered Rebekah's dirty face. She looked into her daughter's swollen eyes and asked, "Why would I hate you, my child?"

Rebekah lifted her fallen chin. Peering at her mother with swollen eyes, she made a stunning and disturbing statement. "Because, Ima, I have broken God's law, Yahweh, will bring wrath on me." Silently, she told herself, *The worst is that I might be with the seed of an unholy union.*

With a grimace, Tikva implored, "I don't understand. Please, explain?"

Rebekah's voice was a mere whisper, and her eyes were downcast as she confessed. "Mother, I don't know what came over me. I had an uncontrollable desire, and I hate myself. I placed Ephron's hand on my breast. I saw the heat in his eyes, and, in the absence of words, his body sought to satisfy me."

The neurons in Tikva's brain began to misfire. Her daughter's startling admission took several moments to sink in. Tikva felt sick to her stomach. Traumatized by the horror of her daughter's words, she gaped at the straw ceiling. As she burst into tears, her cries echoed hauntingly around the rooftop. Rebekah reached out to console her mother, but Tikva pushed her hands away. "Don't touch me, child," she hissed. "I have to think."

Tikva was astonished and crestfallen when she left the rooftop, and she remained profoundly uncomfortable for quite a while. She wanted to understand what had motivated this wickedness. She felt like lashing out, reprimanding her daughter with a beating, but, instead, she asked a burning question. "Rebekah, I must know the truth. Did Ephron force himself inside you? Did he pass on his seed? Are you taking full blame, lying to protect your half-brother?"

Though deeply ashamed, Rebekah's mental ghost took control of her thinking. *How can I disclose the shock of the sensations I had felt for the first time in my life—the erotic, electric tingles of sexual intercourse?* Her head still lowered in shame, she answered, "No, Mother. He did not *force* me. I alone am to blame for what happened at the grazing land."

"If I ever get my hands on Ephron, I'll skin him alive for lying down with his sister," threatened Tikva. It didn't enter her failing mind that her marriage to her uncle (her father's brother) was equally sinful in the eyes of their God.

"... *Any other than kin* ...."

With Ephron missing, yet again, Tikvah began treating Rebekah with herbal remedies and more—savory, cypress, hellebore, and goat's urine—attempting to abort a possible pregnancy. No *mamzerim* (bastard) would be allowed in her family, she fumed. Her children had committed *Mishna* by having sexual relations with a sibling, and that was punishable by death, but Tikva could not accept losing both her children. That outcome would crush any mother's heart.

Tikva's potions failed. Rebekah's swelling tummy was noticed, and tongues began to wag. She had prayed for a miracle, the merciful miscarriage of this child, but it seemed that God had other plans for this family who had brazenly broken His laws. It wasn't long before an outcry from the living ensued.

One evening, when confronted by a mob of angry women outside her courtyard, Tikva hung her head in shame. The two sisters

Tikva had observed returning to their yard on that horrid night of discovery were particularly vocal. "I saw them with my own eyes, lying together *naked!*" She emphasized, "*Lo-ey-vah* (disgusting)."

"Yes. I can vouch for that," stated the other.

Their mother stepped forward. With a bony finger, she poked Tikva's chest. "Your daughter is condemned by Yahweh and must be punished," she declaimed.

"It is our ancient right to stone her," the matriarch healer woman added.

"Your daughter and son have shamed our people, and that will surely bring the fury of God upon us," affirmed another elderly woman.

"Where is your son hiding?" another demanded.

"It doesn't matter. Yahweh will find him," the sisters' mother concluded.

"Summon your daughter now," the matriarch commanded. "We all know she hides on the rooftop."

Tikva, legs apart, held a warrior stance. "I will not. I will never let any of you hurt my daughter. Go about your own business and leave me to mine!" she commanded angrily.

"It's Gods' law, woman of a sinful daughter," the matriarch stated. "At daybreak, she will be taken to a spot of my choosing, and a hole will be dug. Our laws declare that you will be ordered to cast a stone."

Tikva shot her a hateful glare. *That will never come to pass,* she vowed silently.

࠰

Long before daybreak, beneath damning black heavens, Tikva, Rebekah, two cousins from the father's bloodline, and three goats crept stealthily from their hillside settlement and walked off into the wilderness, taking only what they could carry. Fear of the unknown had not yet entered the minds of these outcasts. Their journey of a thousand miles began with a single step.

Their travels would transport them into an abyss of challenges, death, and punishment.

CHAPTER THREE

- PRESENT DAY -

New Desert Beginnings

*"No one born of a forbidden union may enter
the assembly of the Lord ..."*
—DEUTERONOMY 23:2

Aphalanx of biting flies and bothersome moths drove the Israelite nomads to quickly erect their communal tent away from the pesky night creatures that patrolled the watering hole. Outdoors, as they ate sparsely of dates and figs, the fatigued travelers tried to protect themselves against prevailing winds by nestling up against ground-hugging shrubs. Afterward, in the tent, they curled up on their sleeping mats and welcomed a long, overdue slumber.

Night after night since their journey began, Rebekah, the mother-to-be, had not slept well. She tossed and turned with violent emotion. Anxiety, sadness, and anger raced out of control, causing sleep deprivation to knock at her door. She would nod off for a few minutes, and then the nightmare would begin. *What have I done? It is all my entire fault! If only I hadn't been so curious about the sexual act!* Ephron had not been a willing participant. She had shamelessly seduced him. The weakness of the flesh had blinded her to potential consequences.

"Wake up," Tikva ordered, jolting her daughter's arm.

When Rebekah's weary eyelids opened, pulling her out of a fitful sleep, she saw her mother standing over her.

"Your screaming woke me up!"

"I'm sorry, Ima."

Tikva sat beside her daughter. "It is going to be okay. You must try and put the past behind you, even though it will probably trouble you for the rest of your life. Think of the life growing inside you. Be strong for your son of our new blood."

Rebekah did not respond, but she did think, *What if it is a daughter?* Her mind dismissed that thought and shifted to what lay ahead. Her mother had never discussed with her what happens during birthing, but Rebekah had seen many sheep and goats deliver. She thought, *When my time comes, I will sail through with only a few bleats.*

Alone in the tent one sunny afternoon, Rebekah was completing her daily chores when she felt a popping sensation followed by a gush of warm yellowish fluid followed by the pain of a sharp contraction. The compulsions brought her to her knees. Rebekah yelled for her mother but soon realized that she and her nieces were out planting seeds from the olives, figs, dates, and citrus they had brought with them. Near the watering hole, Tikva, about to insert a seed into a hole in the ground, heard her daughter's shout and stiffened. An icy shiver ran down her spine. *"Rebekah!"* she cried. Tikva turned to her companions. "I'm needed," she told the wide-eyed, curious girls. "Finish the planting, and I'll see you back at the tent."

Tikva tucked her floor-length robe up to waist level and sprinted toward the distant black canopy. Inside the tent, experiencing acute labor pains, Rebekah was relieved to see her mother. "My pain is bad, Ima. The baby's presence is too soon."

"Don't worry. I am here now," Tikva consoled.

A few moments later, the scent of aromatic herbs permeated the birthing space.

Rebekah squatted to more easily push. She braced herself against her mother and cried out, "Yahweh, help me."

An answer to her prayer would not come to pass!

Labor began with a rush, and the baby's breech position and premature delivery threatened to rip Rebekah's insides apart. With no training in high-risk deliveries, Tikva intuitively knew something was wrong with the baby's position. She used both hands to try to turn the infant's bottom, but time was running out for this vaginal breech delivery.

Twenty hours later, Rebekah, on her knees and elbows, gave birth to a five-pound daughter. But the infant was not breathing. Tikva quickly whisked the baby away, placed her flat on her back, tilted the head, took a deep breath, and exhaled hard into the tiny mouth. The baby responded with throaty, piercing wails. Tikva tied the cut umbilical cord with a thin strip of goat hide.

"She is so beautiful," the proud grandmother proclaimed. Tikva bent low and handed the baby, now wrapped in woven goat hair, to her exhausted daughter. Instead of shedding tears of joy, though, instead of feeling love at first sight, Rebekah let out a demonic yell. Overcome by revulsion, tears pooled as she wailed, "Mother, my daughter is *cursed*. She has yellow goat eyes. Look at her skin. It is darker than a slave's, and she has an ugly mark on her left cheek, and her hair color ..."

Rebekah's sobbing ended her flow of words.

Tikva *had* noted the differences but had decided to keep such thoughts to herself.

Generally, the Hebrews had black hair, yet this child's hair was thick and blond. She was as hairy as a dog. And the baby had amber-copper eyes, a color they had never seen before on any human. Yes, the newborn's skin was the color of black mud, but then so was theirs. The skin tone of the Hebrews was very much like the skin tone of the Egyptians. But the facial defect—an oval dark sienna stain that spread down the baby's left cheek—was not typical. What most concerned Tikva, though, were the child's legs, crooked with knees projecting distortedly. Tikva asked silently, *Will this girl be able to walk on her own?* She understood there was no simple explanation for the child's differences, however, being profoundly religious, she had to question, *Is it unfair for God to punish children for the sins of their parents?*

From that day forth, it became evident that this child's first imprint on earth and her inherited *curse* from her biological parents would not be pardoned. Tragically, there would be no deliverance; the effect of sin *would be* passed down mercilessly from one generation to the next until its ending in the twenty-first century. Or would it not?

Thus it began. Living, dying, and repeating with unimaginably tragic events for the sinful act committed by the first foremother, Rebekah. Or was the first immoral act—committed by grandmother Tikva, who married her relative—the real curse of these tragic reincarnations?

CHAPTER FOUR

- Twenty-Four Hours Later -

In the New Desert Beginnings

"More than one soul dies in a suicide."
—Anonymous

The tiny, malformed infant captured Tikva's heart, but her biological mother did not feel love at first sight. Drowning in guilt, Rebekah was overcome with self-loathing, leaving her blinded to the needs of her newborn. She turned her back on her child, wouldn't look at her, breastfeed her, or hold her when she wailed. These parental duties were performed by kindhearted Tikva, who fed the baby goat milk from a spoon, trying desperately to keep her alive. Tikva was saddened and angered by Rebekah's lack of affection, but she knew her daughter, once headstrong, was now fragile. No amount of scolding or sweet-talking could encourage Rebekah to love this "unholy" child. However, one question still demanded an answer. "My daughter," asked Tikva, "what name shall she be called?" When Rebekah didn't respond, Tikva declared, "This baby girl will be named *Lala* (Desert Flower) and will bring us joy."

Rebekah raised her eyebrows and shrugged her shoulders in an I-don't-care attitude that expressed more than words ever could. Tikva sighed heavily. Deep in her soul, she felt the darkness that consumed her daughter, and she knew of no antidote or herbal medicine that would alleviate Rebekah's dismay at a consequence she had brought upon herself. It saddened Tikva to understand that the blood of both her son and her daughter would not receive parental affection or recognition. She, the grandmother, would have to become the glue that held their family together.

In the days that followed Lala's entrance into the world, Rebekah, overwrought with anguish, embarked on a path that led her into a deep, dark tunnel. She withdrew from her daily chores, and when she lay on her sleep mat, she hoped never to awaken. She had no interest in food, seldom washed at the pond, and was quick to anger and tears when spoken to. Rebekah had no contact with Lala, and so, the raising of her child was left primarily to Tikva, who was assisted by her two nieces. All of them were disturbed by Rebekah's refusal to interact with her child.

Tikva embraced a positive outlook: "Lala has three other loving people in her life, and that is all that matters."

Rebekah buried her head under a cover and responded in a broken voice, "Then I have no reason to rise."

Well into the night, while the other occupants of the tent were sleeping deeply, Rebekah, her lovely smile forever erased, lay awake.

She couldn't hear anything but the beating of her heart. She wanted to *feel* something for her three-week-old child but was overpowered by depressing, condemnatory thoughts: *What have I done! How will I ever be able to look my child in the eyes and tell her that she is damned for all eternity because of my shameful sin?* Distraught, she recalled a bible verse her mother had cited: *"And surely the blood of your lives, will I require."* In her tortured mind, riddled with guilt, Rebekah could see no happiness in her future. Unable to deal with her self-imposed pressure and without the energy to cope any more, she slunk out of the tent. She tilted her head and gazed up at the radiance of the full moon, forever beyond her reach. Under the silvery illumination, Rebekha made her way to the waterhole. There, she stood staring at the water. Her broken mind insisted she had nothing to lose, so she stooped to pick up a large rock. Clutching the weight to her chest, she uttered a heartfelt apology. "I am truly sorry for what I did and regret it. Please, forgive me and don't punish Lala for my sins. I crave your forgiveness." Serenity infused the night air as she walked slowly forward and submerged herself in the deepest part of the pond. Within moments bubbles of air rose to the surface and vanished. Rebekah's drowning lungs claimed the last word.

At sunrise the next morning, Rebekah's bloated body was discovered by the youngest of her cousins, Abriyah.

Crash!

The clay-baked water receptacle Abriyah had been carrying lay in pieces. The flapping of her sandals and her shrill cries alerted Tikva. "What makes you bray like a demented donkey?"

"She's dead," the trembling girl replied.

"Whose is dead, girl?"

"Rebekah," Abriyah murmured. "Come and see for yourself."

An inconsolable Tikva struggled with the loss of her last-born child. However, she was not going to deny her troubled daughter traditional burial rites even though she had twice violated their laws—first, by breaking the doctrine of "any other than kin," and, second, violating the ban against harming oneself. Tikva understood that her daughter had not been of sound mind when she committed this final act. What disturbed Tikva most, however, was that her daughter would never hear the words "Mother" or "I love you" from Lala's mouth.

Rebekah's bloated body was washed and dressed in clean linen. In the absence of a cave, a hole was dug, and many rocks were placed atop. Tikva performed "ee-sheh," a sacrifice. She put a dead lamb in a blazing fire and implored aloud, "Yahweh, please accept this fire offering as forgiveness for my only daughter. Take her in your arms and love her as I have."

The previous night, before falling asleep beside Lala, Tikva had experienced icy chills of forewarning, but she had not been able to make sense of them at the time. Even so, nothing could have prepared her for her final parting with her daughter. She blamed herself for not understanding or wanting to understand, Rebekah's desire to depart.

Had Rebekah's freed spirit sent a message to her mother that she was now at peace? After Rebekah took her life, torrential rain converted the desolate desert into a wonderland of flowers. The morning of that discovery, the cousins stood and gawked at another miracle, a sight they had never seen before—a rainbow arching grandly over their water source.

"See, I told you," Yokova declared. "Rebekah is smiling down on us from heaven. She didn't go to hell's inferno. Why else would there be such color?"

"We miss you, Rebekah," the cousins soulfully intoned.

Goodbyes hurt the most when the story is left unfinished.

CHAPTER FIVE

The Aftermath of Rebekah's Passing

*"If you kill yourself, you're also killing
the people who love you."*
—Anonymous

Rebekah was gone, and there was nothing Tikva could do to repair that. But the sorrow that lived in the wake of her daughter's suicide was lessened by the fact that she was now Lala's surrogate mother, her sole parent. Tikva overflowed with motherly love for the three-year-old. She never knew she could love another person so much, so profoundly. She became the orphaned child's entire world. From the time Lala was born, she had spoken directly to her grandmother's heart. Now, their bond was infinite. Tikva hip-carried the child everywhere, hoping for the day the girl could stand on her own misshapen legs.

Today was the day!

"Ima," Lala exclaimed, "look. I can stand by myself."

Though unstable in the upright position, Lala took her first "baby" steps and did not topple over.

Tears of happiness ran down Tikva's cheeks. "You're so clever, my daughter," she praised. "Ima is so proud of you." In the back of her mind lingered a longing: *I wish your real mother could have seen this?*

From the netherworld came the unheard message: *I do see, Mother Tikva. You are the best mother my child could have. Please grieve for me no longer, for now I am free.*

Time passed, and Lala grew into an outgoing, personable young girl who commanded attention when she entered her tent home. At age ten, Lala glowed with electric magnetism, always smiling, always helpful, a good listener. Her hearty laughter made Tikva and cousins Yokova and Abriyah, forget that they were "incarcerated" in the desert, afraid to return to the land of their birth.

The orphan was yet unaware of her true birth mother. Only Tikva and the two cousins stood between the known and the unknown, and they could not bring themselves to disclose the painful secret they had carried since Rebekah's suicide.

Another year passed, and Tikva and her "daughter" enjoyed a close relationship and a powerful bond. Lala learned from Tikva to be gentle, empathic, nurturing, and selfless. She became an excellent student in the healing arts, which Tikva was teaching her. When she was not tending livestock, helping prepare meals, or performing other mundane chores, Lala spent personal time with her "mother." While Tikva related her family's beginnings, her marriages, and her two children, she hid the painful truth of Lala's conception. Instead, she said, "My son and daughter are both dead. But one day, with God's blessings, we will all be together as a family."

In Lala's eyes, the old woman was a goddess. The two of them had a special bond that stretched beyond words. Then, one day during one of Tikva's many storytelling moments, Lala dropped a brow-raising question. "Will you tell me who my father was? Do I come from your first or second husband?"

Tikva dropped the spoon she was stirring with onto the floor. Deep down, she knew this question was inevitable. "Your father's name is Ephron," she said, with a tight-lipped grimace. "And he is no longer with us."

"So he was your *third* husband, yes?"

"Child, I do not wish to discuss this," Tikva returned in a chastising manner. "It pains me to talk about him. He is long gone."

Lala sensed Tikva's tension and responded submissively. "I'll not ask again."

But the dangling question, the not knowing, would soon to be a *beginning*.

When Rebekah withheld the bond of a mother's love, she unwittingly prolonged a misery that would span many lives to come.

Lala's hitherto uneventful life was about to grab her by the horns.

On a pre-dusk evening shortly before Lala's thirteenth birthday, the weary girl was returning home with her charges, a herd of goats, when she spotted two shadowy human figures moving toward her. Her gaze fixed in anticipation of something terrible. *Who are they? What do they want?* She had previously encountered camel caravan nomads stopping to drink at the water source, but she had never engaged them in conversation. To the contrary, she had always hidden in fear by crawling under the bellies of her long-haired companions.

This time, too, she hid. Once camouflaged, she observed that the two strangers were not Bedouins. They were wearing unfamiliar clothing and were not accompanied by a slew of smelly camels, which was the norm with desert travelers. The older male wore a white *jellabiya*, an Egyptian garment, and a colorful scarf around his neck. His fluffy white beard swayed as he walked. He had a distorted mouth, twisted to one side as if he had suffered a stroke. He was holding the hand of a young boy, similarly garbed but with a dark blue turban on his head.

The older man noticed Lala and approached her. "Don't be alarmed," he comforted the shrinking girl. "Is this the home of Tikva and Rebekah bas Sora?"

Leaping to her feet, she challenged, "Who are you, and what do want with my mother, Tikva?"

His bushy white brows tightened. "What's your name, girl?"

"My name is Lala," she replied, twiddling the braided hair that hung down her back. "I'm the daughter of one of the women you wish to visit. And aunt Rebekah is dead. She drowned in the pond."

With his hands clutched to his chest, the old man emitted a high-pitched, piercing cry.

A breathless Lala bounded inside the tent. "Ima, there are strange people outside asking for you."

Moments later, Tikva's shrieking pierced through the earlier echo of the man's alarm. "My old eyes are deceiving me!"

"No, Mother, they are not."

Tikva rushed up to him, cupped his face, and peered deep into his eyes. "Ephron, Ephron. Is it you? Where have you been all these years?"

Tikva slumped to her knees and wept. Mystified, a frown creased Lala's dark forehead. She rushed to her sobbing mother's side, flung her arms around her, and implored, "Please tell me, Ima. What causes you so much pain? Do you know these strangers? Why have they caused you to cry so?" She felt the man's stare penetrating through her, but she brushed the sensation aside. "Why does this old man call you *mother*? You told me that when Rebekah died, her brother, your son, was also dead."

"I said my son was gone, not dead."

Lala countered irately. "No, you didn't! I have an excellent memory. I can even remember the time you put hot stones on my tummy when it was sick."

Tikva frowned. *How is it possible she can recall that? She was only six months old!*

Ephron, the boy, Abriyah, and Yokova were confounded as Tikva pulled her granddaughter closer. "There is something you should have been told a long time ago. Maybe I will let your *avi* (father) answer for my long silence," she said, looking in her son's direction.

A confused look creased Lala's features. She didn't immediately grasp the word "father."

Ephron made eye contact with his mother. "No. *You* tell her," he demanded. "It is better if the truth comes from you, Mother."

Tikva wrung her hands beset by troublesome musings. It was hard to determine the right amount of truth to divulge. She felt her story was replete with intimate secrets better left to adult interpretation. How much of the past should she keep hidden? How much sharing could she be comfortable with? Of late, Tikva's entire life seemed a web spun with secrets! Her biggest concern here, though, was the potential aftermath. She drew her granddaughter closer and began, "My precious child ..."

An understanding of Tikva's personal disclosures bypassed Lala's young, immature mind. Her immediate reaction silently flowed unchecked. *Father! I'm sure she told me he had died back in Jerusalem. Rebekah was his sister! So she is my mother, not Tikva! Tikva is my grandmother! And Rebekah killed herself. Why?*

The dark secrets, now exposed, felt shameful to Lala. Emotionally ravaged and losing control, she jumped to her feet and fled the tent thundering, "If it's your wish, Yahweh, let me die like my *real* mother, Rebekah!" She inhaled sharply and shouted over her shoulder, "How could you have kept this dreadful secret from me, *Tikva*?" The previously respectful address of *Ima* was replaced with this act of disloyalty. Then a question penetrated the walls of the teenager's mind: *Did her adopted mother love her any less?*

Having led a simple life, young Lala had few coping skills, and until this day, she had not needed them. She wasn't yet an adult, but often she appeared to have an "older," more mature understanding of things. Even so, she was bothered that Tikva, the woman she had always believed was her mother, had kept so much from her.

How could Lala emerge from this confusion intact? If she had known about the devastation wreaked by tornadoes, she would have wished to be swallowed whole by one. When she burst into tears, a pain-soothing antidote appeared. It took the form of a small, warm hand seeking hers. Lala peered into the big brown eyes, searching hers. In a sweet, calm tone, the boy said, "I don't really understand this "sin," but just know that you didn't make it. You are not to blame."

How is it possible that this boy understands my feelings? She yearned to know about this tenderhearted boy, who seemed far advanced in maturity. But she was fighting back an internal conflict that was rising like bile. Hassam seemed to read her mind.

"Please don't be unhappy," Hassam pleaded. "I will be your best friend, and we will be strong together." With that said, he flung his little arms around Lala's waist and hugged her tight.

Lala's body stiffened. She didn't know how to react to his loving embrace. But she had to ask, "Is Ephron your father, because that would make you my brother!"

"No. *That man* is *not* my father! You are *not* my sister!" he said in a robust tone.

"Then why are you here with him?

"I'm happy that you speak Arabic because I can't speak Hebrew," he announced with a beaming smile. "My name is Hassam el-Din. I was captured, just like Ephron and taken to slave in the quarries, breaking stones for Egyptian statues. He helped me escape. For many days we traveled in search of my tribe here in the desert, but they were not where I remembered them being. My family never stays too long in one place. It was during a meeting with another nomad tribe that we learned of Judah women who lived in the desert and remained in one location. Ephron told me that he had a strange feeling, a premonition, that they were his lost family. After days of traveling, we found you. And so here we are."

Ephron, Lala's biological father, had indeed put two and two together!

In the days that followed, the eight-year-old Fellahin (peasant laborer in an Arab country) and the Hebrew, Lala bas Sora, became inseparable. Their relationship was a healing distraction from Tikva's shocking revelations, and the mockery of the happy life Lala had led. Lala had no wish to spend time with her natural father, but Tikva did become *Ima* again. After all, she was the only mother Lala had known. But Hassam, Lala's best friend, was the person the teenager confided in and shared her feelings with. He was the one she looked to for reassurance. "Hassam, do you think I'm cursed by God for *their* sins?"

Hassam grunted like a caveman. "No. Why would Allah punish you? You didn't do it, lie down with your brother—if you had one, that is!" he finished cheekily.

"Then why am I much darker than they are, and why do I have this black mark?" she gestured toward her facial blemish. "Neither Tikva nor Ephron have it. Nor did Rebekah."

A dirty fingernail gently touched her cheek. "In my culture, it is a sign of beauty, and the darker the skin, the more pretty you are. And your goat eyes are adorable!"

Lala grinned from ear to ear.

In the early hours of the next day, Hassam accompanied Lala as she herded the last six goats. She had been the minder of thirty shortly before he had arrived. But scant rainfall had shriveled up most of their garden, which left Tikva little choice but to barter with passing nomads: her goats for dates, figs, and whatever else was offered. Some grasses adapted to the drought, though, slowing their growth to conserve water, and a few of those were on the menu today. What troubled Lala most, though, was that their little group might be forced to migrate if rain didn't soon fall. The drought was affecting their underground water supply, and hardly any water was left. How long until it all evaporated? Could they survive on goat's milk? What if the animals had none to give, their supply shriveled up like most of the desert plants?

In stifling heat Lala and Hassam searched for a *miracle*, a grazing ground. They walked for hours before Hassam spotted a large cluster of grasses in the distance. Together, whooping and hollering, they encouraged the goats to pick up sped. They discovered a large boulder that gave them a temporary respite from the baking sun. Sitting in its shadow, they watched the goats chomping on the crinkled grasses. The friends chatted about this and that, and then Hassam spoke to his friend about how his mother had died. She had been decapitated trying to prevent the Egyptian slave masters from taking her son away, as they had killed his father a few days earlier. Lala couldn't imagine someone being dragged out of their home at the whim of a foreign captor. But she could relate to death—Rebekah's suicide! Not quite as horrific, but nonetheless traumatic. Lala remembered an event that took place before Hassam arrived.

She had stepped into their family tent and overheard Tikva discussing Rebekah's "sins" with cousin Abriyah. "I'm ashamed of my harlot daughter who not only took her brother, my son, into her arms but also took her life by drowning, leaving me, an old woman, to raise her child. Look at Lala? The poor girl is deformed and has the curse of her mother's sin on her face ..."

Tikva quoted *Galatians* 6:8, "Whoever sows to please their flesh, from the flesh will reap destruction; whoever sows to please the Spirit, from Spirit will reap eternal life."

But had not the *Beginning* of time shown that blood relatives did lie down with each other! Did these teachings explain the consequences of having closely related genetic markers? These people of olden days could not have imagined that in the future, DNA analysis would detect problematic genetic markers within chromosomal genes that determine gender and some of the characteristic defects arising from incest and other interrelated activities. Yet in ancient times, the belief in cursed rebirth was spoken in many tongues—a practice that continues today.

With the goat herd in view, Hassam noted Lala's discomfort and changed the subject to their different beliefs. He was a Muslim, she a Jew. Thinking hard, she responded, "Who cares! There is only one God." Lala took a swig from the goat-skin water pouch. "Anyway, the Jewish God does not favor me, so I don't suppose it matters if we are friends!" She took another swig and nearly choked when Hassam announced with a big cheesy grin, "Well, I don't care either because I'm going to marry you one day. You have stolen my heart, and we'll have lots of children that won't be *cursed!*"

Lala's amber eyes twinkled with amusement. "Mad boy!" she laughed. "I'm much older than you, and even if you were of age, Tikva would never allow it. Do you forget something, little man?

I'm a Jew. Tikva is extremely religious, even though I'm not." With arms akimbo and wearing a doubtful smile, she stated, "What am I saying? This is a ridiculous conversation! Can we talk about something else?"

The charmingly irreverent Hassam laughed jeeringly. "Do you want to marry some old goat Tikva chooses for you … or the most handsome man in the land?"

Lala slapped him playfully on the back. "We will see," she said as she smiled broadly. Lala thought how content she was to have a young companion in her life instead of being surrounded only by adults since her birth. She imagined the fun times they would soon share and wished this time would never end.

Careful what you wish for.

When the sun was at its highest, Lala and Hassam snuggled beneath the shadow of the rock for an afternoon nap. But Lala was not ready to sleep. Hassam's snoring was like a raging sandstorm—*Zzz-Zzz!* Lala prodded him hard but failed to disturb his sleep.

By evening, sunset clouds began to drift across the sky, and jerboa—long-tailed leaping rodents—emerged from their daytime hiding places. It was time to leave.

The goats obeyed Lala's whistled commands and hurried homeward.

When the hungry herders were in sight of the tent, Hassam lifted his head. "*Mmmm.* That smells good," he remarked, his nostrils twitching. "Tikva is the best cook ever." But he never harped on the fact that Lala's mother was also mean to him!

Tikva had never refused to include Hassam in their daily meals, but his food was to be eaten outside, not with the family. This annoyed Lala. "Just because he is not one of us doesn't mean he is not human!"

"He is an *Arab*, Lala!" Tikva glowered. "He doesn't belong to our people!"

So Lala took her meals outside with Hassam, under the stars.

Lala's bold defiance triggered Tikva to think back. *The apple doesn't fall far from the tree!*

As the sun disappeared into the horizon, the pair—with hands clasped in a soft grip and voices singing a cheerful song—neared the tent. Instantly, Lala released her grasp, as if Hassam's hand was contaminated. Heading toward them at a rapid pace was Ephron. Had he seen the pair holding hands? Would he, like her grandmother, scold her because Hassam was an Arab and she a Jew?

"I've been waiting for you," Ephron announced, grabbing Hassam by the hand. "I have no choice but to return you to the rock quarry."

Two sets of startled eyes bugged out from their sockets.

Ephron made eye contact with Lala. "I have learned that the slave masters are searching for Hassam and me ..."

Lala interrupted, "That's not possible! I haven't seen any other strangers, apart from you!"

"A nomad leader told me that when he left here the other day with his purchased goat, he was stopped by several men on horseback." *A very unusual mode of transport so far into the desert,* the goat buyer had thought.

One of the riders had demanded, "Have you seen any Hebrews traveling through?"

Hassam frowned. "What did he reply?"

Ephron sighed. "He didn't know that the men were *slave masters*, and so they turned up here after you left this morning."

"And?" Lala queried. "I don't see them. Are they inside?"

"No. Not willing to wait, the slavers departed. But before leaving, they warned me that if Hassam and I do not obey and return to the quarry of our own free will, they will come back to slaughter us all."

At first, Lala was speechless. Then, in a firm voice, she spoke. "What are *we* going to do?"

Ephron had failed to divulge that he had been promised his freedom if he would return the boy, who had many more years to serve the Egyptian slave masters.

Hassam's face froze in fear. "I can't go back!" he cried. "I will die there." He swallowed hard. "Please, Ephron, you promised to take care of me. Let's move where they will never find us."

"I wish it were that simple," Ephron murmured deceptively. "You and I will leave in the morning."

Lala clenched her lips in fury. She may be just a girl, unschooled in the inhumanity of slavery, but she had to defend her best friend. Her five-foot-six frame bent low as she whispered in Hassam's ear. "When he enters the tent to eat, we will run away, hide in the desert where no one will find us."

Ephron was one step ahead. "Come, boy, you'll sleep beside me tonight."

The following morning, when the two figures—Lala's biological father and the love of her life—were no longer visible, she put her head between her knees and prayed: "Hear, O God of Israel. Bring giants to kill the slave masters and save my Hassam, the only man I have ever loved."

Her prayer ended with darkening clouds and thunderclaps. Heavy rain accompanied the storm that collided with the drought-stricken land. With a torturous pain twisting her heart, Lala lifted her sodden head heavenward. "Thank you, God. You heard me. I guess you're no longer angry with me, right?" Tears rolled down her cheeks. She felt simultaneously empty and heavy! But she was confident that even if God had sent the rain, he would also return Hassam. She believed in Him now, and her crushed heart began to fuel with hope. Lala picked up a stick and carved a tip on it with her knife. In an elegant font, she scratched in the sand, *"Lala and Hassam forever."*

Two weeks later Ephron returned to the desert alone. There was no point in asking him where Hassam was. Lala knew that he was *never* coming back. God had lied to her!

When Ephron announced he would not be staying, Lala was pleased. "I have some business to attend to, and I'm not sure when I can return."

Lala lost track of time. She felt only emptiness like she was sleep-walking aimlessly, always awakening with a hole in her heart. Hassam's brief appearance in her life had been emotionally fulfilling, and without him, Lala felt hollow inside. She mourned, but she was not going to receive condolences from her Jewish family. Hassam was just an Arab!

Alone with her goat charges, Lala often burst into angry, tearful fits. *So I am cursed! Taking Hassam away from me is your punishment, isn't it, Yahweh?*

The teenager tried not to dwell on the loss of Hassam, but it was not easy.

Lala became a tiny boat bobbing aimlessly on an outraged sea. Perhaps the Hand of Destiny would commiserate, feel her overwhelming pain, and allow her to relive in another life all the happy memories they had shared in their brief time together.

Perhaps!

CHAPTER SIX

- A MONTH LATER -

Lala Suffers Further Loss

*"Life tore us apart, but so glad I had the chance to
call you my beloved one."*
—ANONYMOUS

A s usual, Lala began her day well before sunrise. She put on
a tunic fashioned from two goat-hair squares sewn together
with an opening for her neck. It had been lovingly crafted
by Tikva. Lala's veil was held in place with a thorn pin. She was
unaware that her outfit had previously belonged to her biological
mother, Rebekah.

Lala stepped outside the tent to breathe in the cold dawn air
before it morphed into a furnace. She looked back at her dwelling,
divided into two parts, one for males and the other for females.
However, this abode hadn't glimpsed the male sex since Ephron and

Hassam had left. Lala stepped inside to share her thoughts. "Ima, why do you hold on to the notion that part of our tent is for *men* who will share our lives? If we dismantled the partitions, we, the *women*, could have more space. Like Rebekah, Lala didn't wish to belong to a man. And the thought of breeding like the goats made her stomach heave. But there were random moments when she wanted a man who could carry some of the heavy workload.

Cousin Yokova read her mind. "Women do all the work anyway, Lala."

"So get used to it," Abriyah added.

Lala loved her cousins and laughed. "Yes, we girls must do all the heavy work. Tikva is too old now."

"I heard that!" was Tikva's playful response. "I'm not too deaf or too old to take the switch to you. Now go fetch water, or we will miss the first meal of the day."

"I'll go, aunt," said Yokova.

Later, Yokova returned, gripping two overflowing water containers, one in each hand. She set her loads down and called out to Tikva. "Aunt my hand is itchy, and it's burning."

"Let me take a look."

The rash was noticeable. When Tikva touched Yokova's swollen hand, the girl winced in pain.

Tikva thought, *Has something sunk its teeth into her flesh?*

"Were you bitten?" she asked.

"I'm not sure," Yokova responded, wailing in pain. "It wasn't a snake. I have been watchful for dangerous things. Tikva, please make the pain go away with your healing herbs."

Tikva put the soothing oil of a rare desert flower onto the inflamed area. The blossom had similar healing properties to lavender. Then she tightly wrapped Yokova's hand with strips of leather hide.

"Go lie down," Tikva ordered. She then addressed Lala, who was looking worried. "Put water on the boil, and I'll make Yokova a warm healing tea."

Twenty minutes later, Yokova, writhing in pain, began vomiting. In less than two hours, she was dead. The walls of her red blood cells had ruptured. Necrotic venom from an aggressive brown desert recluse spider, donning three pairs of eyes, had been her assassin!

Tikva wanted to pack up camp and move to a safer spot, but she knew that finding a new water source in this desert, the harshest environment known to man, would be madness.

Now there were *three* Judah exiles.

Lala, Tikva, and Abriyah, cried for days.

CHAPTER SEVEN

- TWO MONTHS LATER -
Lala's Abduction

"You may not control all the events that happen to you,
but you can decide not to be reduced by them."
—MAYA ANGELOU

The desert sand shone like gold as the rising sun garnished it with warmth. Lala put some dried dates into her pocket, collected her goats, and headed out. As she neared the watering hole, she wasn't surprised to see branded dromedaries and their owners drinking greedily. The earlier rainfall had fueled the desert bloom.

The water source, the soul of living things, had been energized by the replenishing rainwater. Green grass and sedge sprouted prolifically. Wild edibles displayed the colors of health.

Enjoying the beautiful day, Lala was not concerned when she

saw the silhouettes of the camels and their riders at the wellspring. She usually tried to keep her distance, waiting for the visiting parties to leave, but today her charges were thirsty. And so was she.

As she approached the water's edge, her brows creased in puzzlement. Nearby she noted square tents adorned with palm fronds that hung over the dwellings to deliver shade. She observed three women dressed in long white tunics. They wore masks that covered their entire faces, except for their eyes. She didn't know what to make of the scene.

Outside one of the tents, a woman shook a tattered carpet that, presumably, covered the sand floor. Lala was filled with curiosity. She had seen countless nomad men come and go as travelers of the night, navigating beneath the stars, but she had never seen a camp before. Up to now, only Tikva had bartered, trading goat meat and hides for wheat and other cereals.

More dark clouds are forming overhead; perhaps a gift of more rain, Lala mused. Was that why the desert people had made camp, to gather extra water supplies for an onward trek? Lala dismissed her thoughts and was ready to herd her goats elsewhere for grazing when a hand tapped her shoulder. Startled, she reflexively started to flee, but the hand gripped her firmly. "You are a pretty one," the aging man asserted. His unfamiliar tongue eluded her, but the fear coursing through her veins didn't. With gutsy spirit, she spat in basic Arabic, "You scared me! I don't understand your strange language! Just leave me alone!"

The short man spun her around to face him. Lala gasped. He removed the camel-hair cloth that had protected his face from sandstorms. He had a pointy nose, a look as fierce as a raptor, and soulless eyes. His salt-and-pepper beard was thrust forward like a dagger.

His chortling resonated in her ears as she unclasped his grip and ran as fast as her crooked legs would carry her. Hot on her heels were her six bleating companions.

A panting Lala burst into her tent as if the Devil were pursuing her. "Ima, a desert traveler frightened me."

"There, there," Tikva soothed, touching Lala's sweating face. "Tell me all about it."

Tikva didn't seem to be overly alarmed. "Seeing that the desert man didn't harm you, child, I wouldn't give it another thought. Just avoid them when they are at the watering hole."

Lala slept fretfully that night. She couldn't get the old man's face out of her mind.

What would have happened if I had not taken off running? Has he followed me to see where I live?

The following day Lala was hesitant to herd her friends, so she asked her cousin, Abriyah, to accompany her. "I don't want to see that scary old man again, but the goats must drink and eat, or they will die."

"I can't, Lala," Abriyah stated. "I must help Aunt Tikva prepare our winter food so that *we* don't starve."

With her head lowered, Lala began her familiar trek to the oasis. But this time she sent the goats on ahead without her. Hiding beneath the rock overhang she had shared with Hassam, she tried not to think about her emptiness without him and instead concentrated on what was happening at the water's edge.

A sigh of relief escaped Lala's lips when she saw the visitors' tents were dismantled, and the camels were loaded with their belongings. Now she could return to a healthy life, unafraid.

Later, as the light faded and her foe was nowhere in sight, Lala whistled as she rounded up her charges. It was time to go home.

Several hours later Tikva stood outside peering into the starless night. *Where is she? Why are the goats roaming freely?* Tikva's stomach knotted. *Had something happened to Lala?* She stepped back inside. "Abriyah, go and look for Lala. Something may have happened to her. She has never been this late coming home."

The worried woman gripped her tunic tightly. With a grave expression etched on her old face, she watched Abriyah retrieve a candle and slip out of sight.

An hour later, a breathless Abriyah returned home clutching a head veil in her hand. "I can't find her, Aunt, but I found this," she announced, handing over the cover with red stains. Tikva put the soiled headdress to her nose. Her deafening, despairing wail echoed through the cool night air, sending distressed goats bleating like screaming humans into their paddock. Abriyah touched her arm. *"What ..."*

Tikva butted in. "It's definitely blood." *Lala's blood,* she thought. "She is injured and lying out there. Quickly, we must go in search."

"I did just that," Abriyah protested. "I followed her usual path, and she is nowhere to be seen. And it is too dark now to search properly. We will have to wait until daylight and hope we can find her."

"No," Tikva retorted impatiently. "It can't wait until morning. I must find her *now!* Yahweh, our God will help us. Light more candles, Abriyah."

Abriyah sighed heavily but did as she was instructed. She remembered hearing the conversation Lala had had with Tikva the day before. "I'm scared, Ima. I had a horrible dream. I dreamed that I was taken to the slave camp, like Hassam."

"It's just a nightmare, my child," Tikva soothed. "Don't let it worry you. Tonight you'll sleep with me. I will protect you from bad dreams."

It was a promise this caring mother couldn't keep.

Was Lala's desert lifestyle a thing of the past?

Only the sands of time held the answer.

CHAPTER EIGHT

- SAME DAY -

Somewhere in the Vast Wilderness

"We draw our strength from the very despair in which we have been forced to live."
—CESAR CHAVEZ

S unrise transformed the sand dunes into a vast sea of black, wavelike shadows, except Lala, bound and sheathed, couldn't see it. When she awoke, she fought desperately to breathe. When her rhythm became more regular, she tried to focus through half-closed eyes, on the darkness that hung around her like a shroud. Her head hurt, and she felt as if she were being shaken like goat's milk when it redefined itself as cheese. And what was that awful smell causing her nostrils to pinch so tightly? *It must be a dream. It's not real!*

Riding a camel isn't a Lawrence of Arabia fantasy for a girl trussed up like a Sunday roast. Disorientated, Lala held on for dear life as she tried to come to grips with her predicament. She did not know that during the calm of her afternoon nap, she had been beaten on the head with a blunt object. The brutal blow had sent her into an unwelcomed dreamworld. Unbeknown to her, a man had lifted her unconscious body, slung it over his shoulder, and headed toward the camel caravan waiting near the watering hole. Eighteen-year-old Malik said, "I did as you instructed, Father. Here she is. Should she ride with you or me?"

"Roll her in a blanket and strap her behind you," the older Bedouin replied.

The dromedary with Minnie Mouse eyes was decked in bright red and blue blankets. It blew bubbles of foam from its mouth as it carried its two passengers to an unknown destination.

The pungent odor of urine was overpowering, yet the waddle of the camel's gait failed to alert Lala that she was being kidnapped. Anxiously, she tried to wiggle free of the restraining blanket, but she was wound up tighter than an eight-day clock. Finally, it hit home. She was being *abducted*! With her eyes the size of saucers, Lala vented a series of earsplitting screams, each sounding powerful enough to puncture the rising sun.

Whack! Whack!

A knotted wooden club rained down on her. "Be quiet, girl, or else!" hissed Malik.

The intensity of Lala's panic worsened her blinding headache. A multitude of anxious thoughts flooded through her pain. *Why am I strapped to a camel! Where am I? Where are they taking me? What are they going to do to me? The last thing I remember, I was napping.*

Where are my goats? Have they been taken? What will Tikva do when I don't return home? Will she and Abriyah look for me? If Ephron had returned to their dwelling, would he search for his missing daughter? Will I ever see Ima again? Tears rolled down Lala's dirt-encrusted cheeks, and then onto her eyelids, which were closed in fatigue, bringing her the blessing of sleep.

Crossing the desert seemed to take an eternity. As the nomads' journey finally came to an end, the camel driver commanded the large animal to kneel. The kidnapped girl tumbled from the enfolding blanket. *Fwoop!* Lala landed headfirst on a sand dune. Most egregious was the sight of her bare bottom exposed for all to see. A mortified Lala wormed out of her entrapment, but before she had time to gather her thoughts, she was surrounded by several females. Lala noted eyes decorated with kohl and calloused hands bearing henna patterns. Silently, two of the younger women lifted the dumbstruck Lala to her feet. The unsteady girl finally found her voice. "What's happening? Why have I been brought here to this strange place? Where are you taking me?"

The only answer the heavily breathing Lala received was tittering as the females gripped her arms and marched her to a cluster of black tents. Outside, a feast of camel and rice awaited the bride and groom to be. The plan to kidnap Lala had been well orchestrated. Earlier that day, a camel had been sacrificed in celebration of Malik's sixty-year-old father, Abdul-Rahim, and his *fifth* marriage.

Beneath a peaceful night sky, adorned with a shower of bright stars, hardly a word was spoken. Only when the small, hawk-nosed man, whose eyes were wrinkled by years of squinting in the brutal sun, licked his fingers, did the tribe stop eating. And only when

Abdul-Rahim stood, did the rest of the group rise, except for Lala. Even though her stomach had growled with hunger, she had refused to eat. Even though she was not yet aware that the feast was made in *their* honor, fear coursed through her jangled nerves.

The innocent teenager could not have imagined the nightmares that lay ahead.

With the tranquility of her former life now reversed, she had no choice but to straddle two cultures to stay alive. She instinctively gathered that she was Abdul-Rahim's trophy and that this influential man was all about control and power, especially over life and death.

The next morning, a sexually violated Lala wanted to end it all, to set herself on fire.

A dead body and a living body have been united in loathsome and horrible communion. There would be no tribal authority to judge this Hasana tribe member for kidnapping and rape. Abdul-Rahim *was* the elder!

The loathsome man hadn't just robbed Lala's innocence; he had also stolen time from the person she loved most, Tikva. Lala sighed heavily, coming to realize that killing herself wouldn't serve any useful purpose. Death was not her way out. More than anything else, she wanted to survive, escape, and find her way home to Tikva.

Would this horrible nightmare be the end of the line for Lala?

Unlike Lala's previous more sedentary existence, these desert dwellers were always on the move. At sunset the next day, while the nomads were preoccupied with taking down the tents and packing their possessions, a battered and bruised girl took the opportunity to flee. "Bad legs, don't let me down," she muttered as she bolted into the wilderness. She had no clue where to hide in the barren landscape, but she was committed to giving this escape her best effort. With her long hair flowing in flight, Lala ran until her lungs felt about to burst. She collapsed onto cooling night sands. Just as she began to gather a second wind, she heard the rumbling high-pitch growls of a camel hot on her heels.

Lala took off like a bat out of hell, but was no match for the desert racer whose slobber now covered her. Being pursued by a four-legged creature wasn't fair; neither was Malik's chilling laughter.

Every muscle in Lalas' body stiffened in fright. Her teeth chattered, and her heart fluttered. As her breath rushed in and out too rapidly for coherent speech, she felt overpowered and threatened. "If you try to run again, you will be hacked to pieces, and we will feast on your flesh!"

Lala resumed her dreadful life but never gave up hope of one day reuniting with Tikva. Her thoughts were with her family and the happy life she had left behind somewhere in this vast desert wilderness. Lala longed for Tikva to embrace her, to recite Bible stories and recall family memories. These reminiscences were all she had now. The captive Lala missed her older cousin, her goats, and the idyllic life they had all shared. And she grieved for the Fellahin boy who had captured her heart.

Eventually, Lala formed a close bond with fourteen-year-old Nisba, a North African slave girl, a dark-brown beauty who was Abdul-Rahim's fourth wife. Like Lala, Nisba was abducted from her village the year before. Lala learned from Nisba that it was customary for the nomads to marry their relatives, but adolescent, foreign black girls were preferable and much desired by the older men in the tribe. Even so, Abdul-Rahim had struck gold when he set his eyes on Lala's thick blond hair. She was the cream of the crop.

In their new encampment, Lala helped the heavily pregnant Nisba feed and milk the camels and prepare meals. Only men tended to the herding. Older wives were responsible for erecting and dismantling tents and taking care of the tribe's twelve children. As the clan continually traveled onward seeking "greener pastures," Lala settled into their nomadic lifestyle. She dressed like them, wore kohl eye makeup, and stained her hands with henna dye. She was now *accepted* by all the women, who treated her well, but not so much by the menfolk, especially her husband.

After a year had passed and no child had come from their union, Lala's husband turned sour against his fourteen-year-old wife. "You are as worthless as camel dung!" Abdul-Rahim said, "I have not chosen wisely, goat-eyed girl. I'm no longer respected as a man. If you do not give me a child, you will be left behind, or I might sell you to a trader, who won't care about having children but only about ravishing your Jew body!"

Having quickly picked up the Bedouin dialect and their belief in malevolent spirits, which they called *jinn,* an incensed Lala fired back, "The jinn are going to punish you for taking me away from my mother. You are holding me against my will to serve your sexual needs and your demands for a child."

At just the mention of the jinn, Abdul-Rahim took umbrage. In a drooling rage, he firmly seized Lala's shoulders, shook her violently, lifted her off her feet, and hurled her down. The back of the teenager's head hit a rock. The impact of her brain crashing inside her skull tore at the fibers of her nerves. Though Lala was still conscious, she was dazed, and her vision was blurred. Suddenly she began to vomit. Lala's hands cradled her bloodied head as she tried to compose herself. With coma-like fatigue, she attempted to rise, but her impaired sense of balance sent her backward to the ground. Blinking back tears, her contorted face was creased as she groaned, "Ooooh."

"That will teach you never to disrespect me again," the pitiless Abdul-Rahim roared. "If I don't get a trader to buy you, I will take another wife, and you will be her servant."

The traumatic injury to Lala's brain had lasting effects. She experienced acute muscle weakness and spasticity paralysis from the waist down. Unable to move her *dead* limbs, she dragged her body along close to the ground, like a slug. But even that movement was restricted by a rope around her ankle. Lala was now at her husband's mercy and that of his other wives, who were warned to keep their distance from her, except at mealtimes. Their daily visits with offerings of camel's milk and a bowl of food were the only generosity offered her. Late one night when everyone else was dead to the world, Nisba crept out of the marital tent and brought Lala milk and extra food, which she had hidden beneath her pregnant belly when no one was watching. Beneath dark skies, the girls whispered, laughed, and spoke about their days before capture and about one day fleeing their jailors. But soon Nisba would have a baby to care for, a child she could love amid her enforced incarceration, and that became her sole focus. Lala understood this reasoning. Tikva had done the same for her.

The next secret rendezvous between the stolen brides brought alarming news. Nisba had overheard a conversation at the campfire. Abdul-Rahim intended to move locations in the morning and sell Lala to a trader who had many foreign sex slaves working for him.

Lala panicked. She was beside herself. She had to think fast.

When she saw her obnoxious husband the next morning, she begged him not to execute his plan. "I'm young. I can bear you many children. Please give me another chance."

The control freak reluctantly agreed, but with conditions!

Lala was subjected to her husband's "pleasures" for the next couple of months, and when it was evident that she was barren, her husband mocked her. "You, the goat-eyed woman with hair the color of vomit, are a *cursed* Hebrew, but I'm sure the trader will not care."

Tears flowed. Lala cried out in pain as Abdul-Rahim tied her hands behind her back. "Have mercy," the tortured girl pleaded. "Let me go so I can return to my mother."

A slap about Lala's head was his response.

The next morning Lala woke to the sun warming her face. Rubbing her eyes, she looked around and blinked. Was she still in a dream state? Not a soul or tent was in sight. Her nomad *family* had vanished into thin air. She was a light sleeper. Why had she not heard a sound? Then it dawned on her.

The tea given to her the night before must be the reason she had not heard the hustling and bustling of tents being dismantled. But why had Nisba *doctored* her nighttime drink? Words could not express her fear of being stranded in the desert alone. How could she escape her wrist bonds? At least she hadn't been sold to a sex trader.

Lala rotated her wrists back and forth to loosen the rope restraint, but it would not give way. She felt enraged. Feisty Lala was back in control. She wasn't going to die tied up like an animal ready for slaughter. She had to find a way to untie herself. Lala raised her knees to her chest, curled up like a hedgehog, and pulled her tethered wrists forward under her bottom. In terrible agony, she used her teeth to pull a strand of rope, and it worked. She was free, but not from the pain of having her arms nearly wrenched from their sockets. Something glinting in the sunlight caught her eye. It was a small knife. Had Nisba left it for her, or had someone simply dropped it?

Lala found a water container filled to the brim, dried camel meat, and a small number of dates. *"Thank you, Nisba, my dear sister. May your god watch over you."*

Courageous Lala wasn't about to let the vastness of the desert or her "slug" legs stop her from trying to find her way home. She hoped that she would come across some decent nomads who would help her, not enslave her. Once before, she had tried to solicit the help of visiting nomads, but the *curse* had had other plans.

The visitors had betrayed her, and she had received a vicious beating from Abdul-Rahim.

After traveling at night for days on end, Lala never did find her way home to Tikva. The girl felt a lonely misery before she finally gave up. "I carry you in my heart, Ima because in there you're still alive," she whispered, looking up to the heavens.

Over time Lala experienced the hospitality and compassion of other *good* nomads, who fed and clothed her. But they all moved on without her, saying they did not want a confrontation should they come across her original owner. The truth was that she could not do her share of the work because of her disability. At the mercy of random drifters, Lala languished in the desert for the rest of her life. Eventually, she would die of starvation.

The day Lala took her last breath, she heard the noisy, guttural croaks of a raven. This species of bird was unknown—unseen in this era.

The raven hovered on wings of purple iridescence and then soared ever upwards into the clear blue skies. Was it a portent of a dark prophecy or a reflection of Lala's spirit?

Over the millennium Lala's bleached skeletal remains scattered, then entombed themselves among the dunes of this unforgiving, inhospitable land she once called home. It was now her final resting place.

Eventually, this flower of the desert became a legend. Lala's life story enthralled the young and old around nomad campfires.

According to folklore, she had lived to127 years.

Abdul-Rahim got his comeuppance, stabbed to death at a watering hole by a member of another tribe over the abduction of his daughter weeks earlier.

Nisba found her way home, taking with her the two sons she had produced with Abdul-Rahim.

Tikva died of a broken heart a year into Lala's disappearance.

Cousin Abriyah perished not long after, buried under mountains of sand that had built up after the worst sandstorm the Judean desert had ever known.

Lala's father, Ephron, was never again seen in those parts. He was brutally beaten to death by Hassam's uncle not long after the little boy was handed back to Egyptian slave masters.

While Hassam el-Din survived his forced labor under appalling conditions, he had witnessed significant loss of life. He never stopped loving or weeping for Lala, the love of his life. He could not have imagined that, on another level, they would never be separated, but would, instead, be reunited in a world that hadn't yet begun.

The love of Lala's life died at age 100. She had outlived him.

Death leaves a heartache no one can heal. Love leaves a memory no one can steal.

Yahweh's *curse* of rebirth for laws broken would continue relentlessly in times to come. No mercy would be shown to the descendants of the bas Sora bloodline.

CHAPTER NINE

- THE PTOLEMY ROYAL DYNASTY, BC -

The Enemy Is Among Us

*"From the hour of their birth some are marked out
for subjugation, others for rule."*
—ARISTOTLE

At the break of dawn on a summer's day, forty-nine-year-old herbalist Debowrah (a distant cousin of Tikva bas Sora); her much older husband, Jacob; her four adult sons; and most of the occupants of Beer-Sheba in southern Israel were awakened to the sounds of stomping feet. The Egyptian army quickly surrounded the urban settlement and ordered the inhabitants to gather out front. Fearful cries from young and old infiltrated the rays of the rising sun. "Yahweh, help us," an old woman begged. "Our enemy is among us. Why does this happen? Are we not *Your* chosen people?"

Debowrah's youngest son spoke up. "Woman, if we *are* the chosen ones, then, pray tell, why the enemies of our people are here?"

"Hush," his mother said, fearing God's wrath. "He will save us!"

The boy disagreed and tightly curled his lips.

After many days of traveling on foot, the roped captives, now slaves, arrived at the great city of Alexandria on the Egyptian coast. The weary, dirty, hungry, and thirsty prisoners gawked in amazement at their surroundings. The opulent splendor was inconceivable to them when compared to their dreary homes constructed of sun-dried mud bricks and terra cotta roofs.

The royal palace spanned 200 feet. It was constructed of enormous limestone blocks and giant red granite columns crafted from single monolithic pieces. A giant statue of the goddess Isis loomed over them. The two humongous sphinxes guarding the palace entrance unnerved the simple folk. This palatial residence was a far cry from their last living quarters.

The thirsty captives stood motionless in the stifling heat, waiting to learn what was to become of them. An hour later, the Pharaoh's high-ranking slave master made an appearance. He was a commanding, frightening dark figure. Over six feet tall, the prematurely gray-haired man had a concrete jaw, angular cheekbones, titan shoulders, and stone-cold onyx eyes. Speaking in their native tongue, he bellowed orders to separate the men from the women.

Segregated from their menfolk, the panic-stricken women, with long braided tresses hidden beneath their veils, wailed loudly as they prayed for deliverance. The parting caused much distress to Debowrah, a protective mother and wife. Shuffling in her ankle tethers, she made her way to her husband and sons, who were visibly distressed. Debowrah flung her arms around her beloved Jacob. "I would rather die than be parted from you and our children!" she cried hysterically, addressing her husband's bowed head. Jacob wanted to spare her the tears of helplessness, but in a flash, the burly slave master was at her side.

With brute strength, Debowrah's arms were forcibly unlocked from her husband, and the distraught woman was thrown to the ground among other kneeling women. The guard's sinister intent was clear. "If you give us any more trouble, Hebrew woman, and do not obey your new owners—Pharaoh Ptolemy and Queen Cleopatra V Tryphaena—your husband and children will be killed instantly."

Ptolemy XII Auletes was a former general of Alexander the Great. Ptolemy took over Egypt when Alexander died. He married his older sister, Cleopatra Tryphaena, who gave birth to a daughter, Berenice IV, the legitimate heir to the throne.

With eyes downcast and brimming with tears, Debowrah's head bobbed up and down.

A captive bystander, a mother who also had her menfolk taken from her, heeded the warning and said, "I know that my words will be no consolation, but we will have an easier life if we do as we are told."

The men and boys were taken to the limestone quarries. Their sleeping quarters were in the open under the stars. The females were put to work inside the palace as servants. They slept in an abandoned and dilapidated horse stable with stars twinkling through decaying roof slats.

The palace had many servant-slaves working as cleaners, cooks, laundresses, and errand runners. With a firm resolve to live and be reunited with her loved ones, an unhappy Debowrah began performing her duties—tending to every whim and need of the younger royal family members: Berenice, Arsinoe, Cleopatra (whose biological mother was unknown) and two younger half-brothers, both named Ptolemy. The first Ptolemy was birthed by a woman from a Memphite priestly family, and the last Ptolemy was birthed by a woman of Greek origin. The only thing that these offspring had in common was their natural father, Ptolemy Auletes.

In the coming days, Debowrah developed a fondness for sixteen-year-old Cleopatra VII. But it was the youngest royal child, Ptolemy XIV, whom Debowrah most deeply bonded with. He reminded her of her youngest son. This nine-year-old boy, seeking to distinguish himself from his other half-siblings, was self-assured, intuitive, sensitive, humorous, and talented. He could play the flute like his father, who was known throughout the palace as The Piper. Also, the boy was a chatterbox. He never let Debowrah get a word in edgewise. The pining mother missed the growing-up stage she had experienced with her own children, and she was drawn to the boy.

Unbeknown to the forty-nine-year-old Debowrah, she was with child.

A few months later, the spunky boy's life came crashing down on him. His father, whom he adored, and his mother, the aging Queen Cleopatra Tryphaena, were driven from Egypt by threat of a popular insurrection. The couple took refuge in Rome. Shortly afterward, Berenice, the King's legitimate daughter by their royal marriage, was proclaimed sole ruler. She, like the rest of her bloodline, was the last of the Macedonian Greek dynasty that had ruled Egypt from the time of Alexander the Great's death in 323 BC.

Berenice's consuls forced her to marry, at the age of twenty, a Syrian monarch, Prince Seleucus. Less than a year into their marriage, Berenice had her spouse strangled to death, a deed reportedly orchestrated by the young Cleopatra.

Bernice was beheaded at age twenty-two at the hands of her father's men, or so it has been documented. Did Cleopatra orchestrate Bernice's death, as well? This remains unsolved.

The Egyptian laws and tradition decreed that Pharaohs marry siblings. The now eighteen-year-old Cleopatra married her fifteen-year-old brother and became Queen of Egypt. Only days into their marriage, her sibling resented the fact that his wife tried to control him and was determined to dispose of her. Ptolemy allied himself with Arsinoe, and their devious actions were reported to the reigning Cleopatra. Reportedly, her brother-husband drowned while attempting to cross the Nile. Most in the royal palace who were familiar with the vengeful side of Cleopatra's character strongly believed that the young Queen was responsible for the boy's sudden death. And they were not wrong!

Immediately after the boy's embalmed body was entombed, and, again, in keeping with Egyptian tradition to marry within the family to preserve the purity of their bloodline, Cleopatra married her ten-year-old brother and ruled *her* kingdom with an iron fist. But when her position of power was threatened by those who wished her removed, she used sex appeal as a political weapon. Cleopatra eventually seduced Gaius Julius Caesar, the Consul of Rome, with her irresistible charm and appeal. Teaming up with this powerful, egotistical lover, Cleopatra executed her sister, Arsinoe, whom she considered a potential rival to the throne.

On the day after Cleopatra's second marriage, to ten-year-old Ptolemy XIV, Debowrah's water broke. Thankfully, it happened outdoors in the courtyard when she was hand-washing linens. No one else was near. She rushed to her sleeping quarters, where she squatted over the moldy hay in the horse stables. She pushed, pushed, and pushed some more, without once releasing a cry of pain, even though the birthing was tearing at her insides. None of the other servants had yet returned to the stables. They were busy cleaning up after the marriage celebration. Debowrah glanced up at the stars and supplicated, "Please, merciful God, take my child to your kingdom. Don't let my child suffer the disgrace of being a slave to nonbelievers."

Plop! The newborn girl birthed directly onto the hay. Debowrah cried with joy, but her happiness was tinged with sorrow. She hadn't seen her husband or other children since being forcibly separated.

Dripping in perspiration, the proud mother lifted the tiny, whimpering infant and looked at the hair color and the strangely colored eyes. Debowrah frowned. She knew no one who had eyes this color or hair that shade. These characteristics did not originate from her side of the family!

The infant's wispy blond hair and dark skin were matted with birthing blood, and the black oval skin patch on the baby's cheek made her mother question the origin of another mystery—the child's birth defect. No family member, including herself, had such a marking. Moving on in her inspection, her daughter's misshapen legs made Debowrah inhale sharply. Did this occur during or after pregnancy? Had she pushed too hard and unintentionally twisted her child's limbs? Troubling concerns and dire thoughts pierced Debowrah's reality. *If my bow-legged child is unable to walk, unable to serve the masters, what will become of her? Will they kill her?*

After breastfeeding her baby, Debowrah wrapped the tiny mite in her used undergarments and concealed her between two stacks of hay. *Will my newborn cry and attract attention in my absence? How long can I keep her a secret?* But her most pressing concern was how she was going to juggle her servant duties with the constant needs of a newborn? Would her companions come to the rescue?

Or would they betray her to the Queen?

By now, well overdue in performing her job of turning down the covers of the royal bed, Debowrah rushed to Cleopatra's chambers. There, her flushed face, apologies for her tardiness, and deflated belly did not go unnoticed. "Servant, have you given birth?" Cleopatra demanded in Hebrew. Fluent in a dozen languages, Cleopatra was an educated intellectual and capable administrator. Yet, despite her abilities and efforts, she would eventually fail, and her life would be more of sadness than glamour.

"Yes, my Queen," Debowrah answered dutifully.

"And *where* is the child?"

With bowed head, Debowrah replied, "In the old horse stables, my Queen."

"Is it a girl or boy?"

"I have a daughter, my Queen."

"Bring her here to my private quarters," Cleopatra ordered. "No child should be raised in that old building!" She never considered mentioning that no one should have been housed there in the first place. But then, to the heartless Queen of Egypt, slaves weren't human. They were merely chattel.

Debowrah responded respectfully. "Thank you for your kind offer." She inhaled a deep sigh of relief. "My Queen, I desperately desire a further kindness. Could you please get word to my husband that our fifth child, Leandra (meaning "Like a Lioness"), is in this world."

"I will do what I can," Cleopatra answered, her hooked nose quivering with deception. "Now go and bring your baby."

Debowrah's feeling of euphoria was shortlived.

Brimming with happiness for the compassion shown to her by the new Pharaoh, Debowrah rushed out of the room. With her hide sandals flapping on the granite floor, her bloodied legs couldn't carry her fast enough to the stable. On arriving, she rushed to the haystacks. "Oh, no!" she shrilled with alarm. "Where is she?" *Someone has taken my baby!*

The crestfallen mother felt like she was stuck in a nightmare as she ran back to the royal chambers. There she found Cleopatra relaxing in a bathtub filled with donkey milk, a liquid the ruler believed would preserve her beauty and youthful skin. (Later, it would be historically documented that no less than 700 donkeys were required to provide the quantity of liquid necessary for Cleopatra's daily bath.)

"My queen, please help me?" a distressed Debowrah implored. "Someone has taken my baby. I have looked everywhere. She is nowhere to be found."

The poor woman's raging emotions were soon moderated by the reaction of the woman soaking in the bathtub. "Worry not, mother," Cleopatra soothed, while immersing herself deeper in the tub. "Your baby is in good hands."

Debowrah's pinched expression prompted further explanation. "As you know, my sister, Arsinoe, is without a child, and she has claimed your infant as her own."

Debowrah couldn't breathe. She felt like Cleopatra had reached into her chest and plucked out her heart. Debowrah fell to her knees, sobbing. "I beg you, my Queen, give me back my baby. She is a *Hebrew!* She can't be raised as an Egyptian. It wouldn't be fair for the child not to know her true roots!"

Cleopatra's wry smile spoke volumes, and her attitude was heartless. "You can't be too smart. You forget that you are a slave, and anything that belongs to you belongs to me. Did you honestly think I would not learn of this child being born on my property! One of my other servants saw you giving birth, and dutifully notified me, her queen." Cleopatra shot Debowrah a lightning-strike glare. "I will not hear another word, or you will be beaten until the flesh peels off your body. Now go about your work and forget you ever birthed this child."

Although stunned to the marrow, Debowrah was not to be thwarted. "My breasts are full, my Queen," she said. "Can I at least give her my milk?"

"No," Cleopatra countered adamantly. "Leandra has the best wet nurse in the palace and now the best mother. You are a slave. What more can you give her besides your milk?"

Debowrah's heart-wrenching sobs echoed within the castle walls as she fled the room. Returning to the emptiness of the horse stable, she found some rope, climbed onto a crate, prayed for God's forgiveness, and then hanged herself from a ceiling beam.

Her body, naked except for sandals, was unceremoniously burned.

Debowrah's family was never informed of her death. Eventually, they too succumbed from overwork and starvation.

Baby Leandra was all that remained of this once proud Hebrew family's bloodline.

As time passed in the royal household, Cleopatra had one thing on her mind: Leandra! Were the advantaged child's privileges with her foster mother, Arsinoe, coming to an end? Had the congenital curse that coursed through the girl's veins already mapped out an ill-fated path?

Certainly! When the blood of one person has cursed the road out of Hell, it does not lead up to the light.

CHAPTER TEN

- THE PTOLEMY ROYAL DYNASTY, BC -

Cleopatra's Betrayal

"The slave is doomed to worship time and fate and death …"
—BERTRAND RUSSELL

The drama unfolded.

"Where is Mut?" cried ten-year-old Leandra.

"Your mother is dead," answered the high-ranking servant.

"No, she is not!"

"I tell no lie, child."

Leandra's immature mind could not understand. She went shrieking into Cleopatra's arms for answers. "Aunt, the wicked cleaning woman told me that Mut is dead. Tell me it is not true."

In a frigid voice, Cleopatra replied, "That is correct, Jew child. My sister is dead."

The perplexed child couldn't process this brutal revelation, so she argued, as any child would. "She can't be dead. I saw her last night. I remember things well," she claimed.

"You must have been dreaming because I had her murdered two days ago."

"You killed her!" Leandra shrilled. "Why?"

Although Leandra had been schooled to be respectful, received daily educational instruction—philosophy, literature, art, and music—and spoke several languages, she was no match for Cleopatra's ruthlessness. She was well known to test experimental poisons on her unwitting slaves.

Leandra, unfazed, held her hands on her hips and glared disrespectfully at the heartless, ugly monster with a hooked nose. In a sarcastic voice that sounded mature beyond its years, Leandra said, You are a wicked woman to kill your own sister, my Mut. I will pray for the lion goddess, Sekhmet, to hunt you for the rest of your life …"

Cleopatra slapped Leandra across the face, ending the child's flow of vengeful words. The Queen turned her back on the stunned youngster and commanded her servant, "Get this disrespectful Jew girl out of my chambers. Remove her, take her to the stables, and prepare her for the journey."

In retaliatory humiliation, Leandra pursed her lips in anger. "What journey? And why do you address me as a Jew? I have the same royal blood as you."

Cleopatra's laughter reverberated around the massive interior of her private quarters. "You certainly do *not* have royal blood! Your Israelite slave mother gave birth to you in my stables, and my sister took pity on her … and why? Because Arsinoe was without child, and your mother could not raise you. How was she to clothe you, feed you, and take care of you? She was a slave with no money, and her servitude duties were to me. Anyway, she is no longer on this earth. She hanged herself!"

A subdued Leandra hung her head. Cleopatra's revelation about her biological mother fell by the wayside. "Then what is to become of me now that my adopted mother is dead?"

A sardonic smile creased the cruel Pharaoh's lips. "You are being sent to Rome. I have sold you."

Leandra's first introduction to cruelty made no immediate impact on her, for she was confused. However, after Cleopatra repeated the devastating reality of her intent, Leandra felt icy shivers travel through her body. She knew she was in big trouble. She had witnessed the slave markets, and she tearfully begged, "Please, Queen Cleopatra, don't send me away. I'll be good. I will be *your* slave. I will work hard."

"I have all the servants I need, and you'll fetch a decent price for your innocence," the unrepentant Cleopatra responded.

The innocent Leandra failed to grasp the consequences of Cleopatra's inhumane statement.

"Now leave my quarters!" barked Cleopatra. "There is nothing more to say."

Within the slave quarters, a somber Leandra was stripped of her royal clothing. Gone were the white linen dress and ornate headdress—a solid piece of gold-woven cloth tied at the back of her neck, with lappets that flowed down either side of her dark face. The royal clothing that separated Leandra from the ordinary people was removed. The gold and silver jewelry that had complimented the headdress were gone. The child's long blond tresses were cut short, and her makeup—kohl eye-paint—was washed off in icy water.

Dressed in the patterned fabric dress worn by all servants, a barefoot Leandra was locked in the barn with several other ousted slaves who had received the same gut-wrenching fate.

Leandra smoothed the rough fabric of her clothing as if her hands were a wrinkle spray. A neat and clean appearance, significant to privileged Egyptians, was a thing of the past for the discarded child. And forever gone was the special bond she had forged with Arsinoe, her foster mother.

Leandra had been loved, cared for, educated, and empowered by the unconditional love of this kind woman. She had also been a strong woman, who would never again be able to employ her instinct and prowess to protect her child from harm. When the face of Arsinoe, the only woman Leandra had ever loved, surfaced in her mind, the girl locked her heart and her mouth in silence. Her elective muteness would be the condition that nourished her, an old soul, in the harsh times ahead.

Alexandria was a busy city. Together with the port, it was a great commercial emporium, a picturesque and lively place, but not for a heavy-hearted child. Leandra stared at the glow, the bright golden beam, emitting from the lighthouse. It was fueled by burning fire. Known as the Pharos of Alexandria, the lighthouse was built of limestone blocks and reached 350 feet high. At the pinnacle was a statue honoring Poseidon, the god of the sea. The tower was built to guide trade ships and their sailors safely into Alexandria's busy harbor. Now, it was guiding a different type of trade away from its shores—helpless human cargo.

A hundred hapless people tethered by neck chains were herded onto a ship called the *Corbitas*. It was a round-hulled vessel with a curving prow, capable of traversing the thousands of nautical miles to Rome, on the Mediterranean seaboard.

Part of Leandra's heart died the moment the ship set sail on flame-blue waters, away from the only home she had ever known. Fighting back tears of sadness, rejection, and desolation, she watched the shoreline shrink to a faint shadow. A teenage boy shackled to her queried, "First time on a boat, right?"

Leandra bobbed her head affirmatively.

"Where are you originally from because you don't look like a typical Egyptian to me?"

Leandra fell silent.

But the boy persisted, "Do you have a tongue?"

Leandra smacked her lips in disapproval and broke the silence she had vowed would be her comfort. "Yes, nosy boy! I have a tongue, but it does not wish to talk."

Caleb was persistent. "And why not?" he jeered. "It is a long sailing, and we have lots of time."

Leandra countered, "And how would you know that?"

Caleb lowered his head. "I have been sold twice over there and then returned to my original Egyptian owner. Now I'm going back to Rome."

Leandra frowned. "Why?"

"I'm a sex slave, and my Roman owner has *missed* me," he replied in a sarcastic tone.

"I don't understand these words *sex slave*," Leandra remarked in a puzzled tone.

The Nubian boy, who had only known the depravity of a *pleasure house*, inhaled sharply. "It is when another person uses your body for pleasure."

Her blank expression prompted his next shocking revelation. "You know, poke you in places you don't wish to be poked. But if you don't let them have their way, you are killed."

Leandra got the picture. She gasped in horror. Princess Arsinoe had shielded her from such lascivious knowledge. Just the thought of someone abusing her in that way sent icy chills down her spine.

Unable to rid the nightmarish image from her mind, Leandra turned her head heavenward and prayed aloud, "Isis, Goddess of all women, I beg for your love and protection to spare me from the wickedness the boy suffers. I would rather die than have my body violated."

Caleb instantaneously scoffed. "That's not going to do you any good, praying to someone you can't see."

Leandra pursed her lips angrily and retorted, "What would you know about gods and goddesses? You probably worship a camel!"

The boy's hearty chortle brought a broad smile to Leandra, who was now feeling more perky. She didn't mean to be rude, she told Caleb. He hugged her. "No matter what happens to us, I will always be your best friend."

Leandra sighed with momentary happiness.

The seafarers were taken below deck. Adults occupied the

bunks. Leandra and Caleb snuggled together on the plank flooring and drifted off to sleep. A while later the slaves were jolted awake by fierce winds and heavy rains pounding their vessel.

A lethargic Leandra broke out in a cold sweat. Her face took on a greenish hue as she felt bile rising in the back of her throat. The pitching and rolling of the ship created a malaise she had never experienced before. She felt dizzy and tried to rise to change her position, but the chains that bound her to the boy were too heavy for her to move.

Vomit exploded from her mouth, splattering her partner. Within minutes the sound of others retching and heaving overcame the roar of the turbulent waves whipping at the hull.

A sailor opened the cargo hatch and immediately clasped his hand over his mouth. The stench of vomit and diarrhea was overpowering. Gagging, he informed the captain, who then ordered, "Unchain the slaves and bring them back on deck."

On deck buckets of seawater cleansed his sickly cargo, but not one of them partook of the bread offered at mealtime. Drinking water mixed with wine, though, did soothe their sore throats and rehydrate their sickly souls.

The *Corbitas* finally docked at the Roman stronghold. Its *cargo* was unloaded onto the ramp. Leandra's hair color, gleaming like a gold coin in the sunlight, augmented her beauty and was noticed by the Roman men as desirable.

However, judging from the frowns appearing on the faces of the

Roman slave buyers, her deformity was not appealing.

The bedraggled slaves were herded toward the slave market in the public square. Leandra had trouble keeping up. Her gait—with legs curved inward, feet apart, and knees touching—had not been problematic until today. She was in pain. "Caleb," she whispered. "My bad legs are going to give way, fall down. What should I do?"

Like Lala, the Desert Flower, this child's deformity had no explanation in her time. Ten-year-old Leandra did believe in deities, but the possibility of *you live and die, and repeat* would have seemed like nonsense to her.

Caleb's strong arms reached out to lend support. *Whack!* The whip slashed his bare skin. "No touching!" the Centurion hollered.

Leandra's heart broke. *If I hadn't asked!*

The *Corbitas's* slaves, many suffering from dysentery, were paraded with signs around their necks that advertised their virtues to prospective buyers: "Untouched Pleasure Boys." "Untouched Pleasure Girls." "Cook." "Gardener." "Apprentice Mason." Thankfully, Leandra was to be spared the reality many of the slaves her age were faced with, sexual activity. This harsh subsistence was an inevitable fate for the unfortunate African children being sold at the market that day.

Leandra was bought by a wealthy and powerful Roman businessman named Tiberius Vinicianus, who had outbid numerous potential buyers for this girl's innocent flesh.

During this era, slaves represented the lowest class of society. Often, freed animals had more rights. So Leandra was fortunate. Her ownership would not include depravity, for the moment. To the contrary, she was not being mistreated in any way. She began her dutiful servitude laboring in a workshop making leather goods, articles of silver, and pots and pans. However, she was presented the same warning in this workplace that her biological mother had been given in Egypt: "You will do precisely as you are told, or punishment will follow in the form of a whipping. Many of her coworkers did try to escape, but Leandra had witnessed the executions of runaway slaves in Egypt, and she knew it would be no different in Rome.

Living with 400 other slaves was not idyllic, but tolerable. Now twelve-years-old, Leandra worked hard, learned Latin, and helped those who could not read or write. Tiberius soon learned of Leandra's advanced scholarly talents and summoned her. "I'm informed of your teachings to my other servants. Where did you gain such education?"

Leandra lowered her eyes at the sight of the overweight man with scythe-shaped eyebrows, an imperious Roman nose, and half-dome cheekbones sitting above a square jaw.

"My mother, Arsinoe, a royal princess in the Ptolemy palace, was my tutor, Honorable Lord," she answered respectfully.

Amused laughter peeled from his fat lips. "What tall stories do you tell?"

"Honorable Lord, it is the truth," Leandra countered.

Entertained by this girl's tale, he urged, "Go on."

When Leandra had finished telling her life story, Tiberius no longer responded with hilarity. "Come with me," he commanded.

Leandra dutifully walked behind her owner until they reached his private quarters. She couldn't believe her eyes. Never had she seen such a rich collection of books. There had been an extensive library in the Egyptian palace, but nothing as impressive as this.

Tiberius patted Leandra's shoulder. "You have my permission to come here after your work and read them all if you wish," he offered.

Leandra rushed to his side and kissed his hand. "Thank you, thank you," she gushed.

The truism "Knowledge is power" never occurred to this generous slave owner.

Leandra found peace from her daily hardships in her owner's massive library. She hungrily read many fascinating volumes: classical studies, epigraphy, history, Roman technology, Greek mythology, and sociology. Having been provided paper from marsh papyrus, pen, and ink, she wrote in her beautiful handwriting many comments about contradictions she discovered.

Lala's gift of beautiful handwriting was continuing in Leandra's incarnation. But, tragically, Leandra would not be spared from Rebekah bas Sora's karmic debt.

On her fifteenth birthday, Leandra was summoned by Tiberius.

With a swish of her tunic, Leandra raced from her workplace. On the way to her master's villa, negative thoughts surfaced *Have I done something wrong? Did I not return his books to their proper order?*

When she arrived, Tiberius came straight to the point. "You're to no longer to work in my shop. Instead, you will join my other mistresses here in my villa."

Leandra's brows rose and curved like church arches. In her own time, she had embraced the Jewish religion, and she had learned from its teachings of the male practice of keeping concubines in addition to wives. Leandra knew she would never receive a legal marriage contract, and her body began to shudder from the inside out. The grotesque vision of bedding this obese man made her stomach heave. And she already had a crush on a boy.

A year earlier, Leandra was working hard when she got a prickly feeling that someone was watching her. When she turned and glanced at the newcomer in the workshop, an adolescent boy, his ebony eyes were still on her. Although she received attention from other males working with her, this felt different!

The thirteen-year-old enslaved Arabian boy was tall, had a chiseled jaw, and smooth dark features. His shimmering black hair highlighted his charismatic presence. In Leandra's mind, the adolescent was the most *man-pretty* person in their group. She wasn't aware yet that he was her biggest admirer.

The boy sidled up to her and introduced himself. "Hello, beautiful girl. My name is Harun al Rashid. What's your name?"

Reacting shyly, Leandra blushed. No one had ever called her beautiful. She had always had a negative body image. She believed she was ugly, with her cheek blemish the color of soot, and her freakish, bowlegged deformity.

In the following days, Leandra sacrificed her library visits to be with her companion, who pushed all the right buttons. He was powerfully attractive, fun loving, and thought little of their age difference, he being two years younger. Harun made her feel like the princess she once was! Leandra had a crush. She was smitten with the boy. He had captivated her.

One day, out of the blue, the besotted Harun declared his intentions. "I'm going to marry you one day, my Princess. I'm going to take you away from here. We'll return to my country and live happily."

Leandra jokingly responded, "I'm a Jew, and you're an Arab! But somehow, we'll make it work."

Leandra was physically drawn. Her sexual feelings were aroused. She daydreamed about her marriage to Harun and of saving herself for him.

Tiberius continued bluntly. "My wife has given me only one son during our marriage. I know you may not understand this, but I must increase my prestige by producing more children. Your ripe young body is what I need."

A shaky hand clamped her mouth. Panicked, Leandra couldn't

concentrate. *Breathe. Breathe.* Then, in an angry attitude, she protested. "You've over 100 attractive women slaves to choose from. Why me? What if my ugliness is passed onto your child?"

Tiberius threw a lavish banquet for his new bride. Well known for his sensuous feasts, he was congratulated by all his guests, except for his first wife, Flaviana. The hatred in her eyes was evident.

The next day Leandra wanted to end her life, never again to be subjected to another night of wanton lust by a dirty old man.

At Tiberius's death, thirty-five years later, his wife, Flaviana, sold the childless Leandra to a whorehouse to be used for the pleasure of Centurions. Feeling helpless, wishing for a future that could never be, Leandra endured her lot in life. She wrote her sorrows on parchment, and the paper was stained with her tears as she scribed, "Harun, you will never vacate my broken heart. I feel strongly that one day, maybe at another time, we will be reunited as husband and wife."

Leandra never saw Harun again. She later learned that he had been sold to a Phoenician shipbuilder. At age forty he had sailed with his maritime owner, importing wool to trading ports along the Arabian peninsula. When the ship had docked at the busy port of Aden, Harun had taken the opportunity to escape. He had hidden behind bales of wool that had been offloaded onto the ramp, waited until dark, and fled. Disguised in women's veiled clothing, Harun had traversed the Taurus Mountains until he finally reached Al-Malikiya, his birthplace in Syria. He never married. He lived out the rest of his life among his relatives, but he never stopped thinking of his first love, Leandra. Her name was etched with indigo dye on his forearm.

Leandra lived long enough to learn of Cleopatra's downfall and her subsequent intentional death at age thirty-nine from the poisonous bite of an asp she had smuggled into a basket of figs. The overzealous, cruel Queen had become the enemy of Rome. Her lover, Mark Anthony, also became a villain of Rome. He committed suicide by falling on his sword, stabbing himself, which was considered an honorable way for a Roman soldier to die.

Leandra's ultimate freedom came at age seventy-eight, when Germanus, first-born son to Tiberius and Flaviana, tore down the whorehouse she lived in. From that point on, Leandra witnessed many slave rebellions.

At age ninety Leandra Vinicianus set sail from Rome to Israel.

With the earnings she had *squirreled* away over time for enforced sexual services, Leandra bought a humble, renovated hilltop home on the outskirts of Jerusalem. Unbeknown to her, she had chosen the same abode in which her biological mother, Debowrah, had been born and later captured from by Ptolemy's army those many years ago.

Was it a coincidence?

At midnight, with her pet goat at her side and a raven circling overhead, Leandra died peacefully in her sleep at age 105.

CHAPTER ELEVEN

- 1478 AD -

Medieval Spain—the Spanish Inquisition

"To live is to suffer ... to survive is to find some meaning in the suffering."
—FRIEDRICH NIETZSCHE

King Ferdinand II of Aragon and his wife, Queen Isabella—referred to as *La Católica*, a title given to her by the Spanish Pope, Alexander VI—were the central religious influence during their reign. They chose Catholicism to unite Spain. Because they were devoutly Catholic, they reasoned their best approach was to rid their country of anyone who was not, or at least urge them to convert. Thus began the process of *purification*—the brutal forcing of homogenization—the driving out of Jews and nonbelievers. The Crown ordered all Spanish Jews to convert to Christianity or face expulsion, or worse. The Jews who refused were expelled, and those who hid from persecution lived double lives. Such was the case of Maimon de Spinoza, his wife, Palomba, and their ten-year-old daughter, Laurencia.

Maimon, an educated man, served as a translator. He was fluent in both Latin and Arabic, a rare combined skill that ensured his services were coveted in Ferdinand's court. But on this day his loyalty was being questioned at the Medina de Campo Royal Palace.

"I have been informed that you are repudiating conversion to Christianity, Maimon of Andalusia. Is this correct?" Ferdinand declared.

Maimon, his head bowed, answered unflinchingly. "My King, I have served you well and have asked nothing in return, but I *cannot* betray my ancestors, whose blood runs through my veins, by denying Yahweh, the true God of the Hebrews. He is not just the God of the Jewish people but is a pantheon among many other pantheons. The prophets tell us that Yahweh is God of everything. As we both claim God's word ..."

Maimon took a deep breath before boldly hammering the message home "... is it not then that Judaism is the parent of both Christianity and Judaism?"

That statement set off the dispassionate, voluble Isabella of Castile, adorned in exquisite, luxurious apparel and dripping with rubies and diamonds. She flew into a spate of angry, retaliatory words. "You have *served* us well, Maimon of Andalusia, but I gather there is no convincing you that what you have chosen is wrong. So I will be merciful, considering your many years of service to us. You have until midnight to take your daughter and wife, whom I'm told is your first cousin, a crime against God, and leave our sovereignty. If you fail to do so, you will suffer the consequences," she ended in a threatening tone.

When Maimon returned home, he found an eviction notice on the door of his residence, which was owned by the Court. It was evident that Isabella's merciless Catholic ideology had begun setting its course and was aimed at a familiar foe.

Isabella, born in 1452 with mesmerizing blue eyes and fair hair, was the daughter of John II of Castile and his second wife, Isabella of Portugal. Their daughter's death in 1504 ended an era of brutal religious witch-hunts designed to convert the Jews and Muslims.

After fifty days of anxious prayer and religious processions, Queen Isabella called a halt to all further negotiation. She knew that she was finished and began to prepare herself for death. Bedridden in her palace in her last months—suffering from high fever, worsening dropsy, sleeplessness, and thirst—Isabella was no longer able to cope with State affairs. She signed her will, a lengthy document in which she declared that her mind was healthy and free.

But Isabella did not die peacefully. She feared the same vengeance the Devil has for his minions—Muslims, Jews, and heretics—to whom she had never given any compassion. Isabella had been the queen of Castile and Aragon for thirty years, since 1474, and joint ruler of Castile and Aragon with her husband for twenty-five. Did she finally have misgivings about her religious intolerance? No. Nor did she express such to her confessor, Thomas de Torquemada, who had been appointed head of the Inquisition. He held a

Holy Cross out to her with the words, "Judas sold his master for thirty pieces of silver. How many will you take for this cross?"

Queen Isabella was buried in the Franciscan monastery in the Alhambra, and there Ferdinand would join her after his death in 1516.

When Maimon, bearing age wrinkles that marked his sixty-four years, returned home and broke the grim news to his wife (his first cousin) and his daughter, conceived later in life, an unruffled Palomba announced, "Pay no mind, Husband. We will leave. We will go to Barcelona, where we'll be safe from this lunacy."

That same night the Ashkenazi family snuck out of the court-owned home under a moonless sky. They departed with only the clothes on their backs—laborers' attire. Hurriedly hand sewn by Palomba, these modest tunics—made for the three of them from undyed wool—and hemp bonnets—made for mother and daughter—were designed to help them blend in with the peasantry. Simple leather shoes with rounded toes accentuated their disguise. They left behind their fancy linen undergarments, as only the affluent could afford such luxury. Now, dressed as the lower class, they had a chance at freedom.

The displaced Hebrews from the Kingdom of Castile traveled by night on donkeys (horses were only for nobles). By day, they rested under leafy groves of umbrella pines replete with large cones.

Days later, unaware that thieves and murderers roamed the area where they slept under thick, concealing foliage, the family was oblivious to the two men secretly assessing them.

Garbed in long, thick, brown cloaks and close-fitting clerical hoods, the strangers stood silent for a moment. Then the more slender of the two coughed loudly, which prompted the family's eyes to open.

Bolting upright, Maimon was the first to speak. "Who are you, and what do you want?" When he spotted a knife raised and ready to strike, he said in a calm, passive voice that defied his quaking insides, "Why are you brandishing a knife? Do you intend to do us harm?"

Corvalán, the portly leader, retorted aggressively, "Hand over your valuables or suffer the steel of my blade!"

"Surely," responded Maimon, "you speak madly. We are poor laborers from the City of Castile. We have nothing but the clothes on our backs, a couple of donkeys, and little food."

Laurencia, highly intelligent, perceived something that forced her brows to crease. Something about this man's speech didn't sit right with her. Real clergymen had command of the Latin language.

Laurencia rose up and released herself from her mother's tight embrace. She pointed a challenging finger at the intruders and hollered with raging wolf eyes, "Leave us alone, bad men. My father has told you …" the girl inhaled sharply with indignity, "… we have nothing for you!"

The slender villain darted forward, grasped Laurencia's arm fiercely with his left hand and wielded a Moorish-looking dagger in his right. "I like a girl with spirit," he mocked. Then it will be another *virtue* that must be taken."

The no-nonsense girl savagely bit his restraining hand.

Her aggressor backhanded Laurencia to the ground then lifted his monk's habit, exposing his genitals.

Fearing acute panic at the imminent rape of his daughter, Maimon reached for the money hidden under the belt of his tunic. "Here is what you seek," he shouted. "Take it and leave my daughter alone."

The robbers began to argue.

"Grab the stuff and let's be gone," Corvalán urged his partner, who was busy raising Laurencia's garment above her waist.

"We will leave when I have had my way," the other announced.

"Are you mad?" growled Corvalán. "Can't you see the witch has the black mark of Satan on her face? She is *cursed!* Do you wish for this spell to follow you to the end of your days if your seed is left in her?"

The would-be rapist stared at the black, oval blemish on Laurencia's face, then sprung away. He made the sign of the cross and snarled, "You will burn one day, you witch of evil, mark my words!"

"You Jews will pay the price when I tell where you are hiding," Corvalán sneered. "Did you think I didn't know? I realized the minute I came across you that you were runaway Jews hiding secret wealth!"

With that said, the thieves swiftly departed with their spoils, including the donkeys, leaving trails of dust behind them.

When the men were out of sight, Maimon raised his hands in the air and again questioned God. "Why have you forsaken us? We could have been killed, and, worse, my innocent daughter could have been ravaged." While Palomba had no words to add to her husband's pleas, her thoughts raced. *How can we continue our travels when we no longer have transport or money to buy food or shelter in Barcelona?*

Maimon read her mind. "God has not forsaken us, Wife. He will provide."

Laurencia's expression could have knocked him down dead if he had seen it. But her pious mother nodded in agreement.

The fugitives begged food along their way, rested under bushes, and finally reached Barcelona after traveling on foot for forty days.

Though weary and worn, they gazed in awe at the majestic, imposing cathedral of Santiago de Compostela, with its twin towers and Baroque façade. The family had seen nothing like it in Castile. Maimon observed that new construction on one of the faces was underway. Workers were busily moving to and fro bearing large stone slabs, and what looked like bags of dirt. Maimon turned to his family. "All is not lost. I will ask for work."

"Father, you can't be serious. It's not right," Laurencia stated. "It is a *Catholic* place of worship. Hasn't this deity taken enough from us?"

"Daughter," Palomba interjected, "be reasonable. We have no money. We will starve to death without food. Your father is right. He must find work with them but not worship their God."

"You are *too* old," was the deflating response given by Atiq, the artisan in charge of the cathedral renovations. "If you have young sons, *they* can work, but I fear you will not last a day at your age." Observing Maimon's long, drawn, helpless face, he added, "You could search out farmers. Many farms surrounding this city may need an extra hand."

Maimon protested. "I'm strong, have many years left in me to work hard. Please, I need to work to feed my family."

"Begone, old man," Atiq said in a gentle tone. "I cannot hire a man who will fall dead on me."

"Please, we have not eaten for several days," Maimon pleaded.

"You are a believer in our faith, yes?"

"Yes, yes, yes," Maimon glibly replied, hoping for a change of heart. A concern sprung up at the back of his mind. *What if he asks me to quote from their holy books?*

Atiq shook his head doubtfully. He had a strong suspicion that Maimon had not spoken the truth. Now, with apparent distrust, Atiq queried, "Where are you from?"

"The City of Castile," Maimon answered truthfully.

"What brings you and your family so far?"

With his conscience weighing heavily, Maimon sighed. He could no longer hide the truth. "We are Hebrews fleeing from persecution. I was told that here in Barcelona we could find freedom."

Atiq scoffed. "No one is *free* if you are not of the Catholic faith. But you will be treated less harshly if you do convert to Christianity."

"I can't do that, betray the only true God of the Hebrews."

Atiq warned, "Then, Hebrew, you will be hunted down by the monarchs who rule this country."

Tears spilled down Maimon's dusky cheeks. "I know that, but for the time being, me and my family need to survive."

The Moor's heart filled with empathy. "You will work from dawn to dusk for only food and shelter. And be warned, slaves here are not protected by the law, so if you displease me, you'll be punished."

"Thank you, Your Lordship," Maimon responded in a grateful voice.

A broad smile creased Atiq's dark lips. Straightening a brimless felt hat that was shaped like an ice cream cone, the foreman admitted, "I'm not a noble and never will be. I'm a slave, just like you. My Muslim family have been slaves since they were overthrown by the Spanish armies. You will address me by my Muslim name, Atiq."

"Thank you, Atiq," Maimon said. "May I ask if you converted?"

"Yes ... and no," he replied with a dispirited expression. "Yes, I became a Christian to survive. No, I do not believe in their faith. I practice the teachings of Allah behind closed doors. So we both have secrets to share and protect."

Maimon quickly made his way to the river, where his wife and daughter were washing clothes. "We are saved," he announced happily. "I've obtained work, shelter, and food, but, alas, no money. The artisan, Atiq, has given me free lodging, but he would not allow anyone else to stay at the workhouse."

Palomba's eyes grew wide. Was this the husband who had vowed to take care of her and Laurencia? "How are we to survive without money to buy food or lodging?"

"Don't fret, Wife," Maimon consoled. "I will bring you both my food every day, and you can remain here by the river until we can all be together again."

Palomba flung her arms around her beloved spouse. "Oh, Husband, you will not survive hard labor without a morsel to sustain you. I will find cleaning, washing, or any other work to feed Laurencia and me. And you will take whatever is offered you."

"I'll work with you, Mother," added Laurencia. "Don't worry, Father. Everything will work out in the end. I just feel it."

Maimon, with a hurting heart, hugged his family and returned to the workhouse.

Not far from the river, a converted Hebrew farmer took pity on the mother and daughter and let them sleep in an abandoned goat shed. The widower was kind to them, supplying food, as well as materials to make better clothing. The women repaid his generosity by cooking, cleaning, tending his sheep, and planting his gardens.

Maimon visited his family as often as his work schedule allowed.

Suddenly, their simple, pleasant lifestyle came crashing down around them.

The kindly old farmer was found lying dead among the prickly thistles of an artichoke patch.

After the farmer's son ousted them from his newly acquired farm, Palomba and Laurencia were back on the streets again.

"Be gone with you, dirty Jews," was the man's pitiless parting statement.

Maimon begged Atiq to allow them all to stay in the stone warehouse, out of sight. But Atiq's position was clear. "Your womenfolk won't stand a chance with the male workers. They will be violated. Neither you nor I can protect them without bringing attention to your Jewish origin. No. I'm sorry. You cannot stay here. And if Bishop Domenico were to find out, we would all be doomed to the fires."

Was this family already ill-fated?

"... *Any other than kin ...*"

The ancestral curse flowed through the veins of this rebirthed family, never to be set free ... until God decided to free them.

Soon, the radiance of a second chance would course through a tunnel of hope.

Domenico de Molina—a middle-aged, short, portly, bishop— was influential with the nobility. He collected the church taxes and was put in charge of the new building extensions of the Santiago de Compostela. He appeared to be a kind, jovial man but hid a dark secret—his lust for young boys.

One day the holy man spotted the eleven-year-old, five-foot-six Laurencia at a nearby fountain. She was wearing boy's clothing. With his robe trailing on the ground, he asked in a voice that could melt butter, "What ails you, boy? Why do you cry?"

Laurencia instantly thought of correcting his perception of her sex, but she held her tongue. Internally, though, her mind screamed,

Boy? Domenico's gender confusion gave Laurencia food for thought. Daily she had witnessed boys being hired to labor on the cathedral extension. Could this ruse work? She had to try. In a voice that was barely a whisper, she answered him. "I weep, Your Lordship because I am hungry and cannot find work."

The bishop patted Laurencia's shoulder. "We can remedy that. What is your name?"

"Maimon, "she said without blinking an eye.

"Then follow me, young Maimon. I will give you food, and then you can start working for me. Would this end your sadness?"

"Yes, indeed, Your Lordship. May God bless you," Laurencia intoned, trying to sound sincere.

The holy man smiled. "Bishop Domenico is my title, boy. You are in good hands, God's hands now. All will be well."

Laurencia followed him into the church, trying not to let her disability give her away. Born with muscle weakness in both legs, her gait was an uneven step-and-a-half. Domenico handed her a loaf of bread and some olives. "Eat boy," he instructed. "You are going to need nourishment to undergo the demanding work that awaits you. Now, I have a pressing matter to attend to, so I will leave you momentarily, but I will return soon.

Laurencia waited and watched until the fat man was out of sight, then she fled the vestry. She rushed back to her mother and father. Laurencia handed over her food and told her mother that she had been offered work. She omitted that it was under the pretense of gender.

But it was what her mother said next that triggered Laurencia's squint.

"This is the blessing we have been waiting for," Palomba said. "Become one of them, if you must, and worship their God, and know that we will not suffer if food and wages are given to you."

Laurencia had a caring heart, but what was being asked of her caused her alarm. If she were discovered, what would happen? Would she hang from a beam, as she had witnessed with others who had *duped* the mighty Catholic Church?

Was God frowning at the audacity of this desperate Jewish girl?

Did she care? No, because it was dog eat dog in these cruel and heartless times. Simple survival was foremost in her mind. The well-being of her aging parents was utmost.

With her long blond hair shorn into a boy's hairstyle, Laurencia was put to work scraping trenches by hand for the new stone foundation. Blood dripped from her hands as she worked from dawn to dusk for food and a pittance, which she handed over to her parents. Laurencia's emaciated frame soon came to the attention of her foreman. "Boy, you are way too thin," the craftsman remarked. "You will be provided with extra bread to fatten you up, or we will be burying just bones."

Laurencia smiled happily. *Now I can partake of some life-sustaining meals and not feel so morally obliged to feed my parents.*

In the days and months that followed, Laurencia became well liked by her unsuspecting coworkers. One boy took a particular interest in her: "A few of us are going to the Festival of Santa Maria on Sunday. Would you like to join us?"

Laurencia politely refused, "No, thank you. I have other plans."

"But you must," Francisco insisted. "It is the only day we have off. You can eat as much as your stomach can hold. The pilgrims from other parts bring lots of food to give to the poor. And ..." he said smiling, "... *money* is cast at the feet of the statue of the Virgin Mary."

That piqued her interest. Her father was emaciated and sickly. But it was her mother who raised the most concern.

On her last visit to her parents, Laurencia had noticed her mother's eyes were drawn and watery. And her rattling cough and green sputum were worrisome to the teenager. Palomba complained of pain in her chest and a bad taste in her mouth. She had no energy and no appetite. The thought of buying medicine for her mother was paramount in the girl's mind. So she accepted the boy's request. "Yes, I would love to join you."

The winter religious festival wasn't to Laurencia's liking but dashing to collect tossed coins while unobserved was thrilling. At the end of the day, with her pockets full of small coinage, Laurencia's eyes moistened when Francisco handed her his coins. "This is for your mother's medicine," the orphan boy stated with a caring, loving smile.

"I can't take this," Laurencia protested. "You can buy anything you like from the market. No, I insist. Keep it."

"What are brothers for but to help one another?" Francisco demurred.

Laurencia wanted to confess that she was a *girl* and would love him forever. Instead, with a sigh of gratitude, she took the proffered coins and added them to her horde.

The following day, after much exertion and toil, Laurencia discreetly sought out a Moor medicine woman. The happy *boy* bought the decongestants she hoped would loosen her mother's chestiness. With the precious herbs wrapped in cloth and tucked under her arm, Laurencia hurried to the abandoned animal shelter that was her parents' home and was met by a weeping Maimon. "Father, whatever is the matter? Have you lost your work? Is mother all right?"

"No, child. Your mother died in the night," Maimon sputtered, trying to control his sobbing. "I held her as she took her last breath. Now I must find work to give her a respectful burial."

Lost for words, Laurencia stared at her mother, now stiff with rigor mortis. Tears gushed as her shrill cries burst through the rafters of the old shed. "No, no, no!" *I was too late! If only the festival had been a few days earlier!* Laurencia turned on her heels and fled from the abode toward the underground herb dispensary.

There, a tearful Laurencia begged for a refund. The compassionate healer did not hesitate as she sadly passed the money over. She placed a few extra coins into Laurencia's hands, saying, "I'm so sorry for your loss, son. Your mother is with Jesus Christ now!"

Laurencia scowled as she left the woman's premises.

A dutiful Laurencia handed the money to her father, saying, "I hope it's enough."

"My precious daughter, your mother, will have a decent burial."

The following day Palomba's body was gently placed in a plain coffin, covered with leather, and tied with cords. A small metal cross was set on the lid, but when out of sight of the coffin maker, Maimon discarded the Catholic artifact and replaced it with a menorah he'd fashioned from sticks. Later, with Atiq's help, the coffin was carried through torrents of rain to the outskirts of Barcelona, where the only Jewish cemetery was located.

The day of the burial Laurencia and her father left Barcelona and headed for the City of Seville, where they were told life would be better for them. However, after months of near starvation there, they returned to Barcelona hoping that Laurencia could regain her work at the cathedral and keep them both alive. Laurencia was not happy about her father's decision to return, but she dutifully agreed. She loved him dearly and would have done anything to see him smile again. Back in Barcelona, she wanted to reunite with Francisco. She had never wished to bid farewell to him.

"God is in no hurry, boy," Bishop Domenico commented to Laurencia. "He is happy to have you back. Your hard work will be rewarded in heaven, once his cathedral is finished."

Laurencia would not see the finished church in her lifetime. Nor would her father. The Roman Catholic Basilica of Las de la Sagrada Familia remains unfinished to this day.

Much to Bishop Domenico's delight, his potential "victim" was back. His sexual advances were frequent, but, so far, the shrewd Laurencia had rebuffed them. "I love a servant, Your Holiness. We are to marry one day."

This disclosure didn't prevent the pervert from trying. At every available opportunity, Domenico came to her workplace. Laurencia avoided conversation with him and used a litany of excuses about not being distracted from her work—God's work!

One day Laurencia heard sounds of distress coming from the vestry. She opened the door and saw her friend Francisco bound to a chair, his buttocks exposed, and Bishop Domenico sodomizing him. "Get off him," Laurencia shrieked. "Untie him now, or I will run to the Archbishop's home and let him know what I have seen."

Laurencia saw the rage in his eyes. The bishop picked a double-edged broadsword from a marble counter, and menacingly approached her. She tried to duck, but the sharp blade made a forceful impact. Blood spurted from the deep slash to her face. Her cries of pain echoed out as Francisco broke free and knocked the depraved bishop off his feet. Out of control, the defiled young man snatched the sword out of the prelate's hand and began stabbing the holy demon in the groin, stomach, chest, and head. Finally, Francisco raised the weapon and plunged the point directly into the bishop's heart. The sound of Domenico's death gurgles and the sight of copious amounts of blood pooling around his prostrate body brought the stunned and injured Laurencia back to reality. She clasped her hands over her mouth to stifle her screams. Francisco did not give her time to think further. Gripping her trembling hand, they both fled through the rear door of the vestry and into the open air. Workers gawked at the bloodied pair exiting the vestry. Despite muscle weakness, Laurencia kept up with Francisco as they bolted like hunted animals.

Moments later, loud wails erupted from the vestry. "They have killed the Bishop!" a stone worker yelled.

"Who are *they*?" inquired a stunned priest.

"Francisco and the new boy the Bishop hired," the witness replied.

The two fugitives were caught on a trading boat as they were attempting to leave Spain and head to Africa. Francisco immediately confessed. "I alone murdered the filthy bastard. Maimon had nothing to do with it."

Previously, on their flight to the docks, Laurencia had disclosed her true gender. To her surprise, Francisco had responded, "I've known all along that you are a girl, but I didn't wish to slip up when we worked together. Know that I have loved you from the moment we met."

Laurencia had cried tears of relief. "I love you, too, Francisco. When we are free in Africa, we will marry."

There proposed life together was not to be.

Francisco was tortured and hanged that same day.

His decomposing body dangled in the town square for fourteen days before it was removed and left on the street for the scavengers to feast on.

Following her capture, Laurencia was taken to prison. There it was discovered that she was a girl. She was tortured into admitting that she was of Jewish faith. Bound in chains, she was paraded through the streets of Barcelona with a sign around her neck: SATAN'S WITCH MAIDEN WHO HAS FALSELY MASQUERADED AS A BOY.

Laurencia walked through an angry mob of spectators. They mocked the desolate girl with hatred, ridicule, scorn, and laughter. They hurled rotten tomatoes at her. "Burn the witch!" a group shouted in unison.

"His Excellency, the Grand Inquisitor, will do just that," another person voiced.

Laurencia was none the wiser about to whom they were referring. Only later would she come face to face with the most feared man in the land: Thomàs de Torquemada, the Grand Inquisitor appointed by King Ferdinand and Queen Isabella.

Thomàs was the most intolerant man in an age of intolerance. But far worse, he was a sadist who became sexually aroused during his brutal torture sessions. A Jew by birth, born into a family of converts, Thomàs had turned most of his fury against the Jews. Laurencia was one such unfortunate victim.

Inwardly Laurencia cried for her father. Unknown to her, Maimon had returned to Palomba's gravesite when Laurencia had returned to work. There, he neither drank water nor partook of food. He survived for five days.

Dragged into the Inquisitor's presence, Laurencia stared at the bulbous man attired in black. A massive silver crucifix hung at his waist and sparkled in the candlelight.

Thomàs's interrogation began.

"Do you confess that you are a Jew?" he demanded.

"No, I cannot. I'm a good Catholic," Laurencia piously returned, her knees trembling.

"Liar," Thomàs spat. "You are the personification of evil and the enemy of the true God and humankind. Confess and repent your sins! Plead guilty, and you will be spared the torture that waits should you fail to do so."

The brutal interrogation lasted four hours.

A mentally exhausted Laurencia pleaded, "For Christ's sake, show mercy!"

The Inquisitor's cheeks flushed crimson. "Do not mock Christ with your lies, Jew girl," he growled. "You will now suffer His wrath." He turned to his fellow torturers. "Take her away."

Laurencia was forcibly dragged to a dank dungeon. There she was hung by her arms until they were pulled from their sockets. Later, her cruel interrogator appeared, lifted his silver cross, and placed it on Laurencia's forehead. "In the name of Jesus Christ, do you confess to heresy?"

A weak reply surfaced. "I have nothing to confess."

Laurencia's head was held in a fierce grip by one of Thomàs's henchmen while she was forced to swallow copious quantities of water, almost to the point of drowning.

"Do you confess?" demanded her tormentor.

Swaying in and out of consciousness, Laurencia's waterlogged larynx remained silent. Thomàs wasn't finished with his victim. "You, witch, bear the mark of a demon on your cheek. In the name of Jesus Christ, I condemn you to the fires of hell."

Undoubtedly, the fires of hell would burn most brightly when they eventually received the souls of the most evil men in Spain.

The next morning, wearing a new placard around her neck—HERETIC JEW WITCH MAIDEN—Laurencia, with a sword wound visible, was again paraded through the streets, this time to a square where a wood pyre was being prepared. The fire, as ordered by Thomàs Torquemada, was to be small and burn lazily.

Laurencia was clothed in an undyed linen dress smeared with pine pitch (a runny, clear tar-like resin), which was intended to burn slowly. Her arms and legs were bound tightly, and she was secured in the pyre. Several torches were lit.

As the flames rose and the red-hot embers flew skyward, the bloodthirsty Christian observers cheered. Laurencia screamed as descending embers burned her like thousands of sharp needles stabbing her flesh. Laurencia begged for a quick and merciful end. "Oh, God of the Hebrews, help me. Help me!"

Thomàs Torquemada shoved his crucifix, now mounted on a long pole, into the face of the sixteen-year-old. "Repent, Jew girl."

Mercifully, Laurencia lost consciousness, and her brain shut off her pain receptors. She suffered for some minutes before her lungs were seared by the extreme heat. The agonizing pain suddenly ended for this disabled girl, who would never marry, have children, or enjoy a ripe old age. Her young life had been meaningless.

Neither fire nor wind, birth nor death can erase virtuous deeds … but a *curse* can!

↜↝

Historical fact: This inhumane method of execution by fire—purportedly by God's will—was performed by religious fanatics of the Roman Catholic faith beginning in 123 A.D. and ending in 1826.

CHAPTER TWELVE

- 793 A.D. -

The Kingdom of Northumbria, England

"The inherited sins of our ancestors dwell not as a lodger for one night, but dwelleth forever."
—ANONYMOUS

The spring rain glistened like angel's tears on the rock-hard earth of winter past. This brought joy to childhood sweethearts, Lyveva, and Raziel. It was grazing and planting time. These descendants of a monotheistic Semitic tribe from the Middle East—companions for thirteen years—were born and raised in the northeast coast of Anglo-Saxon England. Their parents, not permitted to own land, leased a small farmstead on Insula Sacra, the Holy Island of Lindisfarne, inhabited by Benedictine monks. Jews and gentiles lived side by side on this 400-hectares settlement. A few of the Jewish families had converted to English Christianity, but not

Lyveva's or Raziel's parents. They practiced their Judaism secretly.

The Lindisfarne monastery, founded by the Irish monk Saint Aidan, was built in 635 A.D. The stone building, with its rainbow arch, was flanked on either side by soaring turrets with cross-shaped arrow loops. An adjacent stone building provided living quarters for thirty of the holy men. On this glorious spring day, the outer courtyard, the gateway to both the church and the living quarters, reverberated with unholy footsteps. For the monks, and even more so for Lyveva, it would be the darkest day ever.

Lyveva's long blond hair bobbed down her back as she herded cows through centuries-old sprawling trees to an embankment overlooking the North Sea. Grass shoots were plentiful there for munching. Her lovely singing voice stilled as soon as she spotted some unfamiliar images.

The onslaught had already begun. No one saw it coming.

Sailing at high tide were longboats adorned with blood-red sails and pole masts as tall as yew trees. Many oars protruded from their sides. Lyveva's blood ran cold. The omen of foreboding that had woken her in a cold sweat this morning served as a portent of evil. The teenager did not linger to affirm her premonition.

Rapidly and in fright, Lyveva pulled up her long linen pinafore dress to waist level and fled on two feet that pointed inward, pigeon-toed. She had not outgrown this deformity. Lyveva's mother had tried to rectify her walking problem when she was two by bracing her daughter's feet with strips of leather, but the rebirth curse had triumphed. All the same, Lyveva's malformed feet did not prevent her from running faster than ever on this day.

All four of her bovine charges turned their heads as if their herder had lost control of her senses.

On reaching her one-bedroom home, Lyveva burst open the door. Hyperventilating, she wheezed incoherently. "Mother, father, *bad* men are coming. We have to hide!"

Lyveva's elderly mother ceased her spinning. Lyveva's father put down the stone he was using to sharpen a knife and frowned. "Child, what are you babbling about?"

"I saw them!" blurted Lyveva. "Men, with long, bushy beards, painted faces, and horns on their heads, like Balaam, the wicked, the evil counselor from the Torah."

Lyveva's father closed his eyes. His only child had demonstrated a vivid imagination ever since she could talk. He considered her previous ramblings. 'Last night in my dreams, I saw a *shakhor* (black) little girl who had broken legs and could not walk. I saw a Hebrew woman named Rebekah, who stepped into deep water and never returned. At this water source, I saw a massive animal with humps on its back that stood as tall as the sky. I saw strange-looking fruit hanging from trees, and a little boy, as dark as burned wood, wearing a strange hat. He was holding the hand of the girl who could not walk. In a dream, I saw this same girl. Her eyes were painted black and gold. I saw her bound at the wrists, being taken from her home on a sailing vessel. Then I saw *myself* with the same birthmark on my face, as these other girls.

Lyveva's parents, first cousins, Abraham and Ester, sighed in unison. But it was the man of the house who put his foot down. "Daughter, you see things that aren't there. Now *go*. Return to the cows and have them home in time for milking."

Derided, Lyveva clucked her tongue and dutifully nodded. The cattle were their lifeline. Their milk, cheese, and meat paid the rent. But before she obeyed her father's wishes, she had a more pressing task at hand.

Doubted by her parents, Lyveva set off in search of Raziel. His parents told her that he had gone to look for her. "Oh, no! I hope I'm not too late!"

Her sixth sense activated, and she quickly turned heel.

Had the soul walker *tapped* into her revelations during her sleep? Was another dire foretelling in progress?" Or had the inherited bas Sora curse reared its cruel head once more?

"None of you shall approach to any that is near to kin to him, to uncover their nakedness."

Not far from the grazing cows, Lyveva halted. The hairs on the back of her neck bristled. Her bronze complexion paled as her adrenalin-driven legs took flight. Eyes wide with fear, she crouched behind the thick trunk of a nearby tree, scared rigid at the sight unfolding. Lyveva watched face-dyed "pirates" wearing long garments, fur-trimmed cloaks, leather boots, and horned headgear disembark. With loud battle-cry shouts in accents as thick as the low-lying storm clouds, these marauders raised long spears and axes and assailed the monastery courtyard. The speed of this attack highlighted their plan. Their strategy was to arrive without warning, loot anything they could get their hands on, and fast. A desire for wealth and social status were the primary motivations behind this raid on English soil. The pagans saw the isolated monastery as an easy target, rich with the gemstones of holy objects.

In times to come, the seagoing pagans, these pirates of the oceans, would become a force to reckon with.

Inside the monastery, dumfounded Lindisfarne monks, standing at tables littered with documents, gawked at the heathens. But one young monk, Berinon (meaning *noble stone*) was brave enough to voice, "Mercy. Mercy! Please don't kill us. Take what you have come for and leave."

A peal of insidious laughter rebounded around the ancient stone walls. "We intend to do just that!"

The monk's life was in turmoil, and no one there was going to put it right!

Berinon was born to impoverished Northhumbrian parents, who could not afford to raise their eighth child. At age five he was handed over to the monastery at Lindisfarne. Eventually, Berinon found happiness, freedom, and joy in serving the Father of his adopted church—Saint Cuthbert. He learned to forget his parents and older brothers and sisters and devoted his life to Christianity. Living at the monastery saved his life in many ways. But, alas, this was not the case for his kin.

Inadequate nutrition and poor hygiene opened the door to typhoid fever. Berinon's parents and siblings died from the disease two years after he arrived at the monastery. The home Berinon was born in was burned to the ground, as were the other dwellings that sheltered people who suffered from this deadly infectious disease.

Upon hearing the tragic news, the grief-stricken child did not return to his previous home. Instead, he said his sad farewells in the seclusion of the monastery chapel.

The warlord Harald Gormsson, King of Denmark and Norway, was surprised that Berinon had pleaded to him in his own tongue. "How is it that you speak my language, monk?" he demanded.

Straightening his back with newfound composure, Berinon calmly replied, "We are encouraged to travel, to spread the word of our God. I speak many languages. But this is no longer your concern. Take our treasures and leave us in peace." Suddenly it wasn't just rich bounty that filled Harald's mind. Cunningly, he reasoned, *This monk could be an asset to future raids on locations and towns that hold great wealth. Maybe* he *is to be the treasure of all treasures.*

The Norsemen plundered the monastery's gold, silver, and other valuable treasures. They also took another highly desirable asset—Berinon. However, before the plunderers departed, they left a heinous calling card! The part of the building that housed the monks religious documentation was now showered with blood. The sole survivor of this brutal massacre was Berinon. With his hands tied behind his back and his head hanging low, he emerged from the gloom into the bright sunlight.

Still hiding behind the tree, Lyveva had heard the cries for mercy but did not know what to make of them. When the murderers emerged from the building, she saw Berinon, his brown habit spattered in blood. She put two and two together.

As her entire body shook from head to toe, Lyveva gawked.

She knew this monk well and loved him. Frequently he handed her sweet treats when she delivered the daily milk and, sometimes, her mother's healing remedies. From the time she could talk, Berinon had tutored her, teaching her Latin, history, and more. But the holy man had failed to convert her steadfast Jewish mind to Christianity. "Jesus Christ is the one and only true God," he had stated.

"No, he is not!" had been her swift reply. "You worship a fable god, but our *true* God of Judah came first!"

Still frozen behind the tree, Lyveva's confusion tumbled around in her head. *Why are they taking this Holy Man? Where are they taking him? What are they going to do to him? And if she spoke up, would they tie her up, as well? And where was Raziel?* Her musings were interrupted by loud, woeful mooing. Without further concern for her own safety, she dashed from her hiding spot toward the sound of the cows' deep distress. What she was witnessing was the nightmare of all nightmares. The plucky girl stomped over to the cow's tormentor. With quivering, angry lips, she spat, "Stop it at once! Why do you kill my cows? I will kill you if you hurt another."

The burly man, whose large chest curved outward, lowered his bloodied ax, grasped Lyveva's scrawny arm, and held it in a vice grip. His bulging, soulless eyes weighed her up and down, giving her more than the shivers.

Mesmerized by the teenager's striking amber-copper eyes, the burly one turned to his companion, who was packing chunks of cow meat into a thick, vine-braided harness. "Look what I found," Lyveva's captor boasted with pride. "This she-wolf will keep me warm in my bed at night, don't you think?"

"You're crazy!" his partner in crime replied. "She couldn't keep an insect warm. There's more meat on this blade than she has on her body."

All heads turned to the causeway.

When Harald let out a raucous command letting all know they were to make ready to sail, Rigsson lifted the screeching, struggling girl and flung her over one shoulder. A rack of fresh cow ribs lay over the other.

With a huge grin, Rigsson headed for the jetty with his most prized possession.

"Harald is not going to like this," his fellow butcher stated.

"My cousin will not say a word," Rigsson responded with a grin.

Lyveva failed to notice the decapitated Raziel, lying behind the carcass of a slaughtered cow. Earlier, her intended spouse had brazenly confronted Rigsson. "What are you doing? You have no right to kill Lyveva's cows!" The outraged teenager raised a shepherd's crook to strike Rigsson. But, tragically, in one swift blow, a broad-bladed weapon beheaded this brave boy.

With no Jewish cemetery on the island, Raziel was interred by his grieving parents outside the Christian burial grounds in an unmarked grave. The life he had dreamed of with Lyveva, to be a husband to her and a father to their children, was not to be—stolen away by cold steel.

The sturdy keel running the length of the Viking vessel made the ship steadier and stronger, better to meet the rough waters of the open ocean. This sailing vessel was the foreboding omen Lyveva's parents had dismissed so lightly. Her eyes misted with tears. "Mother, father, Raziel, my love, will I ever see you again?" she whispered to the wind.

In this new world of menacing adults, Lyveva watched the land of her birth disappear. Unable to control her overwhelming emotions, she wept. Berinon tried to soothe her broken heart. "Do not despair, Lyveva. God has other plans for you and me. He will bring us safely home when the time is right."

The crestfallen girl wasn't buying into the monk's words.

"In the meantime, we are tied up like animals ready for slaughter, just like my cows."

The monk knew her faith did not embrace his, but he gave it his best effort. "There is only *one* God. He *will* protect us."

"Then you pray to *your* God, and I will pray to mine to deliver us from Balaam, the Prince of Darkness, who lives in the hearts of these evil men." At that moment, she wished she had the strength of David, the ancient boy warrior, who defeated an enemy much stronger and meaner than himself.

As the sun crawled below the horizon, crossing the North Sea in torrential rain was too much for the Christian and the Jewish captives. They heaved and retched, much to the amusement of the sea-hardened sailors.

"What did they eat for breakfast?

"Pigs guts!" one pagan mocked.

"I'm not cleaning that up!" another said

"Our women will do it when we get back home!"

"No. The slaves should clean their own mess!" demanded a disgusted sailor.

After four days of sailing against a savage wind, the longboats arrived at Hedeby, Norway. Rigsson shoved Lyveva onto the deck ramp. She bolted. Peals of laughter rang out behind her.

"I see you are going to have your hands full, Rigsson," stated a fellow sailor.

"Good luck taming that one!" said another.

King Harald grinned. "That's if she doesn't claw your eyes out first!"

Lyveva ran headlong into Queen Astrid, who firmly grabbed the teenager. Astrid stared into the eyes that had bewitched Rigsson. "My, you are a pretty one. What beautiful eyes, and you are definitely marked by the gods!" The shield-maiden touched the dark pigmentation on Lyveva's cheek. "What's your name?" she asked.

The teenager glared at the woman, who reminded her of a sheep decked in a floor-length wool cloak.

"I see you have no tongue!" Astrid sneered. "Well, we will soon change that ..."

Harald kissed his wife on both cheeks. "I have brought you a gift."

"I see," she said, still gripping Lyveva.

"No, not *her*," Harald smiled. "She belongs to Rigsson."

"Well, we will see about that," Astrid mocked. "I want her for myself."

Berinon was brought forward, and Harald forced him to his knees. Astrid's full lips curled in scorn. "What were you thinking? I have no use for a Christian priest?"

"He is not just a priest," argued her husband. "He is a traveler, like us. He has excellent language skills and can teach our young son, Palnotoke, the ways of the world. And, Wife, this monk knows the English settlements well. He can lead us to them!"

The haughty Astrid offered no other plans.

"I want *this* girl as my personal slave," stated Astrid, gripping Lyveva's arm. The girl winced in pain. Astrid's claim to Lyveva did not sit well with the impatient Rigsson. "She is mine. I captured her!" he retorted.

"That will be the decision of King Harald," Astrid responded icily.

Harald extemporized, venting an I-do-not-wish-to-intercede sigh. "Whatever pleases you, my love?"

Muttering vulgarities, Rigsson's stomping footsteps thundered as he departed. Those who knew him well understood that this spurned man would have the last say.

That night a celebratory feast was in full swing around the firepit in the long hall. King Harald was a revered leader who had forged a reputation as an indomitable warrior. Overjoyed with his latest success, he allowed his fellow warriors to each take one item from the accumulated loot.

King Harald chose Berinon as his prize. When Harald took the monk to his home, the children mocked his tonsure (short haircut with a shaved bald spot at the back), since most people of their time wore their hair long. That same night, a delighted Rigsson received his *one* item, the five-foot-six Lyveva.

Berinon, weary from the difficult sea journey, tried to sleep atop the animal pelt laid on the floor in Harald and Astrid's log home. But he was kept awake by their noisy sexual escapades. Astrid approached the monk, who was pretending to be sleeping soundly. "Come and join us, priest." When she kicked Berinon's leg, he hastily protested. "I cannot! I have taken an oath of celibacy, and God would know of this sin."

Unaffected by the monk's pious statement, the couple continued their revelries without him. Berinon placed his hands over his ears, attempting to silence their sinful orgy.

Despite Berinon's worldliness—extensive linguistic skills, a logical mind, knowledge of the Bible—he was hopelessly innocent when dealing with other people, especially the ambitious and sexually free spirits of these pagans. Surviving in their strange, cruel world was either do-or-die for the new slaves, Berinon and Lyveva.

That same night of "take one item," Lyveva recoiled with darting eyes from the hulking six-foot-three-inch, 350-pound man. In utter fear, she backed herself against a wall thick enough to keep the abode cool in summer and stop it from freezing in winter. She glared at the man with balled fists. The tension was as thick as a dawn fog.

"Come, my lovely. Undress and lie down," Rigsson commanded, striking his strong hands on a bed covered in animal furs.

Lyveva thought hard. *This is not going to happen!*

Rigsson lunged at her, ripping her dress. He stared at her budding breasts. Mortified and terrified, Lyveva urgently covered her bareness with her hands. She had no knowledge of the desires of men. However, she had seen beasts mating. She thought her companion, Raziel, was still alive, and she piously wished to save her virginity for their marriage day.

Tears dropped from her chin. How could she avert the inevitable? She was to be ravaged against her will, and there was nothing she could do to save her virtue.

Oh, how I wish I had the strength of Goliath.

Lyveva felt the tremendous pain of forced penetration. "Mother, Mother," she cried out. "I am ruined!"

This traumatic event broke her physically and was never forgotten spiritually. It was stored forever in the timeless hippocampus of her brain.

A dawn cockerel crowed, arousing Lyveva. She sighed with relief. Her cruel abuser had left the sleeping area. Where he had gone was of little concern to the violated girl, who was left with her tortured thoughts. *Mother and father, are you grieving for my loss? Raziel, my beloved, I'm sorry. We will not know each other with the depth of marriage. I am ruined. I now belong to Balaam's devil dog! The demon has ripped the goodness in my heart, from my body.*

With a fractured heart, Lyveva wept. Her brokenness over-whelmed her, and her eyelids closed with heaviness. She slept soundly until heavy footsteps forced her awake. Rigsson entered and approached the cringing girl. "You know, I don't even know your name," he said in his native tongue. "Please, tell me so I can treat you as a respectful wife and not as my slave."

Within a couple of silent moments, Lyveva got his drift. She contemptuously bit back in Latin tongue. "As long as I live, I will *never* love you! I do not *belong* to you for the taking. I will end my life this day rather than spend another with you."

Rigsson sighed. "In time, I will learn your tongue, and you will learn mine."

Lyveva's blank expression was her response.

Lyveva's body balled up when Rigsson approached. "Don't be afraid," he said softly, placing a fur blanket around her naked body. Then, with a reassuring hand on her back, he guided Lyveva to the firepit. There, he motioned her to sit down. Lyveva remained stand-ing. She was young but not stupid. From an iron cauldron, Rigsson ladled the stew—boiled lamb bones prepared the night before—into a wooden bowl. Lyveva shook her head.

"You must eat," the burly man insisted. He broke off a chunk of bread from a crusty flat loaf and motioned her to dip it into the stew. When Lyveva refused, Rigsson again reached out. "If we don't fatten you up now, you will not make it through our frigid winter."

A clueless gaze was her only response. The frustrated man jumped to his feet and walked out. Minutes later he returned with Berinon, who cradled the crying girl in his arms. "Oh, child, my heart is heavy for the loss of your innocence to this evil. But we are slaves now, and to survive, we must obey."

Lyveva angrily retorted, "I don't want to *survive*! I wish to die, and you must help me to accomplish this."

Berinon argued vehemently. "I cannot do that. It is a sin to take your own life."

Lyveva argued, "I'm not of your faith, so how can it be a sin?"

"I'm not acquainted with your teachings in the Torah," Berinon stated, "but my religion forbids me to take part in suicide."

Rigsson's head darted from one to the other. "What does she say, monk?"

Glibly, the holy man answered. "She says that she misses her mother and father but will try to be compliant with your wishes from now on."

Rigsson beamed. "Tell her that I love her and want to marry her. I will treasure her as my own."

Berinon's sense of human decency prevented him from translating literally. Instead, he said to Lyveva, "I will try to come and see you as often as I can. Be a brave young girl."

She nodded reluctantly.

After Rigsson and Berinon left together, Lyveva's spotted a knife made from animal bone lying near the cooking pot. Her immediate thoughts were, *Can I do this? Do I have the strength? What will happen if I fail?* Her vengeful head bowed with uncertainty, but she came to the realization that there was no other way out. She imagined the sharp knife thrust into the heart of the barbarian who had ripped her from her loved ones and stolen her innocence.

But could she really murder another person? *Thou shalt not kill* echoed over and over in her fractured mind. Lyveva exhaled with finality. It was him or her! Lowering herself on the edge of the bed, she was emotionally numb. She grasped the knife, her last resort. With tears flowing, she slit her wrists. Bright red blood sprayed from her severed arteries at a rate that would kill within minutes.

Lyveva's consciousness ebbed and flowed. She experienced euphoria as endorphins were released into her bloodstream. Instinctively, her brain did everything it could to keep her alive. "Mother, Father, I am so sorry. I'm not strong enough to bear this awful weight of sorrow. Please, forgive me." She placed a bloodied hand on her chest and murmured, "Yahweh, please forgive me ..." As her consciousness faded, she entered a dream-like state. She heard *Whoosh! Whoosh!* in her ears. Glancing up, she observed a darkly hued bird the size of a large eagle swooping in her direction. As the creature approached, she noted the iridescent plumage of its expansive wingspan. Gliding overhead, the bird turned its glowing sapphire-blue gaze upon her. Then, with an echoing caw, the glorious winged creature ascended into the drifting pale-blue mist of her dreamscape. Was this a phoenix, the mythological harbinger of death and rebirth?

Death throes accompanied her strangled breath.

Unexpectedly, Berinon entered, carrying a basket of fruit. "Oh, no!" he exclaimed. "You cannot die. God has plans for you."

Lyveva now no longer had a voice to express her feelings.

The monk, his heart pounding, galvanized into action. He stripped pieces of cloth off his tunic, then wrapped the material tightly around her wrists to control the bleeding. The fabric became saturated with blood. Berinon applied pressure to the wounds and beseeched, "Almighty Father, I beg you, save this poor child's life."

Will Lyveva's death appease the Hebrew God? Will He now absolve the sinners: Rebekah, Debowrah, Palomba, and Fajcia (Lyveva's mother) for bedding their own blood?

"… Any other than kin …"

Will he accept Lyveva's suicide as reparation?

Will Berinon's Christian god forgive him when he denies his faith and converts to his captor's Paganism?

When the cows come home!

Summoned by Berinon, Astrid watched Lyveva fight for her life. "You no longer have to feel fear. You are my slave girl now. Rigsson will never touch you again. You have my word."

Lyveva eventually recovered. In no time she learned the Norse tongue, but privately she preferred to speak Latin with the monk who had saved her life. Lyveva learned from him that King Harald was preparing to set sail for his next raid and that Astrid was to accompany him. Was Rigsson going, too?

To her dismay, Lyveva learned that Rigsson would not accompany the warriors on this trip. He had an intestinal infection, dysentery, and was experiencing severe abdominal pain. Somehow Lyveva's empathy was stirred. While she could never downplay the gravity of his abuse, she still couldn't let another human being suffer.

She spent the morning gathering whatever anti-inflammatory plants she could find in this part of the world—psyllium, picrorhiza, and lady's mantle—the ones she had seen her mother collect to treat fever and diarrhea. Later she would become the essential medicine woman of this outpost. Ancient healers, like her mother, Tikva, and her mother before, had transferred their knowledge of the healing arts to future souls in their family line, but Lyveva could not have realized this.

She entered Rigsson's dwelling and announced, "I'm here to help you heal."

The speechless man swallowed the bitter medicine she offered, then stared at the girl and asked, "Why are you so good to me? I thought you hated me!"

"I do not hate *anyone!*" she replied. "You need help healing, and my mother taught me well. That's all."

Lyveva bathed him, prepared food, and cleaned the cabin.

Rigsson recovered fully, and in the days that followed, he and Lyveva were "getting along." He treated her with respect and did not push for intimacy. But he had to get something off his chest. "I am sorry I was a beast to you. I do love you, Lyveva. Would you please be my wife? I will treasure you with my own life?"

Lyveva gawked. He was the opposite of her in every way. He was her abuser, and a pagan. Even though she was disillusioned with Yahweh, she was still Jewish. And she had many traits opposite of Rigsson's. She was intelligent and learned. He was illiterate. She was gentle-hearted. He was barbarically brutish. She loved animals. He was a hunter. She was petite, and he resembled a Sasquatch.

Lyveva's next words flowed with passion, "If you love me, let me go." She paused, unsure of his reaction. "Take me back to my family the next time the ships sail for England."

"I cannot do that!" Rigsson argued. "Only warriors' and shield-maidens sail the seas, and King Harald would never allow it. He would suspect my reason for taking you with me."

Lyveva's sad heart sank. She was trapped in a world that was not hers, and she understood she would never see her family or the shores of her birthplace again.

In the end, a cruel joke of nature befell Lyveva. The proverbial falling for a bad boy and opposites attracting had the last say. *Better the devil you know than the devil you don't!*

Their wedding ceremony, sanctified by Berinon, was held in the big hall. Young Lyveva knew the chemistry necessary to carry the relationship any distance was not there, but feeling secure was crucial to her survival, and so she partnered with Rigsson. Slowly they grew closer. She taught Rigsson to read and write and identify herbal plants. He schooled her in Norse traditions and ideology. "Our Norse God, Òdin, is the god of kings and the god of war and the mentor of heroes, to whom he often gives magical gifts, like he does for you," Rigsson grinned. "He lives in Asgard," Rigsson said as he pointed skyward. "That is the home of gods. Our supreme deity is a shapeshifter, roaming the world in disguise, accompanied by a pack of wolves and ravens. He rides on the legendary eight-legged horse named Sleipnir, known for its strength, courage, and tremendous speed."

Lyveva was captivated by Rigsson's ardent storytelling but remained unconvinced. However, over time, she would struggle with her Jewish beliefs, eventually coming to doubt her faith. This would have been unthinkable a year ago.

Life carried on. One day Rigsson announced, "There is someone you should meet. I will take you to him."

Lyveva frowned. "Who is it?"

"Wait and see. You will never doubt our God again."

The sight of the ancient *seidmadhr* (Oracle) chilled Lyveva to the bone. This seven-foot seer—dressed in a long black robe, with disfigured skin—was nightmarish. She could not help but stare at the patches of dark-red leprosy scabs covering his entire face. His loss of eyebrows and eyelashes, his distorted nose and blackened lips repulsed Lyveva.

"Sit, woman," the blind man instructed. Touching Rigsson on his shoulder, the Oracle ordered, "Leave us. I wish to speak to her alone."

Lyveva's inner voice screamed, *No! No! Don't leave me with Balaam!*

The master telepath laughed. "Do not be afraid," he comforted. "I will not harm you, and I'm not Balaam!"

How did he know what I was thinking? the shaking girl wondered.

The Oracle, possessed of supernatural powers, would soon shake the fourteen-year-old to her core.

He began. "You have the black mark, a curse from ancient times for the first wrongful deed of a foremother, whose name was Rebekah bas Sora. She lay with her own brother and then took her life by drowning. Her God, your Hebrew God, cursed future generations to many rebirths, compelling reincarnations to follow in her footsteps. This punishment for wrongdoers will not end until the twenty-first century."

Lyveva's stunned thoughts queried, *Was this real or was she dreaming? This is too much to swallow!*

The Oracle droned on with additional disturbing revelations. "I see only sorrow for you, a young woman who bears this mark of punishment because your parents were blood related. Your union with Rigsson will be childless, as ordained by the higher powers. His own fate is nearing, from death in battle. He will go to Valhalla, the Hall of the Slain. But *you'll* not have entry to Òdin's Asgard. No. The flames of your Hebrew God's fires await you. But you *will* be reunited with the boy you intended to marry, Raziel, in a life to come."

Her love's name caused tears to well into Lyveva's spellbinding wolf eyes. The ancient man had revealed more than the teenager could rationally handle. In a quivering voice, she asked, "Who are you, really? And how do you know of these things?"

The Oracle sighed heavily. "I, too, am cursed, like you. I took my brother's wife to my bed when he was alive. I did not know that she would infect me, and had infected my brother, with leprosy, a contagious disease. What you see is the result of my wrongdoing," he said, placing his gnarled fingers on his face. "I begged Òdin, son of Bor and the giantess, Bestla, to take pity and heal me. I told Him I would be celibate for the rest of my life, never touch another woman again, but to no avail. For my wrongdoing, I have lived and rebirthed over

200 years, condemned to suffer in this same state."

It was too much for Lyveva. She got up from the stool and bolted from the hut straight into the arms of Rigsson. "Take me away from here," Lyveva implored. "He *is* Balaam, a dark entity, trying to trick us …"

The rattling caws of ravens winging above quickened their pace.

That night Lyveva tossed in turmoil. Did she believe the Oracle? Part of her wanted to accept this mystic man's revelations, but another part tried to dismiss it as nothing more than pagan nonsense. But then, how could he have known about her parents and her intended spouse, Raziel?

Two years later, as had been eerily foretold, Rigsson was killed in battle in Wessex, England.

King Harald continued as monarch of Hedeby until his own "temptation," the Swedish Princess Freya, appeared in an advanced state of pregnancy.

Freya and her unborn child were murdered by a vengeful Astrid.

King Harald subsequently died when he was struck in the heart by an arrow shot from the bow of Palnotoke, his only son with Astrid, who supported his scorned mother.

As foretold by the Oracle, Lyveva would eventually meet her doom.

Time passed. Lyveva, now in her late seventies, began stacking resinous firewood in the moot-house she had acquired after Rigsson's demise. Suddenly, the top layer started to shift precariously. Then an avalanche of split wood hurtled downward. With legs crushed and her safety foremost in her mind, Lyveva screamed for help. Boisterous revelries honoring returning warriors after a successful raid in England drowned out her cries. She tried and tried to escape the oppressive weight. She began heaving logs off her body the best that she could. One hit a nearby oil lamp, shattering it. Within minutes the volatile combination of dry wood and burning oil ignited.

Lyveva watched helplessly as the fire's fury consumed furs and other flammable objects. Then, a flagon of buttermilk exploded. That bomb-like sound finally brought the revelers rushing to the moot-house, but it was too late. Lyveva's charred body was all that remained of a Jewish girl who had never asked to be born.

CHAPTER THIRTEEN

- 1847-1939 -

Ireland, The British Isles

"When Melchizedek met Abraham,
Levi was still in the body of his ancestor."
—HEBREWS 7:10

It was the final day of autumn, 1847. Heavy rains fell outside the Wexford country house. The sound complimented the brush of trailing silk as a woman's bulbous skirt moved across the floor. The soft swish of satin slippers tied at the ankle with silk ribbons added to the melodic background. As Molly paced up and down her boudoir, her eyes were pinched with worry. How long could she keep up the deception? What would happen if she were to confess? Deep down, she knew the probable outcome—the end of this period of happiness.

Biting her lower lip, Molly glanced at the floor-length mirror.

Her flaming red hair, parted in the center with ringlets at each side, was fashionable for these times.

Wearing a low-cut satin gown with layers of concealed petticoats, opera-length gloves, and sparkling jewels, she mused, *How have I been so fortunate as to join the upper class?* Her marriage to the aristocratic landowner Duke James Thomas Abercan, forty years her senior, was a dream come true for a teenage orphan previously employed as an under-kitchen maid in his grand home. Molly didn't want to revisit the past, but her overflowing memory bank was unrelenting.

Molly Alice Mahoney, her baby face dusted with freckles, was born in County Cork, Ireland, in 1830. She was the first child of ten, born to dirt-poor farm laborers, tenant farmers who leased a half acre to grow the humble potato, not native to Ireland. (It is believed that Sir Walter Raleigh brought this tuber to Britain around 1570.) No one could have foreseen that this staple, which seemed to be heaven-sent, would eventually devastate the Irish economy and scatter thousands of Irish citizens around the globe.

During September 1845, blight (a plant disease) would cause the potato crops to fail and bring a six-year famine to Ireland. The Mahoney family, like many others, was dependent on this crop and suffered an abiding tragedy. The horrors of their poverty needed only a spark to explode.

Unable to pay rent to their landlord, Duke Abercan, the Mahoney family was evicted. Powerless to shelter and feed themselves, the destitute family had little option but to seek out one of many infamous workhouses of Ireland.

Four days before Christmas, a frostbite wind mercilessly assailed noses and fingertips. With their bellies rumbling in hunger, the Mahoney clan vacated their two-room stone cottage, the only home they had ever known. Mary Alice and her husband, Patrick John, were relatively young and able to suffer these hardships, but not so the most vulnerable—an eight-week-old baby and his brothers, aged four, three, two, and one. Molly, who had just turned fifteen, her sister Eileen, fourteen, and the older male siblings, equally aged apart, helped by carrying the younger children strapped to their backs. The family walked for hours until they arrived at the town of Enniscorthy. There they joined the many other pitiful souls flocked around coaches begging alms. Among them was Mary Alice, carrying in her arms the corpse of her last-born child. "Please, sir, take pity," she cried. "I need a coin to buy a coffin for my dear little son who has surrendered to the bitter cold."

An English traveler dressed in his finery threw coins to the soggy ground. Many hands grabbed at what he had tossed down. Mary Alice retrieved only two pennies, not enough to bury a child, let alone feed her crying brood.

An hour later, a few yards away from the bustle of coaches and throngs of people, a grief-stricken but stoic Patrick hand dug a three-foot square grave in the wet, spongy ground of decomposing peat. Baby Liam, wrapped in Mary's petticoat, now rested in the shadows of a foreboding brick building—the workhouse. The mother's heart-wrenching sobs drifted up into gloomy clouds that were laden with snow.

Mary dropped like a stone to the bog-sodden earth. "I am not leaving my son in this cold grave," she protested. "You might as well bury me with my precious angel, for my life is not worth living when our child is taken from us simply because we are poor."

"Come, Mother," Patrick comforted, wrapping his arms around her. "We all share the sadness of baby Liam's loss." Yet in the back of his mind, he thought, *Liam is in a better place.* He knew not to verbalize these sentiments, for they would not comfort the bereft mother. Instead, he uttered softly, "Look at the sad faces of your other children. They are too young to understand our grief. They need you. Be strong for their sakes."

Mary's wails were heartbreaking.

Molly lifted her mother from the gravesite. "I pray for your healing and peace of mind, Mother," she said softly. The girl placed the only item she possessed, a rosary given to her at her Holy Communion, atop the grave and spoke shakily. "Goodbye, little brother, we will see you again in heaven."

That afternoon a shroud of grief enveloped the Mahoney family as they headed to the entrance of the workhouse and stood in line with other unfortunate souls. This was the last resort for these miserable people, whose only crime was poverty.

Outside the high, foreboding walls of the Portumna workhouse, the most feared institution ever to be established in Ireland, the family joined the seemingly endless line that was flooding in. Crying, broken, and confused people shuffled their frozen feet forward a few steps at a time.

Finally, two hours later, the Mahoney family stood shivering in a cold, damp hallway. The master of the workhouse, a stout, unsmiling man, looked up from his paperwork. "Is this your first registration?"

Patrick nodded affirmatively.

"Then I will require your names, ages, town of birth, and religious persuasion."

Patrick responded. Their fate was heartlessly delivered. "Under the Poor Law Act, you will work for food. Children aged one year or less will stay with the mother, the rest of your family will be kept apart, both day and night with separate yards and work duties. Is this understood?" the master demanded.

At first, it was beyond Mary's ability to comprehend. Then she gasped loudly, heavy with shock. "Mother of God, have mercy," she cried. "I have just buried my baby." She gathered her youngest sons close to her. "My boys need me. They are too young to fend for themselves."

The callous master stated brashly, "Males and females are separated in this workhouse, and only infant *females*," he stressed, "may stay with you. Those are the rules."

The frantic expressions on the faces of older children painted a bleak picture, but none uttered a protesting word.

With mounting tears, Patrick spoke up, "Sir, we have fallen on hard times, but separating my family is against biblical teachings."

The master rose from his chair and made eye contact. "Are you deaf, man? I've already explained. These are the *rules* of this establishment. If you don't like them, then you are free to leave, find another workhouse. But you will meet the same conditions, I assure you," he stated without emotion. Still erect the master pushed the registration ledger forward, which none of them could read. "Now sign here if you want admittance."

A disparaged Patrick clenched his teeth. He knew he had little choice but to accept. Those who were destitute were nothing. He took the nib, dipped it in the inkwell, and made his cross. His action was followed by his wife, Mary, and the older children. The toddlers were exempt!

The unsympathetic former military man continued stonily. "Your possessions, including the clothing that you are wearing, will be placed in storage until you are able to leave. You will be given uniforms, workhouse clothing, and then you will be examined by the medical officer. If the medical officer says you are *not* harboring any disease of the body or mind, you will be put to work."

Another warden, a softer-toned man, directed them to their change booths. "Clothing is in there. Search through the pile, and I hope you all will find garments that fit you."

Concealed by dividers, the family, excluding the little ones, disrobed. Mary and her two daughters, Molly and Eileen, emerged in shapeless, ankle-length black dresses. Draped around their shoulders, threadbare paisley shawls obscured their shabby outfits. Plain cotton bonnets covered their hair. Boots, a size too large or too small, hid darned black stockings.

On the other side of the partition, Patrick and his sons fared no better: rough jackets and trousers, striped shirts, cloth caps, and previously worn boots. His smaller sons, eyes wide with fright, fled the cubicle to their mother. They implored, "Mammy, don't let them take us away."

As her tears flowed like a burst dam, Mary said the first thing that came to her mind. "Do not worry. Be good boys. Now, go with Papa. You will see me tomorrow."

A workhouse employee appeared and disengaged the clinging boys. "Come with me," he ordered.

"I love you boys, and I love you, Husband," Mary called out as her family was being led away.

"I love you, my wife and daughters," Patrick returned in a fading voice.

"We love you, too," Molly and Eileen echoed.

Those were to be the last words they would ever speak to each other.

Mary, Molly, and Eileen's sorrowful wails resonated against the grim, white-washed stone walls of this house of horrors.

Life in the workhouse was harsh and frequently cruel. There were many inhumane rules, and food was scarce. Generally, it was a mix of porridge, milk, and potato peels. Adults received two meals a day, and children three. Only the children got bread. Several hundred women and children walked in circles pushing a large corn-grinding wheel. Adult females—like Mary, Molly, and Eileen—were put to work mending clothes, spinning wool, and performing kitchen and laundry duties. The worst of their tasks was to carry corpses, without coffins, on carts outside the workhouse grounds, where they were thrown into mass burial pits. Every time Mary saw a dead body, she howled. The loss of her last-born child was imprinted deeply in her mournful mind. But the separation from Patrick and her other children is what most devoured Mary's tormented mind and soul.

One day Mary learned that her youngest boys had died from scarlet fever, the older boys from dysentery, and her loving husband from suicide. Overwrought, he had hung himself. A grieving Mary mounted the stone stairs leading to the top of the tall building and jumped to her death. Molly and Eileen were hanging laundry when they witnessed the gruesome end of their beloved mother's life. Neither girl wished to be consoled by the workhouse staff or chaplain. The last of the once-proud Mahoney family, the sisters clung to each other for emotional support during these dark, despairing times. They refused to attend the Sunday service.

Was there to be no end to this family's sorrows?

While handling garments that were removed from the dead for rewashing, Eileen, Molly's sister, eventually succumbed to the deadly scarlet fever epidemic and passed away. Molly was beside herself. "I wish the Lord had given me a clever brain. Then I could have been a fine lady doctor helping these poor people in this pit of death." But Molly's impoverished circumstances had never allowed her to walk through the necessary academic door.

❦

Molly was now an orphan. While she struggled with the loss of her entire family in under a year, Molly would not let fear prevent her from surviving this hostile place and then showing the world how shabbily so many people had been treated. Even so, part of her yearned for death, so she could join her loved ones once more.

As time passed, the workhouse conditions worsened; they became even more overcrowded as the numbers of destitute increased, showing up in droves. The living, dying, and dead were indiscriminately crowded onto the same floor, with nothing to cushion them from the cold earth save a few ragged clothes. Shortages of bedding and clothing led to the practice of collecting clothing from inmates who had died of fever or disease and giving them to new inmates arriving at the workhouse. Every day Molly was fighting to stay alive in unhygienic conditions that invited the Grim Reaper to gallop in and snatch up souls. But *he* would be thwarted. A guardian angel was watching over the last surviving member of the Mahoney family.

For how long would Molly be afforded such divine protection?

One year later, Molly was summoned to the Matron's office. "Put these on," the plump woman ordered in a guttural tone. The woman handed Molly a clean dress, stockings, bonnet, underwear, wool shawl, and shoes. Surprised, Molly gazed at the new clothing. Her parents had never been able to afford such items.

A broad smile crossed the matron's joyful face. "Molly Alice Mahoney, you are one of the lucky ones chosen by the Board of Guardians! You are leaving this place and going to Enniscorthy to become a servant of the gentry!"

Molly frowned. "I know of no such a place."

A scornful look crossed the Matron's happy face. "Ignorant girl, does it matter?" she chided. "You should get on your knees and thank Jesus for sparing you from the fate of the many who have died here, including your whole family. Now hurry. Wash and change. The carriage will be here shortly."

The road to the workhouse—known as *cosannamarbh,* pathway of the dead—a place where indescribable horrors occurred, faded into the distance. Molly could not have been more relieved. She had survived, for now.

Two hours after being informed, a horse-drawn, two-wheeled carriage entered the laneway—a bed of crushed stone worn smooth by ages of use—that led through expansive parkland to the grand mansion. Molly was awestruck. She marveled at the sight ahead, one she could never otherwise have imagined.

The stately residence, with attractive terraces descending from the southern front to the lavish lawns below, was surrounded by pristine gardens and woodlands. The house boasted seven bedrooms over three floors, two formal reception rooms, staff quarters for the servants, and an adjacent row of stables. Indeed, Molly was the lucky one. She wished her family could see her now.

But all was not as it appeared.

The cabby opened the carriage door. Molly's wavy red hair cascaded from beneath her tight-fitting bonnet. She was greeted by an elderly woman with pure white hair poking out beneath *her* hood. "You must be Molly Mahoney. Welcome to Abercan house," she greeted.

With her knees quaking, Molly managed a clumsy curtsey.

"Goodness gracious!" Coleen O'Riley laughed. "No need to bow to me. I'm just the head cook, and you'll be working for me as my assistant. Come," she said, taking Molly's shaky hand. "I'll show you to your room. You can freshen up before you join me in the kitchen. I will make you a nice cup of tea and a bite to eat."

On the way to the staff quarters, Molly was told the rules. "You will rise at five and retire for the night only after all your chores are done. You will not fraternize with any of the other staff, nor address the Duke, his family, or guests. You will be paid nine pounds a year, and if you break anything, it will be deducted from your wages.

Molly's brows arched like the Arc de Triomphe in Paris. *Nine pounds! That's more than my poor father earned! I will save every penny, return to that horrible workhouse, and place gravestones so my family may rest in peace.*

Molly's days were long, monotonous, and exhausting, working from dawn until late at night, with few breaks. She lived at the beck and call of Cook Coleen, who had complete control over the kitchen. Molly's duties were physical and demanding, such as cleaning and scouring the floors, stoves, sinks, pots, and dishes. She also prepared vegetables, plucked fowl, and scaled fish. Nevertheless, the prospect of having a wage kept her going without a grumble.

↩

On Christmas Day, Molly received a small part of her annual wages, and, with permission from Cook Coleen, was given the afternoon off. She traveled on a farmer's hay-filled wagon and returned to the place that had previously terrorized her. As a winter wind blew against her taut face, Molly walked through the unwelcoming gates. Unbeknown to her, the workhouse had been closed by the English health authorities four weeks after her departure. The now abandoned structure creaked in a haunting way. Where had the inhabitants gone? Are they all dead? Is the famine over? Had the survivors of this macabre institute returned to their homes, if they still had them?

Beneath a cold, foggy sky, Molly placed a small, handmade, rectangular piece of wood on the perimeter of the mass gravesite. It had been grooved to hold dried flowers. For the first time since leaving the institution, Molly clasped her hands in prayer. "God of all Irish people, I hope you have welcomed my parents, brothers, and sisters, and all others who lie here into your Paradise, where there is no sorrow, weeping, or pain …"

Molly felt a tug on her coat. She quickly turned around and then felt a warm, tingling sensation and pressure as if someone were stroking her face. Molly wasn't about to attempt an explanation of being touched by dark, earthbound spirits trying to communicate.

Instead, she took flight. As she fled toward the waiting haywagon, she was run down, struck in the head, by the hind leg of a magnificent black Arabian thoroughbred transporting his master homeward.

Both horse and rider ground to a halt.

Molly lay on the ground, unconscious.

When she finally came to, she found herself in a strange bedroom lying in a sumptuous four-poster bed fit for a queen. Molly's head spun with confusion. "Where am I?' she asked the strangers staring at her.

"You have had an accident, but thank goodness your injuries are minor," responded the attending physician.

"I don't recall …" she paused to touch her throbbing, bandaged head. "All I remember is being at my parents' gravesite."

A taller, slim man who was at the physician's side moved closer. His voice was kind. "I'm so sorry. My stallion spooked when you came flying out of nowhere. But I'm glad to hear that you are not seriously injured. Young lady, you may stay here in my private quarters, until you have made a full recovery."

Molly gazed up at the handsome man with mariner-blue eyes as clear and entrancing as a mountain stream, and golden hair streaked with aging. Molly felt her heart beating as she had never felt it beat before.

Who was he?

Could he be her employer?

Molly's hunch was soon confirmed.

"As I said, young lady," he smiled, "you'll remain my guest until my physician says otherwise. Cook has found a temporary replacement, so there will be no kitchen duties for a while."

Duke Abercan, the most handsome man she'd ever seen, was her employer. Molly replied coyly, "Please, my Lord, I don't feel unwell. I am fit for work. It is merely a bump to my head like the physician said. Please, I need to get back to work to pay for proper gravestones for my family, who died in the workhouse."

The nobleman looked down at Molly's bowed head, then pulled over a chair, sat beside her, and took her hand, which he gently caressed with his fingertips. "There, there," James soothed. "I'm sure that I can work something out. Now, tell me, what brought you and your family to the poorhouse?"

The physician's grimace went unseen by the Duke and the patient. Uncomfortable with knowledge of what was at "play" here, Dr. Creighton gave hasty farewells and departed the room. The physician's thoughts weighed heavily as he made his way to his carriage.

James Abercan had long ago formed his opinion of women, and Molly was too naïve to consider that her employer's attention was nothing more than sexual desire.

Seated in his carriage, Dr. Creighton's thoughts were scattered. Having served the Abercan family for many years, he was no stranger to what was sure to ensue in the bedchambers. The tomcat was at it again, seducing his servant with false concern. The physician had witnessed all too many heartbreaks and sudden deaths. Reproaching the Duke with his opinion of this class-division with Molly would not sit well!

Like his predecessors, James Abercan was not really a gentleman. Instead, he was a womanizer—a player—charming single and married women alike throughout his past four marriages. Each spouse had died under strangely unexplained circumstances. Was James just unlucky? Or was he a cold-hearted killer, like King Henry VIII, whose paternal bloodline ran through the Duke's veins? Did his loyal physician actively comply and conceal the Duke's real crimes?

Dr. Creighton never returned to check on his patient. But he did finally retire from his medical practice—when the scandal hit the front pages of the English and Irish newspapers.

The Duke's upcoming betrothal to Molly was shunned not only by his six daughters from previous marriages but also by English and Irish nobility. As a result, his private, chapel ceremony was held on site, and the only wedding guests were ten maids, four footmen, and Cook Coleen. She was the single servant in this grand house to really accept her new mistress.

Coleen offered the new bride some words of wisdom. Take no mind to being tainted as a crafty schemer in trapping the Duke by becoming pregnant, as some are saying. You have the right to be happy after living a life of hell. Now, with the baby coming, you will experience more joy than you have ever imagined."

Confronted by her new role as mistress of the house, Molly spoke to the servants who were now in her employ in a poor imitation of an upper-class accent. But she depended on Coleen for guidance with the household and other related matters, as she would have depended on her mother if she had still been alive. Coleen became her surrogate parent, confidante, and friend.

With the Duke frequently away on business, Molly spent more time in the downstairs kitchen than anywhere else in the big house.

One day, in a fit of anxiety, Molly rushed downstairs to find Coleen. "I'm bleeding," she exclaimed to her surrogate mother, who was busy at the stove. Colleen put down the wooden spoon she was stirring with, turned to Molly, and asked in a concerned voice, "Did I hear right that you are bleeding?"

"Yes," Molly answered, lifting her outer clothing. She exposed the scarlet red stains on her underwear.

Coleen gasped. "Go back to bed immediately," she instructed. "I'll send for the master's physician ..."

Molly cut her off. "No, no! I don't want him near me!" She was unaware that Dr. Creighton was no longer on her husband's payroll.

Coleen's features creased with concern. "Then I'll send word to my sister, Bridget. She is a highly skilled midwife. You'll be in good hands. Now go and get into your bed. I'll bring you a soothing cup of peppermint tea." At the back of her mind, Cook's instinct told her that something was wrong at this late stage in the pregnancy. "Oh, dear," Coleen muttered under her breath, as she recalled what Molly had told her. "My husband is thrilled with the coming birth of our baby. He so wants a son. Sadly, his other wives bore him only girls. But I will give him a male heir. I'm certain of it'"

⟜⟝

Bridget administered pain-relieving chloroform over Molly's nose and mouth. In an induced torpor, her miscarriage was painless. When she finally came too and learned that her baby son had been stillborn, her shrill cries of grief echoed eerily down the vast corridors of the mansion. Servants, who had been going about their usual business, abruptly froze in place. They had guessed something was wrong when they spied the midwife entering Molly's bedroom and, next, hurriedly leaving with something in her hands.

Bridget wrapped the dead eight-months-in-utero baby in a pillowcase. Downstairs in the kitchen, she found a discarded box and gently placed the deceased child in it. At that moment, what she should do with the tiny corpse was the furthest thing from her mind. Molly became her priority. She returned to Molly's bedside, calming the wailing teenager with a further small dose of chloroform, and then busied herself cleaning the birthing blood from Molly's legs.

Downstairs, Bridget discarded the stained washcloths in a wood stove before addressing her concerns to her sister. "I wonder what the Duke will say when he returns from London. Do you think I should try to get word to him?"

Cook replied, "No. That wouldn't be wise! Let her tell him herself. It's a private thing, grief is."

Bridget scratched her head. "But won't he be mad if the word doesn't get to him?"

"We don't know where he's staying in London," Cook returned.

"I must leave," Bridget announced. "I've another poor woman to help. It is her fifth child, so I should not be that long. Afterward, I will return and check on the Duchess."

Cook inhaled sharply. "Do not leave the dead child in my kitchen!"

Bridget gently picked up the box and left.

Four days after the loss of her baby, Molly was crazed with worry as she anticipated the imminent return of her husband. Her mind could not rest. A footman had informed her that he was preparing the carriage to collect the Duke from the wharf at Wexford seaport.

Meanwhile, Molly chose to adorn herself in his favorite costume, one he bought for her shortly after their marriage. "My dear, you look positively regal, so elegant. I will instruct the Jewish seamstress to make similar garments for you," James enthused.

Molly's rise from maid to Duchess was not without its drawbacks. Given their age difference, was she really the love of the Duke's life, or merely an intimate object of his desire? She loved the Duke so much, but did he feel the same depth of emotion for her?

Molly was in denial up, down, and sideways!

Molly's fingers were tightly entwined as she paced around the room in her finery. Her mind was adrift as she considered the rumors she had heard from tongue-wagging staff about James's womanizing. Her anxiety grew as she plodded around the room. Had he cheated on her? Would he forsake her if he learned she was no longer pregnant, lost the baby he desperately wanted? Would her padded stomach suffice as a ruse for the time being?

⮂

The ties of Bridget's bonnet whipped at her face, and her shoes sunk into pools of rainwater that had collected on the cobbled street. Clutching the bundle she held to her chest, hidden beneath her cape, the midwife hurried to the Abercan house. Would she be too late? Was the Duke already there? Would the Duchess be thrilled with her surprise?

Her soaking wet feet picked up the pace.

A few minutes later, Bridget arrived at the mansion, relieved that the Duke's carriage was nowhere to be seen.

Bridget hurriedly searched for Molly, who was still pacing around the room.

"Hurry, hurry. Remove your clothes and get into bed," Bridget implored insistently.

Molly's eyebrows raised in puzzlement. "Oh, my word!" she exclaimed. "Have you lost your mind? Why must I do that?"

"Please. There is no time," Bridget demanded firmly. "Duchess, if you wish to keep your marriage, it would be in your best interest to do what I say."

Molly heard a whimper coming from beneath Bridget's cape, but she couldn't place the sound. Shocked and surprised, she gasped as Bridget reached under her cloak and withdrew an unwashed newborn child. She said to the flummoxed Molly, "I will have my sister make up a milk formula, but in the meantime, place her to your breast as if you are breastfeeding. Your husband will be none the wiser. I will tell him that I have helped you with a premature delivery."

Molly, her eyes wide, was speechless. She gazed at the child in Bridget's arms and shrieked. "James is *never* going to believe this child is *his*! She's dark as Indian tea and has a strange black mark on her cheek." Bewildered, she inhaled sharply. "Dear God in Heaven, who does the baby belong to? Who is her *true* mother? Did you steal the child?" she asked accusingly. "If so, you will return this baby to its rightful mother *now!*"

Bridget wrung her hands. "Her mother, barely a child herself, is dead. It was her first baby, and she ruptured inside. I couldn't save her, but I saved her child by cutting open the mother's body."

Molly felt nausea rise as Bridget continued. "By bringing this orphaned baby to you, I thought I was *saving* you from being thrown out on the streets. My sister, Coleen, overheard a conversation between the Duke and his butler before you became pregnant. Your husband said that if you didn't produce the son he always wanted, he would get *rid* of you!"

In total disbelief, Molly ranted. "You are lying, and I don't know why! But what does it matter if you are telling the truth or not? This baby is a *girl!* He wants a *son!*"

Bridget sighed. "Then you are going to have to use your best womanly charms to convince him that your next pregnancy will be a boy ..."

Her words ended abruptly when Cook threw open the door. "I hope you two can pull this off because the Duke just arrived. I told him that you have given birth. He is as happy as a pig in muck!"

Coleen's face paled. "I pray to God that he accepts this child, girl, or no!"

Cook had worked long enough for the Duke to know that his former wives had not been met with enthusiasm when they brought other than boy babies into the world. But this was neither a boy nor his flesh and blood!

Molly began to cry. "I know both of you meant well, but I'm not clever enough to carry off this deception. Please take the baby away."

"Darling," an elated voice announced. James entered the room. "Please tell me you have given me a son?"

Bridget hurriedly placed the baby into Molly's arms. The sisters' held their breath and slipped away like thieves in the night.

James came closer, bent down, and carefully removed the blanket from the sniffling baby in Molly's arms. The Duke yelled hysterically. "Jesus, Mary, and Joseph. You have deceived me, woman! This child is *not* mine. You have lain down with a negro. It is blacker than coal!"

Molly's body was paralyzed with fear as James continued to rant and rave. "I should have listened to Creighton's sound advice. You *are* beneath me!" he stormed, slapping a nearby glass table and causing Molly to jump with fright. The loud cries of Molly and the baby sent James into a growing frenzy. "You are an adulteress, nothing but a whore! It's my right to annul our marriage and have you punished by law. But I am a merciful man. You have *one* day to pack your things and leave my home for good. I never wish to set eyes on you again." With that said, he stomped out of the room, ranting vulgar curses heard by all his nearby servants.

Pacing in his library, a livid James ordered his butler to bring

Coleen and Bridget to him. Fearing for their lives, the sisters came clean and confessed.

"You are forbidden to leave this house," James spat at Bridget. To his shaking cook, he added, "You have known me since I was a boy, and I can't believe that you could betray me in such a manner. Go to your room and stay there until I send for you."

James turned to his trusty butler. "Lock every exit door, bring me the keys, and summon the Constabulary."

The everyday life all had known in the Duke's residence would never again be the same.

Shortly after the angry confrontation in the library, Molly Alice Mahoney joined her beloved family in death. Empty chloroform and laudanum (a solution of opium resin in alcohol) bottles lay by her side. The traumatized Molly had no strength left to survive.

Not in her wildest dreams could she have imagined being handed a stolen child, or that the love of her life—whom she had believed to be a loving, mild-mannered man—would throw her out onto the streets as if she were nothing more than dirty sweepings from the floor. However, even in death, Molly's lifeless body would be disrespected. She would be thought of as even lower than sweepings.

At the edge of town, the day following Molly's death, tongues of flames leaped into the sky, devouring the abandoned workhouse.

A group of soldiers deployed by the Irish Constabulary battled the blaze. Their policing during the famine had involved grand-scale rioting and plundering, and many suspected them of igniting arson fires.

However, on this day, something more unnerving drew close.

The frantic firefighting scene was interrupted by shouts of dismay. The fire supervisor was alerted by a soldier covered with grey ash. "Come with me. You have to see this sickening sight."

"Jesus Christ!" the supervisor exclaimed, staring at the dismembered body. He swallowed rapidly to prevent losing his lunch as he gazed at the grisly scene. He turned to the soldier, who was equally pale. "Go into town and fetch the head constable," the superior soldier demanded. "Tell him it is an urgent matter, and to lose no time."

The head constable, Bernard Cummins, a forty-year veteran of the Irish Constabulary, had witnessed many gruesome death scenes, but nothing like this kind of evil. Unaware of Molly's death by suicide, he assumed *she* had met with foul play. Who was the perpetrator behind this terrible act? Seemingly, someone skilled with a blade had perpetrated this heinous crime! There, scattered atop the old workhouse burial ground lay Molly's dismembered body parts. A clump of red hair attached to her crushed skull was all the remained of the rags-to-riches story of a young girl named Molly Alice Mahoney.

Bernard scratched his head. Who could be capable of such evil? Who could act in such a cold and inhumane fashion? Eventually,

Bernard's crime scene drawing would be exhibited to officers of the newly formed Scotland Yard, in London, England.

(The sentence structure has been changed as not to confuse Molly's suicide with murder.)

An autopsy revealed that Molly's body had been drained of blood *before* dismemberment. Why this act was carried out left the law enforcers shaking their heads.

By 1849, the mass gravesite at the workhouse ruins was excavated. The remains of the dead were reburied in unknown graves at a Catholic cemetery. Molly's dismembered corpse was not one of them. Her remains resided in the custody of the Irish Constabulary at the mortuary. It took years before the circumstances surrounding the demise of the Duchess of Abercan were revealed.

The Duke's butler had locked all the doors, as ordered, and left the kitchen area. He was unaware that Coleen had a spare key in her private quarters. In her room, Colleen removed a wad of notes from a biscuit tin and put the money and spare key in her apron pocket. She returned to the kitchen, where Bridget sat crying.

"Here," Coleen said, handing over the money. "Take this and leave Ireland. When you are safe, and only then, send word that everything is fine."

✑

The Irish Constabulary located Bridget attempting to flee by boat to England. Where was the baby? Had she disappeared from the face of the earth, never to be seen again?

After six hours of brutal interrogation, Bridget confessed.

"I have been practicing midwife skills for forty-five years, and I routinely save lives. But in this case, in a fit of madness, I took it upon myself to steal a dead women's baby to help the Duchess, who had lost her baby to premature death and was terrified of her husband's reaction."

Cummins continued his questions relentlessly. "Where's her dead baby?"

"I burned the box. I placed the boy child in the cookstove fire," she said through tears.

"And where is the stolen child?" Bernard Cummins demanded. "And what is the name of her mother?"

Unaware that Molly was deceased, Bridget replied, "As far as I know, the Duchess has her. And I don't know the real mother's name," she answered truthfully. "I was asked to go to the Jewish sector to assist in a difficult first delivery. I was told I would be paid well. I had never been there before. I was shown the way by an older woman who told me she was the girl's mother."

(It is common knowledge that a small population of Lithuanian Jews had settled outside the county of Wexford. They were accepted into Irish life and lived in relative tolerance.)

✑

Two years earlier, twelve-year-old Gabija, her mother, Zita, her uncle, and two cousins had landed in Ireland with nothing more than the clothes on their backs. Gabija's father had died while fighting Russian rebels. Fearing for their lives, her uncle arranged for the family to flee. He became the head of their family in Ireland. Life was hard, but they made a living by going from home to home offering their services: sewing, cleaning, and gardening, whatever a household desired.

Eventually, elderly Zita, a descendant of the Ten Lost Tribes, became a sought-after seamstress by wealthy, noble ladies who competed for colorful Russian-designed clothing. Young Gabija, a quick learner, followed in her mother's footsteps. She, too, was coveted for the intricate silk-ribbon footwear she hand sewed by candlelight.

At age fifteen, the prearranged marriage to her uncle, the head of their household, was accepted without question. This honorable Russian daughter could never have gleaned that a cursed first baby would end her life, as well as that of its departed foster mother, the Duchess Abercan.

With her head lowered, Bridget continued. "When the girl died, I panicked. I'd heard strange stories about these Jew people and wondered if I would be blamed for the girl's death. I do not know what came over me. With the family members waiting outside the home, I slipped out the back, the baby hidden under my cape. It's the truth. I tell no lie."

Bridget was sentenced to ten years for kidnapping and an additional ten years for unlawfully removing a baby from its mother's womb. Two days into her incarceration, she was beaten to death by an inmate who accused her of being a baby killer! Colleen was heartbroken when she learned of Bridget's demise. The next day, without giving notice, Coleen walked away from the Abercan residence and bought passage on an ocean liner bound for America.

The former cook eventually died of old age in the home of a cousin, but not before telling the story that shook her relatives to the core.

"I saw Dr. Creighton, the Duke's retired physician, and two other men unknown to me enter Molly's room after she had killed herself. I heard a terrible racket like someone was sawing wood, but I couldn't make sense of it. A good while later, I saw the men carry some large, bloodied flour bags to the Duke's carriage to be hauled away. And still, it didn't dawn on me. It wasn't until recently when I was reading a magazine article about the gruesome dismemberment of an Irish noblewoman named Molly Abercan, that I connected the dots. "I cried for days. I loved Molly dearly. She was the daughter I never had."

Bernard Cummins reunited Gabija's baby with her shocked father and grandmother. She was immediately named Lidiya Gabija, after her dead mother.

As time passed, and neighbors were none the wiser as to Lidiya's horrific origins, Grandma Zita raised the spirited girl and taught her everything she knew about the sewing trade. The girl was as gifted as her grandmother and her deceased mother. Despite her misshapen legs, a condition passed down from generational rebirth, young Lidiya peddled the streets, selling hers and her grandmother's handmade garments. She was stared at and often treated as a freak, but none of that disturbed her.

One cold winter's day, a tall man and a well-dressed pregnant woman approached Lidiya's market stand. "Oh, how lovely," the woman gushed, lifting a lace shawl.

"I will buy it for you, my darling," offered the man. Then something caught his attention. With lightning speed, he grabbed Lidiya's arm and pulled her closer. He stared at the visible birthmark on her face. His thoughts swam hauntingly. *No! It cannot be! Creighton told me he had terminated her life!* He grasped the girl's arm more firmly.

Lidiya groaned. "You are hurting me, sir. Let me go!"

"How old are you?" the man asked.

"Ten, sir," she politely replied, while her insides shook.

"What's your name?"

"I am named Lidiya, sir."

"Where do you live?"

Even for a ten-year-old, his questioning seemed out of place, but she boldly answered anyway. "I live with my father and grandmother in the Jewish quarters, sir. Will you pay for the garment or not? I haven't got all day to stand around and wait while you make up your mind!"

The nobleman was taken aback by the child's articulation, but then the revelation of truth pierced through his guilt. James Abercan threw coins on the market table, took hold of his wife's arm, and scurried away. James's thoughts were unbridled. *That cad Creighton lied to me! I should have gotten rid of him, as I did Molly and Bridget!* James had paid an assassin to end the midwife's life.

James' scurrilous thoughts returned to reality. *She hasn't any inkling who I am, or of Molly or Bridget or what happened in the past, so let it go.* But the sadistic James brooded on his return to the mansion. He put a diabolical plan into motion that same evening.

James's loyal butler was sent to the Jewish quarters, where he knocked on a tenement door.

"I'm here on behalf of the Duke of Abercan," he announced. "His wife, the Duchess of Abercan, requires a private maid, and the Duke was most impressed with a girl named Lidiya, whom he met at the marketplace. His Lordship is offering her a position in his home and will pay well."

"She lives over there." The woman gestured to a modest house at the end of the tenement row. "Her father died, you know. And her grandmother is ill with a fever. The little girl works hard to care for Zita."

Lidiya answered the rap on her door. She stared at the butler. Mistaking him for a client, she queried, "Are you here to pick up the dress for Mistress Calhoun?"

"No. I'm here on behalf of the Duke of Abercan," he responded.

The butler stated his employer's proposal, and Lidiya adamantly refused. "I will not leave my grandmother for all the money in the world. She is ill and needs me. Please thank the Duke for his kind offer, but I cannot leave."

↷

Lidiya honored the tradition of taking care of her only surviving family member until Zita's death, ten days after the butler had knocked on the door. She had been the dressmaker the Duke had mentioned all those years ago to his young wife, Molly.

Like her grandmother, Lidiya became a popular seamstress to the rich. She never married. She died in her sleep on September 5, 1939, at 4:45 A.M., the same hour that 1.5 million Nazi troops invaded Poland across its 1,750-mile border with the adjacent German-controlled territory.

The Duke's sixth wife vanished from the face of the Earth following the birth of her second daughter.

James, like his ancestor King Henry VIII, died from syphilis. He was declared insane and took his dark secrets with him to the grave.

Coleen had sailed on a ship filled with Irish immigrants eager to start a new life in Boston, America. There, she had worked as a cook for wealthy folk until her death at age eighty. Before she died, she went to the local police station and told them about the sordid events she had witnessed back in Ireland. "I was told to clean the room and keep my mouth shut if I knew what was best for me. That was the Duke's warning. Oh, my word. I had never seen so much blood! I knew that the Duke, with the aid of his physician, had done away with poor Molly in a wicked way."

The astonished police officer asked, "Why did you not go to the police back in Ireland?"

"No, no. I couldn't," Coleen stated, "because the Duke and his doctor were both in on it." Her story seemed unbelievable, but, nevertheless, the officer felt he had to pursue it further. He lifted the cradle of the telephone.

"Scotland Yard," the voice at the other end greeted. "How may I direct your call?"

CHAPTER FOURTEEN

- SEPTEMBER, 1939 -
Poland

"You have no right to live."
—RAUL HILBERG

ucja Mandelbaum's life was to change forever on her thirty-first birthday. An encounter with evil loomed on this autumnal day when a conquering force of Nazis entered her hometown of Będzin, in southwest Poland. At the onset of World War II, this municipality boasted a flourishing Jewish community of over 20,000.

The settled lives of these fearful Będzin Jews would soon vanish. What lay ahead of them in the coming days and years would be unimaginable cruelty. They would suffer the highest degree of inhumanity and oppression: demoralization, eradication of human rights, physical duress, brutal torture, social alienation, and more. These evil strategies would strip the villagers of all humanity.

The suffering that was to be inflicted upon these Jews and others was beyond comprehension. What motive unleashed such demonic evil?

Nazi ideology deftly crafted the Jewish people as "undesirable and unnecessary," making it acceptable to demean them as the lowest of creatures. In times to come, many wealthy Jewish families would flee their homes seeking the promise of safety. Those less fortunate were listed as *enemies* of the Third Reich. Lucja's father, Josek, refused to take the German invasion seriously. He commented snidely in Yiddish, "The schlubs (worthless oafs) didn't win the 1917 war, so I doubt these losers are going to be victorious in this one!"

To Josek, Będzin, where he was born, was Shangri-La, heaven on earth. But it would not be long before his imagined paradise would be transformed into hell on Earth. The gates of Hades were held open for the tyrannical ruler of the "promised" Thousand-Year Reich, who was determined to give birth to horrendous mass genocide.

Born April 20, 1889, in Braunau am Inn, Austria, Adolf Hitler (who allegedly had some Jewish blood) came to power in 1919. He argued that Germany was weak because of the insidious Jewish influence. Hitler blamed the Jews for everything wrong you could imagine. He believed that the Jews sought world dominance, that they had stolen victory from Germany in the First World War and left that country with a shameful defeat. He believed the Jews conspired to control the world and that they would stab Germans in the back whenever it suited them. He believed the Jews were responsible for the great depression in Germany because they managed a lot of important merchandise and fields of financial expertise.

Hitler concluded that Germany was weak and in decline due to the Jewish influence. He began hating the Jews very early in life, after a Jewish doctor, Eduard Block, unsuccessfully treated his mother, Clara, for breast cancer. Hitler is also alleged to have experienced maltreatment while previously working for Jewish families.

Hitler's heightened aversion to everything Jewish developed while he was working as an artist in Vienna. Twice rejected by the Vienna Art Academy, Adolf sold his modern art sketches and postcards for a fraction of the value realized by favored Jewish artists, who were accepted into this prestigious institute. As a twenty-year-old spurned artist, he barely eked out a living, and he grew to believe that the Academy endorsed only Jewish painters! This sent Adolf into a psychotic rage, and, ultimately, to his obsession with ethnic cleansing.

Adolf Hitler, a self-proclaimed anti-Semite, did not invent Jew hatred. Jews have been victims of persecution since the fall of Judea under the authority of the Seleucid. The Jewish people were deemed responsible for the death of Jesus and were labeled as Christ killers. From the fifth to fifteenth centuries, they were stereotyped as greedy usurers and blamed for the "Black Death" epidemics. Horrifically, they were also accused of drinking the blood of Christian children!

↭

Hitler's heinous crimes challenged the human spirit. Life would never be the same for the Jewish populations of Europe. The Mandelbaum family was no exception. At the end of the war, Lucja would be the sole survivor of her dignified Jewish family.

Lucja was born in Będzin to an Orthodox Jewish family, the only child of Ashkenazi descendants, Josek and Bronislawa Mandelbaum. From the time of her birth, she shared her home with her parents, her widowed grandmother, Agnieszka, and her widowed aunt—Josek's older sister—Maja. Their two-level penthouse was in the heart of town in an affluent area. The ground floor accommodated a large kitchen, a spacious living room, and workrooms. Stairs led to an upper level consisting of four bedrooms and two bathrooms. A morning room was endowed with a balcony affording panoramic views of the town center. Josek, a well-known shoemaker, ran his business from the ground floor of the building. Lucja's mother and aunt were textile artisans, craft weavers, who worked by hand at home-fashioning beautiful blankets, tablecloths, and napkins, which were sold in the shoe shop.

Eighty-year-old Agnieszka, the matriarch of the house, was a coveted herbalist. Herbal balms, tinctures, and potions were compounded from aromatic plants grown behind the residence. Sadly, Agnieszka's remedies failed to save her husband. He died in an influenza epidemic ten years earlier.

On this lovely autumn evening, the sidewalks filled with people waiting for a parade to march down the town's main street. Lucja was the only member of the family who was enthusiastic about the German arrival.

Gripping a walking stick to stabilize her awkward gait, she made her way uneasily across the morning room carpet. Her instability was the result of a clubfoot that had presented itself at birth. The top of her right foot twisted downward and inward but caused her no pain since Josek had crafted special walking shoes and slippers for her.

Were Lucja's foot disfiguration and facial blemish genetic inheritances passed down from the sinners of her forewomen ancestors?

It could well have been!

With her braided long blond hair tucked beneath a headscarf, the five-foot-six Lucja headed for the French doors that opened onto the balcony. She was stopped abruptly by her father's command. "Lucja, do *not* go outside!"

Lucja frowned. She had never heard her father raise his voice to her with such intensity. She questioned, "Why not?"

Josek sighed. "For once, my child, do as you are told."

"Tata, the Germans are not going away anytime soon," Lucja announced with foresight and conviction. "I might as well welcome them here to Będzin."

Her discourse raised eyebrows the length and breadth of the morning room. Josek shook his head vigorously. He couldn't muster an adequate response. His headstrong daughter had always been a "conquering force," frequently undermining his authority as head of the household. But then, she was also a blessing.

The gates of Josek's memory banks swung open.

Following miscarriage after miscarriage, Bronislawa, age thirty-eight, finally birthed him a child. But the birth bought unexplained and shocking surprises. The baby's dark Mediterranean skin tone served as a backdrop to many discolored, dark-brown patches scattered over her entire body. The most noticeable was a black, oval blemish on one cheek. And the infant's amber-copper eyes and fair hair color did not match those of her parents, who both had brown eyes and jet-black hair. These anomalies would remain a mystery until some years later when Josek and Bronislawa's shameful secret would finally surface.

The new parents adored their shy and a highly intelligent little girl, but when she reached her teens, everything changed. A new side of her character began to emerge. One day the strong-willed child displayed a defiant temperament that astounded her doting father. Josek had declared rules for his family to live by, but Lucja rejected the laws of *Kiddushin*—the union of man and woman in matrimony. Most teenage girls dreamed of marriage to a good man, of having children and living happily ever after. After Lucja spoke her mind, Josek, as head of the family, unloaded his anxiety. "Daughter! It is unnatural! Marriage is fundamental in Judaism! You are breaking the laws of the Torah and denying us the right to grandchildren. To whom will I pass on my trade and accumulated wealth? I have no male heir, and because of your stubbornness, no grandson, either."

Although Lucja had a special bond with her father, she didn't know how to answer him. According to their faith, she would be required to be subservient to a chosen husband, and she knew she couldn't comply. With an unshakable belief in herself, she was sure her role in this world was as an "earth angel," here to help less fortunate people.

If Josek and Bronislawa had a religious belief in the good works of nuns, that would be one thing, but their Judaism presented them with a challenge. In the end, though, Lucja's parents did come around and accepted their daughter. "God has sent us this special child to challenge our faith, so we will yield to her reasoning, for she is doing God's work."

A warm smile creased old Agnieszka's mouth. She understood that her granddaughter was one of a kind.

Lucja was quite content to be an unwed woman, and she actively dedicated herself to helping others. She handed out loaves of bread to the hungry, minded children when their mothers were ill, gave away her own clothing to those who were cold, and often "liberated" footwear from her father's shop for impoverished schoolchildren, whom she tutored after school hours. She had earned a degree from Jagiellonian University in classical Hebrew and Arabic history, and she delighted her students with her ancient tales.

Shortly after her graduation, Lucja casually remarked to her parents, "I believe I may have lived in these past eras because I have had many dreams of *myself* in those times. What sad times, what pain and suffering were borne for the dark sins of others. Are either of you withholding secrets that I should know about?"

Her question brought a sigh of resignation from Josek and Bronislawa. Yes, Lucja was different. Her daughter's request for "secrets" was not something Bronislawa cared to broach. *Her* mother would have slapped her hard for displaying such audacity. Sadly, Bronislawa wouldn't live long enough to unravel Lucja's genetic evolution. Another person, though, could have revealed the shameful "secret" hidden in the attic of her old mind—Josek's mother! But Agnieszka would maintain her silence for now.

With humor and self-criticism, Lucja had the last word on marriage. "Anyway, my dear Tata, I don't think suitors are likely to come knocking at our door, not with my hyena patches, wolf eyes, and frog foot!"

On a picture-perfect fall day, as the setting sun decorated the sky with orange-red rays and the promise of new dawn, Lucja watched from her family's balcony as German soldiers strutted by, goose-stepping (swinging alternate steel-straight, rigid legs back and forth) to the sound of military music. Adorned in sleek black uniforms, the fighters were followed by the death squad, the *Einsatzgruppen*, who flaunted swastika flags that loomed upward like mythical *Harpies*, the carriers of punishment in Greek mythology. It seemed otherworldly to her. As the din of hobnailed jackboots faded, foreboding shivers ran the length of Lucja's spine. She drew her lightweight cape tighter around her shoulders and stepped back inside her home.

"How was it?" her aunt asked.

"Quite impressive," Lucja replied.

"They are up to no good," her grandmother proclaimed. "I'll never trust Germans. They have always been dark, underbelly warmongers! Your grandfather would have agreed. He fought alongside them in the First World War. He told me they were born evildoers."

"We must trust in God," Josek announced. While other women echoed his holy words, Lucja did not. Although she had been strictly raised in the Jewish faith, she had doubts. Was *He* real? Or had a mere mortal simply fabricated a tall tale to gain power and control over others?

These days, Lucja's instinct signaled that the Creator wasn't going to be in their court any time soon! Yet she still chose to see the good in people. Were the soldiers just following Hitler's orders? Had they been brainwashed into believing his evil doctrine? What if ...?

A few days later, the Nazis were comfortably settled at the top of the human pyramid, relishing control and acting as the masters of death. The first hateful act of their upcoming anti-Jewish program was to randomly murder worshippers in a local synagogue. After Rabbi Yehiel was shot to death in cold blood, the heathens set fire to the Mandelbaum's place of worship. Those who escaped the bullets were burned alive.

Incalculable terror forced worshippers, including the Mandelbaums, to pray only in the privacy of their homes.

Evil was taking root.

On October 8, 1939, Hitler declared Będzin part of the Polish territories annexed by Germany. Hell obliged, willingly opening its doors to this tumultuous, diabolical period in history.

Could it be true?

Could the Jews rise above this crushing oppression?

Who would act as their protectors—the Polish government?

When Hitler's army invaded Poland on September 1, 1939, and started the Second World War, the ill-prepared Polish army soon succumbed, surrendering to Germany's vastly superior forces. The cowardly Polish government officials fled into exile in Romania.

Would the remaining Polish gentiles support racism against the Jews?

Some did. Some didn't. However, most Poles simply regarded the Jews as foreigners living in their midst. Even though the Jews had flourished in Poland since the Middle Ages, they had always maintained their own language, culture, and religious and social institutions, distinct from those of the Polish culture surrounding them.

The German-directed upheavals impacted the Polish population immediately and drastically. In the first month of the war, tens of thousands of Polish intellectuals, including many teachers and religious leaders, were slaughtered. Lucja's name was not on the list, but Josek's was. Lucja's ambition to contribute something significant to the world was never to be.

Two weeks into the occupation, at half-past nine at night, heavy footsteps echoed through the stairwell entrance to the shoe shop. Josek heard an intense, insistent rapping that was followed by a penetrating voice, "*Aufmachen!*" Then the order, "*Schnell!*"

Josek, awake and working late, obeyed the *open the door immediately* orders. He was wearing his badge, which he was forced to display under threat of death. Printed across the yellow felt star located just above his heart was the word *JUDE* (Jew) in black letters.

"Can I help you?" Josek queried in his Polish tongue. "Do you need new boots …?"

He was shoved brutally backward.

"Dirty Jew!" spat the uniformed Schutzstaffel (SS) political adversary. Josek's assailant pummeled him with iron-gloved fists. Josek's wails of terror and pain were unheard as he was dragged bleeding from his shop. As he often worked late into the morning hours to prepare an order, it wasn't unusual for him not to join his family at breakfast.

Shortly after 7A.M., Lucja, clutching a mug of sweetened coffee, headed downstairs. When she saw the store front's window glass shattered to smithereens, her heart began to beat wildly. Lucja gingerly stepped through the wide-open shop door. It was not like her security conscious father to leave doors open. Without considering that whoever had done this could still be inside, she called out, "Tata, I have brought you coffee, and mother will have breakfast ready in ten minutes ..."

Lucja dropped her coffee mug and her cane. She gazed in open-mouthed shock as tears streaked down her cheeks. "What have they done to you, Tata?" she sobbed. Copious pools of blood were splattered across the oak floor. Bloody handprints were visible on the wall. It was apparent a violent struggle had taken place. Her wide, wet eyes surveyed the crime scene. Empty shoe boxes littering the floor. A cash register drawer open and empty. Papers strewn everywhere. Furniture toppled on its side.

In a fit of panic, Lucja rushed upstairs. Bronislawa was preparing breakfast.

"Matka," Lucja wailed. "The store has been broken into ..."

Bronislawa interrupted, "Where is your father?"

"I don't know," Lucja replied. "But I fear that something terrible has happened to him."

Lucja's words brought Bronislawa to her knees.

Days came and went without any word from Josek.

Frantic with worry, Lucja and her mother decided to travel to the German headquarters in Krakow and attempt to get answers. Unknown to them, the new anti-Jewish measures forbade them from entering specific areas of the major cities and railway stations.

↶

The next day the intrepid women, wearing their yellow star

identifications, walked toward the Będzin railway station five city blocks away. When they arrived, Lucja's Mediterranean features drew attention. Two armed Nazi thugs descended upon them like bloodthirsty mosquitoes. One of the men, a whippersnapper barely out of a school, prodded Lucja in the stomach with his rifle barrel. "And what have we here? I do believe we are looking at a pig sow Jew?" he said in a humiliating tone. He then demanded, "Show me your identification and permission-to-travel documents."

A quaking Bronislawa cowered behind her daughter's back. Lucja thought quick and hard. She had to outwit these bullies. Straight-faced, showing no emotion, she responded in German. "We *have* identification, but we didn't know that we *needed* permission to travel on the train." Then, without a second thought, she added, "There are printed rules for us *subhumans* on every lamp post. I did not see one for *travel* restrictions! So where do we get these permission documents?"

Both soldiers' faces contorted with enraged retaliation.

In the snap of a finger, Lucja was hit on her forehead with a rifle barrel. The vicious attack sent her reeling backward, taking her mother down with her. Both women lay motionless on the cold concrete platform. The two power-mad brutes began to kick the hapless women with their steel-toed boots. Lucja shook with helplessness and fear, but also with rage. She cried out, "Stop, please! My mother is old and frail. You are going to kill her!"

Scornful sneers rebuffed her. Neither Lucja nor Bronislawa knew if they would get out of this alive!

The Nazi with hands like baseball mitts growled, "Leave the station immediately, or you will not live to see another day, Jew bitches."

The two women quivered as they crawled on all fours to the edge of the platform.

Mocking laughter shadowed them.

An hour later, bruised, battered, and humiliated, they arrived home and were met with further indignation. Someone had painted red lettering across the Mandelbaum's front door and wall: LEAVE, FILTHY JEWS, IF YOU KNOW WHAT'S GOOD FOR YOU.

Back in her family's penthouse, Lucja's mind whirled with fear. Foremost in her mind was how she was going to protect the aging women in her life from the threat left on the door.

That night Lucja presented them with a daring and risky plan, which could make the difference between life and death. Bronislawa was the first to protest. "No. I forbid it. You'll be caught. I may never see you again. We're living in perilous and dangerous times, my daughter. What occurred at the railway station proves how brutal the Germans are."

Lucja's grandmother added in a scolding tone, "I told you not to greet the evil ones."

But her aunt, having her own personal motives, was more understanding. "Without Lucja's plan, how will we learn what has happened to my brother?"

Bronislawa began to cry, and that prompted tears to cascade down all their cheeks.

That same evening, while her family slept, Lucja slipped out of the penthouse. She realized she was breaking the curfew, 9 P.M. to 5 A.M. It was daring and risky, but she would not be thwarted. She had to get answers. How else could she shed light on the condition of her beloved father?

With her black hood pulled low, obscuring her face, and the tell-tale yellow star removed, Lucja made her way through the shadows of several unlit back streets. At 10:30 P.M. she tapped lightly on the front door of their former maid's, Anna Kendonsky's, ground floor apartment.

Lucja missed chatting with her bubbly friend, Anna, who was about her age, but another Nazi order—NO GENTILE SHALL BE EMPLOYED BY JEWS—prevented that.

The door creaked open, and Anna's jaw dropped. "Miss Mandelbaum, what are you doing? You could be arrested!"

Who is it?" a male voice inquired from within.

"Lucja Mandelbaum," Anna whispered.

Within seconds, a portly man was at Anna's side. "Go away!" he whispered. "You risk your life and *ours* by being here long after curfew."

Lucja made eye contact. "I'm sorry to trouble you. But I desperately need your wife's help, and I'll pay you for it."

"Quickly, come in," Anna's husband urged, his eyes searching to confirm no neighbors had seen Lucja's arrival.

Lucja was offered a hot chocolate, but she politely refused. The sooner she got down to business, the better. She began, "Anna, it's your help I need the most. What I'm about to ask you cannot be undertaken by me, my mother, or my aunt. We are worried, sick. We have not heard from my father in several weeks ..."

"Excuse me for interrupting, but I don't quite understand," Anna said.

Lucja explained what had occurred the morning she had taken coffee to her father.

"Oh, my God, that must have been frightening," Anna exclaimed. "How can I help?"

Anna listened with wide eyes, but her husband spoke for her. "I'm sorry, but it is out of the question. The SS are not stupid. They'll wonder why a German-born woman is enquiring after a Jew."

"Anna can tell them that Josek owes her money, wages, she is unable to obtain from his family."

An idea popped into Anna's husband's mouth. "I have a better plan. Apart from her eye color and dark complexion, Lucja looks Aryan. She won't come under scrutiny if something can be done about those discrepancies."

Lucja squinted, not sure of where all this was leading.

Moments later, Anna's husband handed Lucja his wife's German birth certificate. "This will help a forger to produce an identity card for you," he claimed. Then, with a worried expression, he thought of their three young children. "If you're caught with this deception, my wife and I will have little choice but to say you have stolen it."

"I understand, and I'm eternally grateful. I'll return the certificate as soon as possible."

Lucja handed over an envelope containing the equivalent of one year's wages for maid services.

"Thank you so much," Anna said. "This is going to help us buy food."

Lucja hugged her former maid and shook the husband's hand before hurrying home beneath the cloak of darkness.

⮂

In the final few months of the war, Anna was arrested by the Gestapo. She was charged with aiding and abetting enemies of the Reich. It seemed as if Lucja wasn't the only person Anna had handed official paperwork to. Lucja's fake ID was turned over to the Gestapo after Anna's home had been looted by Polish citizens.

Anna died in the prison's torture chamber. She never revealed the true identities of the Jewish women she had helped.

Shortly after Anna's arrest, her husband fled with their children to Sweden, a neutral country during the war. He never tired of telling the story of the courageous woman, Lucja, who had inspired his wife to help so many others.

Two days after her meeting with Anna, at 10 A.M., Lucja walked into the dreaded railway station. Would her disguise work? Or would she be apprehended before she reached the ticket booth? At Anna's suggestion, Lucja wore a brightly colored Polish folk costume decorated with rich embroidery. Thick rimmed tinted glasses obscured her distinctive wolf eyes. Her blond hair was concealed, held in place beneath a plain cotton *babushka* (scarf). Several applications of off-white powder lightened her dark skin and concealed her facial blemish. Having exchanged her father's handmade shoes for Polish footwear, flat shoes with elastic straps, she concentrated on walking without losing her balance. As she looked around, she saw the platform was crowded with blue-eyed Poles and armed German guards.

Mimicking Anna, Lucja used a step-and-a-half gait to make her way to the station's ticket booth. There she put on a thick Polish accent. "A ticket to Krakow, please."

"One way or return?" the ticket master asked.

Lucja, trying to speak as little as possible, gave a short response. "Return, please."

"I'll need your identification card," he stated.

With a sweating hand, Lucja slipped the *Volkslisliste*, personal identification card for Poles of German ancestry, under the glass partition. *Please, God, let this work!*

A tidy sum of money had been paid to an "underground" fine arts student whose unique talents had created the *Ausweis der Deutschen*. It had a black-and-white photo of Lucja on the left side of the document.

While the ticket master examined the document, Lucja's peripheral vision detected the two Nazis bullies who had previously assaulted her. Her stomach muscles tightened into knots. Thinking quickly, she attempted to avoid further scrutiny by turning around and greeting them in perfect German. "Good morning," she cooed. "What a wonderful autumn. It makes one want to sing and dance," she added as she hummed to the tune of Wagner's "Ride of the Valkyries," which was playing over the platform loudspeakers.

Lucja was fluent in several languages, including Old Prussian and Aramaic. But would her disguise and German conversation fool these Jew haters? With her exceptional memory, Lucja had planned every minute detail of the role that she was playing, that of Frau Anna Kendonsky: birth date, place of birth, school records, marriage license number, and the names of the children and the schools they attended. Lucja breathed a silent sigh of relief when the soldiers moved on, striding further along the platform. Before they moved on, they gave her an enthusiastic greeting. "Heil Hitler."

"Heil Hitler," she returned with concealed loathing.

Purchasing the train ticket had been an unnerving ordeal, but "slumming it" in third-class on a punishing wooden bench for three and a half hours was almost more than she could bear. True to her ruse, though, it was all that a lowly "servant" could afford without raising suspicion!

The train was cramped, noisy, and dirty. Lucja blocked out the wretched conditions by envisaging her next course of action. If Lucja Mandelbaum could have wound time forward, she would have seen that this train was a luxurious mode of travel when compared to what was to come. The promise of the new dawn Lucja had witnessed on the balcony in September, heralded, instead, the darkest days yet to befall the Jewish people.

During the train ride, Lucja rehearsed the speech she had prepared before leaving home. One word out of place, and it would all be over.

Anna arrived at Number 2 Pomorska Street, the SS headquarters in Krakow. After waiting two hours, she was ushered into an office and was facing the massive form of SS-Oberleutnant Max Müller. The shiny buttons of his pristine black uniform looked as if they were about to rocket-launch off the stretched fabric at any second.

"Sit," Müller said, flashing perfect white teeth. "And what can I do for you?"

Lucja boldly made her case. "I worked for the Mandelbaum family in Będzin for over twenty years, but no more. My husband says *they* are nothing but vermin," she said with a serious face. "I am a simple woman. Times are hard, and all I want is my wages ..."

A steely voice cut in. "Get on with it. I haven't got all day."

"I'm told that Josek Mandelbaum is in your custody. Could I speak to him? I just want my money!"

Suspicious eyes stared at Lucja, and she felt their intensity. It gave her the creeps. He was checking her out. She had to think fast. "Oberleutnant Müller, I hope you don't mind, but may I compliment you on your uniform. It's the finest I have ever seen, and your office is very well appointed."

Had her bootlicking tactics worked?

"Well, thank you, Frau Kendonsky." Müller beamed at her flattery. "And may I say that your costume is delightful. You must tell me where I can obtain garments like yours for my daughters."

"I will give you the telephone number of the maker of these fine costumes," Lucja returned glibly.

Müller nodded. "Now, we must conclude business. I'll need some information: full address, full name, age, occupation of your previous employer."

Lucja was careful with her responses. After all, she was just a cleaner! Müller scribbled on a notepad, then stood up. "Wait here," he said, "I will see what I can find."

The wait in his office, adorned with Nazi paraphernalia and a framed picture of Hitler, was the least of Lucja's discomfort. She was desperate to use the bathroom! She noticed the sound of black boots squealing under excess weight.

Müller towered over the sitting Lucja. "Josek Mandelbaum of Bedzin is no longer with us," he announced, showing Lucja a copy of Josek's death certificate: "Died of natural causes in prison while awaiting trial for assaulting a German officer."

Lucja fought hard to conceal her shock, sorrow, and doubt. Presenting a passive face to hide her devastation, she responded, "Thank you, Oberleutnant Müller. It seems that I'll not be getting my well-earned money from the filthy Jew!"

"You should fill out a work application at the reception desk, should a cleaning position come available here."

"Thank you," Lucja said with a bitter taste in her mouth. "I will do just that."

Lucja left the building, found a nearby bench, and cried until her tears dried up. Her father did not have a savage bone in his body. He had *never* lifted a hand to anyone. He wasn't a criminal … in any way. How was she to break this tragic news to her mother?

Back at the SS headquarters, Müller felt uneasy. Something without an explanation sat heavily on his mind. An intuitive sense flooded his mind. He yelled to his private secretary, "Did you make a copy of Frau Kendonsky's identity card?"

"I did," he answered. "Do you require it?"

"Yes."

"Go downstairs and see if she is still in the building. If so, bring her back to my office."

"*Jawohl*," answered the secretary, affirmatively.

Müller's finger pressed out a telephone number, and he spoke to the voice at the other end. "I'm sending you a copy of an identity document that I believe may be false."

From that day onward Lucja resolved not to give up her quest to learn what really happened to her cherished father. It wasn't until after the war that the circumstances of Josek's demise would be brought to light.

Lucja learned that her father had been viciously attacked at the shoe shop because of his failure to report to the *Generalgurverne-ment*, which was required of all Jewish males. They were to be registered as unpaid labor.

The morning of the attack, at the SS station, his hair and beard had been shaved off, and he was ordered to strip naked. He was tortured until he lost consciousness. Barely alive, he was shipped off to a nightmarish place—Mauthausen-Gusen–a concentration camp north of Linz, Austria.

Prisoner 33207 slaved from four in the morning until eight at night in a granite quarry for an SS company, German Earth and Stone Works, which was created to manufacture building material for State construction projects in Nazi Germany. The idea was simple: Work them until they can work no more. Prisoners too weak, tired, or ill to work were executed on the spot.

After eight days of this brutal labor, Josek joined the pile of dead. He did not die from his back-breaking slave labor or at the order of the heartless Camp Commandant, Franz Ziereis. Instead, he was killed by a Soviet political inmate who accused Josek of stealing his bread ration. The Cossack stabbed his so-called bread-thief to death.

Josek Mandelbaum's body was one of the thousands buried in a mass grave in a nearby forest.

On December 6 just before dawn on Hanukkah, the Jewish Holiday of Lights, the Mandelbaum women were frightfully woken by a loud banging at the front door and a loud *Sich Eröffen!*

Lucja, her mother, grandmother, and aunt descended the stairs to find the front door had been smashed in. Standing in the doorway were two Nazis pointing Lugers at them. Both hollered in unison, *Raus, Jude. RAUS!*

With knee-jerk resolve, the feisty Lucja demanded in German, "What's going on? Why are you demanding us to get out …?"

A searing pain flamed through her. The barrel of a Luger struck the girl squarely on the head. Lucja's mother, Bronislawa, defensively bellowed a protest in Yiddish. "You despicable German *beheyme* (beast)." She froze when the same soldier raised his weapon to strike her, but his intention was suspended in air by the words of his comrade. "Stinking Jew bitch, move, or you will die where you stand!"

With passive resignation, Lucja cradled her sore head. Clinging to each other in their sleepwear, the three women were roughly herded by armed soldiers onto the street. Although it was dawn, bitterly cold and sleeting, the road was already filled with Jews lined up in rows: women with babies and little children in one line, men and teenage boys in another. Shrieks of fright permeated the frigid air as some of the children were separated from their parents. Dog handlers, restraining snarling, salivating Rottweilers, screamed their orders in German. "The first rows get into the truck."

Comprehending the German language meant life; not understanding it, death.

Women, whether young or old and small children who did not march quickly enough to the German commands, were instant targets of abuse. Shouts, kicks, and violent blows furiously assaulted them. A sledgehammer blow to Agnieszka's old, curved back sent Lucja's ninety-two-year-old grandmother crashing to the street. Her horrified granddaughter sprang into action. "*Bubbe* (grandma), put your arms around my neck."

"Leave me here, granddaughter," Agnieszka's tearful voice responded. "I've had a good life and am ready to go to God. Take care of my daughters, Bronislawa and Maja, and tell Josek, when you see him, that he is the best son-in-law I could have hoped for."

Lucja firmly protested. "I'll do that anyway, but you are coming with me, even if I have to carry you like a baby."

"No. Do not try to lift me," Agnieszka argued. "I think my back is broken. But there is something that you should know, darling granddaughter, before we are separated."

Lucja frowned. "Tell me later, Bubbe. I *must* get you to your feet. I'm not leaving you here for this evil *beheyme* to hurt you further."

In a barely audible voice, Agnieszka confided. "Do you remember when you wanted to know if there were any withheld family secrets?" She inhaled sharply. "Well, there are. Your father, Josek, is your mother's half-brother. They broke God's laws."

"*… Any other than kin …*"

Before Lucja could react to Agnieszka's shocking disclosure, an attack dog viciously sank his teeth into her forearm. Lucja cried out in pain. The dog handler chortled, then ordered the animal to release its bite. The youth cocked his gun and yelled, "*Raus!*"

Lucja shot him the evil eye and refused to budge. Her aunt,

Maja, trembling in fear, urged her niece, "Come away *now* before we are all murdered. There is nothing you can do. Please, I beg you, listen to me!"

The deafening and merciless *crack* came swiftly.

The bullet entered Agnieszka's temple, ending the life of this precious wife, mother, and grandmother. Numbed with shock, Lucja, Bronislawa, and Maja climbed into the back of the transport carrier. Lucja's bleeding lacerations and skull-splitting headache locked her grandmother's disturbing revelation about her parents in time and space, for now.

Jammed together on the truck bench, Lucja tightly embraced her sobbing, grief-stricken mother. "Try to be strong, dearest Matka. One day this murderous, evil race will pay for their crimes; you mark my words. We will survive this and bear witness."

A young woman at the far end of the wood bench contradicted Lucja bitterly. "No. They won't be punished. They believe they *are* Gods, higher than our God of Israel!" A woman holding a crying baby added, "The world is falling apart!"

"I don't want to be Jewish. It is a death sentence to be Jewish," said a teenager.

"I'm frightened!" a five-year-old moaned.

"Trust in God," consoled an elderly woman.

A mother clutching her baby to her breast added bitterly, "There is *no* God! Look at all *His* dead people lying in the street. I agree with the young girl; I do not wish to be Jewish, either."

Loud gunshots outside the truck silenced the bereft prisoners.

Etched in Lucja's mind was the vision of her beloved grandmother's crumpled body. A pair of red satin slippers lovingly crafted by Josek lay strewn nearby. Lucja was in the present, the here and now. She inhaled deeply. Her Bubbe's last "confession" had not yet sunk in. Although she had lived with secrets and lies, her mind was now blocking out past tragedies.

Would the ghosts of the past eventually reveal Agnieszka's truthful secret?

Lucja's thoughts now meandered to happier times. So much of her grandmother was a part of her. She would never again enjoy the aromas of her grandmother's healing herbs simmering on the kitchen stove. Her ears would never again delight in Agnieszka's infectious laughter or her beautiful singing. And her arms could no longer embrace the old woman she loved so dearly. Assailed by a kaleidoscopic of flashbacks, Lucja swirled in a host of emotions: love, grief, anger, disgust, hate, and loathing. But mostly *contempt* for the German race that treated Jews as subhumans.

Past and present events would not be erased by time.

Worryingly at the back of this transport carrier, Lucja's photographic memory loaded the images of dead bodies lying in the street. She stored them alongside the memory of the fateful evening she had "welcomed" these leather-clad creatures of hell.

Were the Jews simply scapegoats for the lost war of 1914-1918? Or was Hitler's ideology viler than anything visualized in Dante's *Inferno*?

Lucja and the other victims of racial discrimination riding with her offered no resistance. They were merely lambs on their way to the slaughter, packed as tightly together as sardines in a can. Their truck journey was filled with loss, remembrance, fear, and helplessness. The captives did not know where they were going, the distance to be traveled, or what lay in store for them when they got there. They had suffered much trauma by this time, but nothing could have prepared them for the hell that lay ahead!

Lucja experienced a sudden rush of anxiety. She couldn't breathe, and her heart felt like it was going to burst out of her chest. She wore a blank stare ... and then she was no longer conscious.

CHAPTER FIFTEEN

- 1939-1942 -

City of Lodz, Litzmanastadt Ghetto

"For the dead and the living, we must bear witness."
—ELIE WIESEL

The Lodz Ghetto, the second largest of its kind, after Warsaw, was established in German-occupied Poland. It was intentionally set up in the most rundown area of the city, a poverty-stricken slum district isolated from surrounding areas.

Within its macabre enclosure more than 165,000 Jews, expelled from other parts of Poland, were forced to subsist in an area less than four square kilometers. For the 20,000 Będzin prisoners, being incarcerated in this barbed-wire-enclosed restricted space with no electricity or clean drinking water was like living in a grave.

The prisoners—tired, sore, thirsty, and hungry—shivered in a frigid Polish winter that chilled them to the bone. The bedraggled inmates were ordered out of the transport carrier by their new lords over life and death, who derogatively addressed their captives with screams of "Dirty Jews! Scum of the earth! Bloodsuckers! Vermin!"

Not adequately dressed for winter's icy breath, the Mandelbaum women looked aghast at the holding pen that was to be their new home. Aunt Maja was the first to speak. "*Take meyn got* (oh, my God), what *is* this place?" She held a hand over her mouth and nose. The putrid stench of human waste overwhelmed them as it trickled through the strewn garbage. The place was a nightmare.

Bronislawa shrieked, "*Take meyn got!* There are dead bodies lying in the street!"

"Don't look, Mother," Lucja begged, turning her mother around. When their eyes met, the barefoot Lucja changed the distasteful subject. "If I don't find footwear or even a pair of wool socks, frostbite will take my toes. Or worse, I'll end up like them, dead from hypothermia." *This place is a sure death sentence!*

Bronislawa and Maja had managed to slip on their warm house shoes when they had heard the soldiers banging on their front door, but they were numb to the memory of Lucja being dragged out of their home barefoot, or of her brutal dog bite injuries. Bronislawa groaned, "I would rather die like my mother than live in this disgusting place ..." Her speech lingered as another thought crossed her mind. "How will Josek know where we are?"

Aunt Maja shook her head. Their previously privileged lives were becoming nothing more than fading memories. She doubted they would survive another day without warm clothing, shelter, and food. Maybe her gold wedding ring, which she had concealed from the Nazis by hiding it in her sleep-bra, could become a bartering chip.

Shortly after their arrival in ghetto hell, several more transport trucks appeared. The street where they stood became filled with chaotic scenes of Jewish people desperately seeking a place inside the overcrowded ghetto. Maja urged, "Lucja, I will wait with my sister here, and you go and see what you can find for us." Placing a hand into her bra, she withdrew the wedding band. "We have no money, but this might help in securing a place for us to live."

Lucja sighed deeply. Maja had risked her life, hiding this valuable. Before entering the truck, the SS had ordered them to hand over all valuables on their person. Anyone caught hiding valuables had been shot on the spot. Lucja was unaware that gold jewelry and other valuables could mean the difference between life and death in this godforsaken ghetto.

Lucja now stared in disbelief as elderly and disabled Jews were dragged out of trucks and onto the street by sadists wielding un-limited power. *Why not kill them in their beds, rather than transport them?* Lucja's musings were dispelled by a flashback from the trip.

While they were being ordered from the truck, she overheard a little boy say, "I will ask God to teach me how to fly so I can rise over these bad walls." Lucja lifted her head toward the dismal gray skies. *If you hear me, give me and that little boy our wings.*

Beyond the crumbling tenements of the ghetto, Lucja could see roads, businesses, and decent apartment buildings, places where Jews had been free to walk, work, and live only months ago.

Lucja knew in the days to come, they had to fight fatigue and the encroaching cold, and satisfy their hunger and thirst. So she left her mother and aunt huddling outside for warmth and climbed the stairwell of the nearest rundown building. Most of the apartments— tiny, unheated damp spaces—were already occupied by several families. Arriving at the top floor of the tenement block, Lucja spotted a curtain divider separating what seemed to be two living spaces. With hope brimming through her broken spirit, she drew back the drape. "Hello," she greeted a thin man and short woman. On a wood pallet behind them sat five children with dirt ruts on their gaunt faces, running noses, and rags clinging to their shrunken bodies. Lucja noted the mist expelled from their lungs as they released moisture into the chilly air. Abraham Joselzon stared at the visitor and said, "As you can see, we have little space. There isn't room for you ..." A look of concern crossed his pale face as he observed the blood-soaked sleeve of Lucja' robe. "Oh, Holy God, you are injured. I am a doctor. What happened?"

Lucja explained, "I was savaged by a Rottweiler in the Będzin roundup. I don't feel any pain because my arm is numb with cold."

"Let me take a look," Doctor Abraham said. He lifted Lucja's arm. He feared a bad infection. The lacerations were deep, but her tendons were intact. Somewhat surprised, considering the depth of the wounds, Abraham saw no significant damage to any major blood vessels. "I'm sorry. This may hurt," he said as he pressed on the lacerations to make them bleed, hoping to flush out any infectious nasties. Without antibacterial ointment, sterile bandages, or clean water to wash the cuts, the doctor felt her chances of recovery were slim, but he improvised as best he could.

Abraham sprinkled grains of salt over the lacerations, causing Lucja to wince for the first time. Then the forty-year-old medical practitioner wrapped her wound with a strip of material that his wife had ripped from a bed sheet, at his request. "I can't promise that this is going to work, but it will give you a fighting chance," Abraham said.

"Thank you. I'm very grateful," Lucja replied. In hindsight, she wished she had studied medicine instead of ancient cultures. This aspiration would manifest again down the road when she would be accosted with maladies offering little hope of recovery.

"I'm curious," Abraham uttered. "Are you a Roma?"

Slightly affronted, Lucja assured him, "Definitely not! I'm *no* gypsy. I'm a Jew just like you. My name is Lucja Mandelbaum."

With knitted brows, Abraham recalled. "Are you, by any chance, related to Josek Mandelbaum, the shoemaker?"

A smile crossed Lucja's pain-filled face. "Yes. He is my father."

Abraham smiled. "I knew well your gentle father, before this …" Abraham gestured toward their dingy surrounds. "Josek made shoes for my whole family, and he always gave me a discount. Is he here with you?"

"Sadly not," Lucja replied. "He was taken away in September, and I believe he was murdered by the foul Gestapo."

"I'm saddened by this," Abraham said softly. "He was a great man."

Lucja had to ask, "How did you end up in this awful place?"

"Ah, it is a long story, but I'll cut it short. A patient of mine, who was serving in the Luftwaffe, died. I was charged with medical negligence. So here I am with my whole family." Abraham shook his head dismissing the recollection. "To change the subject, I'm sure we can accommodate one more person."

"There are *three* of us," Lucja emphasized. "My mother and aunt are with me. They'll freeze to death if I can't find shelter for them. We were forced out of our home in our nightwear, and that's the only clothing we have." Lucja gestured to her numb, bare feet. "And my feet are frozen."

Rebecca Joselzon gasped as she stared at Lucja's blue feet. The doctor's wife immediately rummaged through a pile of rags and handed over a pair of old wool socks. "Until footwear can be found for you, put these on."

In another kind act by this couple, Bronislawa and Maja were given one of the two wooden pallets, where they could lie head to toe. The four younger children occupied the other one. This compassionate family refused the offering of Maja's ring as payment.

That night Lucja snuggled under threadbare blankets with Abraham and Rebecca. Before bedtime, the Joselzon family had shared what little food they had. A small portion of moldy bread and a thin slice of cooked potato was the first taste of nourishment the Będzin inmates were offered since the roundup. Abraham's oldest son provided some brackish water taken from the communal faucet four blocks away. Though it equaled no more than a few sips, it sufficed to quench the burning thirst of the new arrivals. In times to come, Lucja would learn that there would be no respite from their constant craving. It would assail their throats like rabid dogs.

⮎

As the Nazis restricted the food supply to the ghetto, hunger was rampant. An underground black market developed into a thriving business. Food was smuggled into the ghetto daily. Those with money or jewelry could purchase quality foodstuffs or anything else they desired. But those who had nothing to barter had to scavenge daily for enough scraps to keep them alive.

Smuggled diamonds, gold, furs, and other valuables were exchanged for a loaf of bread.

The following day Maja's wedding band was bartered for three loaves of bread, a bag of potatoes, lentils, antibacterial ointment, tattered winter coats, boots, hats, and mittens for each of them. A cobbler made a leather insole for Lucja's clubfoot, which temporarily relieved her step-and-a-half gait.

The three women shared their meager bounty with their gracious hosts.

The children told Bronislawa that she made the best potato soup they had ever tasted. But with so many hungry bellies, it didn't take long for the food supply to vanish. Nights later, Lucja lay awake listening to a chorus of rumbling stomachs suffering from starvation. A flashback transported her to a horrific incident.

While the prisoners were systematically being deprived of food, sick amusements were conducted by the ghetto guards. On this day, an obese SS-Untersturmfuher guard threw a bucket of potato peelings into the crowd. The brute stepped back in a fit of laughter as a horde of ravenous souls pushed, shoved, and clawed their way to the vegetable scraps. In this frenzy to survive, many were injured, and some were trampled to death.

Food was survival.

Lucja wrote in a notepad, "I know now that *hell* exists." Some years later, after the war, her partially burned journal was discovered among a pile of ghetto rubble.

The spring of 1940 blew in and out of the timelessness of the ghetto. With a death clock ticking, the Mandelbaum women tried frantically to maintain a semblance of ordinary life, an impossible task under their nightmarish circumstance. Starvation remained the principal cause of death. Their food—bread mixed with sawdust—was causing severe digestive problems. Though in dire circumstances, Lucja didn't fall for the deadly ruse that was offered as an escape from their ghetto misery. The Germans printed and distributed notices to the inmates: "You will be offered two loaves of bread, some margarine, sugar, and a bowl of soup if you report to the *Umschlagplatz* for work detail."

The notices were part of a diabolical plot to gather men, women, and children for German labor camps. Those who had been taken in by this wicked deception were never again seen on the ghetto streets.

Barely existing on 209 calories a day, Lucja dreamed of fresh bagels, stuffed cabbage rolls with a side of potatoes, and mouth-watering Hamantaschen cookies filled with jam, all Ashkenazi delights lovingly prepared by her grandmother. She recalled Agnieszka saying, "You are so skinny. You need to eat more. Finish off those biscuits."

The memory of her dead grandmother lying on the street, never to receive a decent Jewish burial, brought on a rush of tears. Overpowered by the edifice of inhumanity she was living in, Lucja succumbed to an emotional meltdown. *I'm not human. I am an animal. It is clear as night and day.* She leaned against a filthy wall and wept.

Lucja felt a touch on her shoulder. "Pray to God, my child," the unknown person advised.

Bitterness tasting like bile rose in her throat. Lucja glared at this Torah teacher, who wore side curls and a large, rectangular prayer shawl. He reminded her of her father. Since Josek had disappeared, the Sabbath and Holy Days celebrations had quietly ended. Lucja didn't bother to pray, feeling certain it would be pointless.

Lucja vented at the stranger with a rush of angry words. "Tell me where God is! I have studied our ancient Hebrew culture, and it seems *we* have been forgotten, from the moment time began. So, please, explain why *our* God turned *His* back on the suffering of *His* people. Is He on vacation? Or have we, His Jewish people, been duped, brainwashed into believing that there *is* a mighty being! It's a doctrine that is taught to us. We were not born with it! And it seems that you, his disciple, have been thrown to these wolves, as well!"

The rabbi glared at Lucja, astounded.

Lucja didn't give him a chance to respond. She rushed away as if he had the forked tongue of an evil serpent. Denying religion, Lucja knew *she* had to act swiftly if she wanted to keep her family alive. She learned from Abraham that the Jewish Law and Order organization—the Jewish Police Service members who were responsible for public order in the ghetto—had placed an advertisement for an interpreter. She gleaned that the members were controversial figures, often given extra privileges such as bicycles, meager food rations, and contraband from the ghetto smuggling operations. The Jewish police mandate was to guard the ghetto gates alongside the Nazi guards and their collaborators, to curb beggars in the ghetto, and to safeguard community administration. But there was a dark side to their functioning, which Lucja would soon discover.

In times to come, many in this policing establishment would face moral dilemmas, as they were often compelled by Nazi officers to perform appalling acts against their fellow Jews. Over time, members of this local law enforcement agency served willingly as collaborators, securing deportations to concentration camps for their neighbors.

Was there evidence that Jewish policemen were killed by fellow Jews as revenge for their treachery? Yes! These traitors deserved no less! They had it coming!

On a bright spring morning, as Lucja was making her way to the Jewish Law and Order Service, she spotted a thin, dark-skinned boy clothed in rags selling cigarettes.

Lucja approached him, and the small vendor sprang into action. "Two zlotych," he offered in Yiddish, lifting a single cigarette.

"I don't smoke," Lucja replied. "But I'm curious. You are young to be selling cigarettes. Where did you get them?"

With a broad, impish grin, he answered, "Ask no questions and hear no lies!"

Lucja didn't know yet that smuggling food and other necessities was primarily performed by kids. Their reality was as harsh as everyone else's, but they risked their lives to succor others and to enhance their chances of survival.

Lucja smiled. He was cheeky. "What's your name? And how old are you?"

"My name is Chaim el-Din, and I'm twelve years old."

El-Din! Lucja's mind raced: "You have an Arabic last name. How does an Arab with a Jewish first name come to be in a Jewish ghetto?"

The boy's smile vanished, replaced by a drooping bottom lip. "You got time, lady? Because it's a long story?"

Although Lucja felt pressed to reach her destination, her natural curiosity overcame her. "I have all the time in the world," she replied.

Chaim began, "My mother's Jewish and my father is Egyptian. They were archeologists and met in a place called Luxor. They were married in Egypt, but after a while, my mother became homesick, so they immigrated. It was a big mistake!"

A customer interrupted. "I'll take two," he said to Chaim, who pocketed the money, handed over the cigarettes, and continued. "I was born in Poland, and we lived in a nice house. My mother got a good job at the museum, but my father couldn't find work. He stayed home to take care of me and collect me from school. Then *they* came! The Nazis took my mother and me to a sports stadium, where I was separated from her. And I don't know what happened to my father."

Lucja's own experience of being dragged from her home flashed vividly before her eyes and mingled with Chaim's ongoing tale. "The

Nazis began shooting people. I was so scared that I ran to a wall, climbed over it, and hid in a thick bush. When the shooting was over, and I was sure no one was looking for me, I returned home. But my father wasn't there, and our house had been ransacked, by who I don't know. But everything was taken. Not even my bed remained. I stayed in that empty place for days, but I was so hungry, I went in search of food and a safe place to stay. And here I am, in a place that the bad people would least suspect." Lucja saw tears welling in his sad eyes as he softly muttered, "I miss my mother and father so much."

Lucja's heart was breaking for this sorrowful boy. Her arms reached out. Holding him in a tight embrace, she asked, "Where are you staying?"

"Here on the street."

Lucja sighed. He was one of the hundreds of homeless people who had to sleep wherever they could find a spot.

Chaim looked straight into Lucja's compassionate eyes. "I like you, lady," he said, smiling. Then he frowned. "But can I trust you?"

"Of course," she replied. "And by the way, my name is Lucja, not Lady. Chaim, I know there is no consolation I can offer because I'm a victim, just like you."

Chaim nodded his head in acceptance, and divulged, "I'm a smuggler. If you've money, I can get you anything from the other side—food, medicine, clothes, and *cigarettes!*" The cheeky boy chuckled, knowing full well that his confidant was not a smoker.

Lucja had to smile. She said, "Chaim, even if I had money, I would never ask you to risk your life. You can be shot if they catch you."

"Well, I'm not dead yet, so I must be doing something right!"

Lucja shook her head, but time was of the essence. "I'm happy to have met you, brave boy, but I must go now. I need a job to support my mother and aunt."

"What job?" Chaim queried.

"I'm going to the Jewish Law and Order Police. They need a translator …"

He cut her off. "My backside!" he snorted, wiping his runny nose on a sleeve. "The Blue Police (named after the color of Polish Police uniforms) pay the Jewish Police to recruit *informers*, to rat on ghetto people. I know, they tried it on me. The Polish and Jewish Police are hated. The shits collect ransom payments, personal belongings, and valuables and hand over their own people to the Nazis for their labor camps. Feh! The *bupkis mitkanuchas* (shivery shit balls) are not here to protect us. Oh, no. They are here to send us to the grave with a bullet, or to work us to death."

Lucja's brows rose in alarm, stunned by the mature, knowledgeable dialogue flowing from the mouth of a twelve-year-old. But was he believable? She had to find out for herself.

"Goodbye, Chaim," she said tenderly. "I will come and spend time with you tomorrow if you are here at this spot."

"I'll be here, all right. This is my home," he said, pointing to the dirty pavement.

Without a second thought about Chaim's warning, Lucja ascended a concrete stairwell and entered the dimly lit office of the Jewish Police.

Two hours later, with her dirty fingernails protruding from tattered yellow mitts, Lucja sat opposite an older man displaying a Jewish armband, yellow star, and name tag identifying him as Romek Linsky.

"Please forgive my ragged appearance, Mr. Linsky, but I have come to be interviewed. I believe you require an interpreter?"

Romek patted her trembling hand and casually commented, "I've seen worse. What's your name?"

"Lucja Mandelbaum, Miss," she returned.

Romek reached across his desk and retrieved a form. "Fill this application out," he instructed nonchalantly, handing over a pencil. Romek's brown eyes searched for a reaction. "I must warn you, there are lots of applicants. But I like you," he said flirtingly. "We shall see."

Lucja cringed internally as she continued making a solid professional impression. "I'm fluent in German and five other languages, including Yiddish. Please, I need this job." Hunger was no longer new to her, but she had to stress the urgency. "My mother and aunt are dying from starvation. I have no means of supporting them."

Romek exhaled loudly. "While I sympathize with your plight, thousands are starving, and there is little the Police Service can do about it. If you have gold, jewelry, or any other items of value, I suggest you sell them for food," he advised.

Lucja wasn't about to give in. "We weren't given a chance to remove any items of value or retrieve my university qualifications, Mr. Linsky. I'm begging you to give me this job."

Romek deviously thought, *She is an attractive blond, tall and elegant, and could easily be mistaken for an Aryan, except for one noticeable trait—her very dark skin.*

Suddenly, Romek jumped to his feet, his leather boots clicking to attention.

From behind Lucja, a stern-looking SS officer addressed Romek. "Don't keep me waiting for the list, or you will end up on it!" the officer threatened.

"*Ya*, Mein Commandant," Romek replied in a pacifying tone. "It will be delivered before sunset."

The door slammed shut. Heavy footsteps were heard thundering away.

Romek's features flushed pale with alarm. Facing Lucja, he asked, "Can you type?"

"Yes," she responded.

"Excellent!"

Romek riffled through another pile of paperwork on his desk and handed Lucja three sheets of handwritten notes. "Type the names, addresses, dates of birth, and occupations on this list in alphabetical order."

"Does this mean I have the job?" Lucja commented flippantly.

"If you complete this task before midnight, I will consider your appointment."

Ignoring Chaim's earlier warning about the true nature of this clandestine organization, Lucja removed her mittens and began to type. Halfway through the list, her fingers froze in midair. Chaim's words suddenly echoed in her mind, *"Informers that rat on ghetto people ..."*

All names on the list were Jewish males, some as young as nine. Was she aiding the Germans by singling out these men for forced labor, or worse? Lucja, fighting to retain her moral dignity, rose from her chair and searched for Romek. She found him swigging alcohol from a bottle.

"Mr. Linsky, I pride myself on being a good Jewish woman with a moral compass, and I need to know *why* these lists are being submitted to the German commander?"

Red with rage, Romek slammed the brandy bottle down. "Who do you think you are to question my authority?" he barked. "Get back to work!"

With nerves of steel, Lucja retorted, "I will have no part in this! Find someone else." She shot him a repulsive look, "I would rather starve to death than hand over innocent people to the evil Nazis." In turmoil, Lucja fled the office and walked away from the building as fast as her clubfoot would allow. Lucja's unique memory enabled her to store most of the names she had typed. Should she try to locate the men and boys on the list? But she wasn't even sure that these males were present in the ghetto.

In the pitch-black darkness of late night, occasionally stumbling on uneven ghetto roads, Lucja walked two kilometers to where she'd last met Chaim. As she approached his nighttime "bedroom" and daylight trading post, her body stiffened as if something predatory was waiting to attack. An ominous sensation came over her. *Where is everybody?* Chaim was absent from his spot, and the many begging orphan children living on the streets—none of whom were fortunate enough to be protected by people or institutions—were nowhere to be seen. It was as if road sweepers had come and swept them all up. Not a sound could be heard. She had never witnessed the ghetto this cemetery quiet, not even in the late-night hours.

Something was dreadfully wrong.

Lucja, her heart racing with foreboding, rushed up the numerous stairwells of the tenement building. Out of breath, she entered the draped quarters. The same graveyard silence assaulted her ears. No snoring or rustling movements were heard. Lucja groped her way in the darkness, trying to calm a looming panic attack. Her hands touched a bed as she called out softly, "Matka, Maja ..." Her words froze in the air when a piece of ceiling panel crashed down, and a living person fell out, scaring Lucja almost to death.

Abraham's eldest son, the water collector, flung his arms around her. "They are all gone, Lucja," he cried. "They took away my family, and yours."

It took a few moments for her brain to work. *Why?* Lucja took a deep breath to calm her nerves and queried, "Gone where? Who took them?"

The Joselzon boy answered angrily, "Nazis! Who else? I was outside on the street when the raid began."

Eyes wide in disbelief, Lucja implored, "And?"

The boy continued. "The Nazi soldiers ordered women and children at gunpoint to get into trucks. The man next to me gripped my arm, and we ran. We hid in a sewer until the shouting and screaming from our loved ones faded, and we could no longer hear the roar of trucks. When I thought it was safe, I came back here and found all of them gone. I hid in the attic until I heard you call out for your mother."

Lucja's dark features paled. She needed time to process this, but she was devastated, and her mind wouldn't give her that luxury. *If I hadn't gone to the Police and Law Offices. They must have been so scared without me.*

The separation from her loved ones and knowing where they had been taken was more than Lucja could bear. She bellowed with emotional pain. "You sick Nazis, you can take anything you like from me but not who I am!"

In the times that followed—despite extreme hardship, constant fear of death, loss of her family members, and the sick games her captors played—Lucja dedicated herself to staying alive. She refused to give up without a mental fight. She had to bear witness to this evil.

Lucja calmed her inner anguish with an irrevocable thought: *I will testify to the heinous, inhumane atrocities committed on those whose only crime was their faith.*

Unable to live in the apartment that held the last memories of her loved ones, Lucja joined her young friend, Chaim, who, craftily, had escaped the roundup on the street. They became inseparable. He risked his existence daily to provide life-saving food to sustain them.

One summer's day Chaim failed to return from a smuggling trip and was never seen again. Lucja was heartbroken. She wept … and smiled … as she recalled his stern expression when he said, "I want to be taken seriously." Then he added, "If we ever get out of this shithole alive, I'm going to marry you." Lucja recalled slapping him good-humoredly. "You're a crazy little man. I'm much older than you, old enough to be your mother!"

"Well, then, we will make a grand couple."

Beneath a veil of memory, Lucja experienced a dejavu moment: She felt confident that her exchange with Chaim had been uttered previously. Lucja could not have imagined that Lala and Hassam el-Din *had* met before. Were their spiritual entities destined to find each other? Yes.

Chaim was apprehended while returning to the ghetto in broad daylight. He was thrown into the back of a transport truck, deported to Mauthausen Concentration Camp on the Danube, the same camp where Josek Mandelbaum had been interned. Chaim was forced to move blocks of granite from a nearby quarry. His daily life was shaped by starvation and violence.

One miserable rainy day, Chaim, wearing ill-fitting footwear, was pushing a heavy load of granite blocks when his shoes clogged in the mud. He fell and was shot to death by a sadistic camp guard for not rising fast enough. Before the bullet ended his life, Chaim uttered his last words: "Lady, I love you, and one day, we will be together again."

Would Chaim and Lucja meet up in another incarnation?

Lucja began collecting bedding from the apartment. She also sought out her journal, which was still tucked beneath a loose floorboard. Her eyes widened when a piece of folded paper fell out.

My dear, beloved niece,

It is with sadness that I write this, but I promised myself that you should know the "secret" withheld from you, should I not live to tell it to you personally.

Unknown to your grandmother at the time, your grandfather had an affair with a librarian. He turned up at the home one day with a thirteen-year-old boy at his side. He explained to Agnieszka that the child belonged to best friends who had passed away and that he had sworn to take care of the boy if something ever happened to them. My sister and I were five and six at that time. We happily accepted our new "brother." It was only when your grandfather knew he was dying that he made his deathbed confession. By the time Agnieszka learned of his infidelity and Josek's blood-tie, it was too late. Bronisława and her half-brother, Josek, were already married. My sister and your father, I believe to this day, never knew about this shameful secret, but I did. I found your grandfather's diary hidden in his traveling trunk, and . . .

The letter ended prematurely. Was the interruption because the Nazis were evacuating the building? Or did Lucja's aunt have "insight" of this event, feeling the need to hurriedly release the burden of keeping the "family" secret from Lucja?

From her religious teachings, "*... Any other than kin ...*" moved to the forefront of her mind.

Of course, Lucja was affected. She had had a loving family, but one with secrets and lies. She carried all the birth defects of their "sin."

Can a shame be hereditary?

And do the actions of others reflect who you are?

CHAPTER SIXTEEN

- 1942 -

Auschwitz-Birkenau Extermination Camp, Upper Silesia, Poland

"The only thing that I dread: is not to be worthy of my suffering."
—Victor E. Frankl

O n the final day of October 1942, gale-force winds lashed at the intense flames that were engulfing the burning buildings and smoking out the ghetto residents.

Crowds of homeless people stood on the streets with woeful hearts and troubled minds, not knowing what the next day would bring.

Days earlier, they had begun to hear terrible rumors. The ghetto talk instilled fear to the marrow. "Any moment, they're coming to liquidate us, ship us off to an extermination camp in Oswiecim to be murdered."

"I'm told that the Germans have built massive ovens in Silesia, to burn us alive."

"I'm told that they are coming with flamethrowers to burn our homes with us in them."

"A ghetto uprising led by resistance fighters will stop the Nazis from killing our people."

"The war is over."

"No, it is not! It has only just begun."

"*Oy vey*! We are all going die in their factories of death."

"There will be no Jews left in Poland."

Lucja was surrounded by these woeful misgivings. She recalled what her optimistic Chaim had once said: "Don't give up hope, lovely Lucja. I have been smuggling weapons for the brave ghetto fighters. Soon there is going to be a revolt."

Lucja's wolf eyes had glinted with resolve. "I want to join the Jewish resistant fighters. Can you arrange this for me?"

Chaim immediately considered her disability. "Lucja, it's dangerous. You can't run fast with your bad foot!"

"Yes, I can. You just watch me!"

Lucja's valiant proposal was rejected by the young boy.

And now these brave plans were going horribly wrong!

The handful of fighters, primarily young men and women, who had on this day fought desperately and valiantly, were vastly outnumbered and outgunned. Nazi soldiers crushed the revolt with automatic rifle fire. Many were killed, but some escaped by breaking through the barbed wire, only to be found, recaptured, and shot on the spot where they stood.

Today—with blustery air gusting around piles of ashes coming from smoldering furniture, clothing, and other flammable items— further pandemonium broke out when a group of army trucks drove into the ghetto. Soldiers jumped out and randomly seized the homeless at gunpoint. Mothers hugged children in their arms and attempted to escape, screaming and trampling one another.

In the days following, the Nazis accelerated their program to liquidate *all* the Lodz prisoners. Over time, 12,000 Jews, including Lucja, were crammed into trucks. The *Final Solution* to eradicate up to 11 million European Jews in death camps was in full execution.

Chilly, penetrating rain savaged Lucja and the other prisoners, who stood motionless on the terminal's platform, like human garbage. No one uttered a word. No one wept, not even the small children. It was as if they had been hypnotized into silence.

Lucja tried blowing warm breath on her frosty hands, but the clouds of vapors clung like icicles to her bare fingertips. As her feet stomped in place to circulate her blood, Lucja overheard a male voice praying, "Hear, oh Israel. God is with us."

Lucja's top lip curled up in scorn. She turned heel to face him. "Shut up, old man!" she commanded. "*He* is not listening to you or to any of us. If *He* were, we wouldn't be here shivering to death in the frigid rain."

Lucja's disrespectful words brought an outraged retort from

the elderly woman standing at the man's side. "Mind your tongue, woman, or *you* will not enter God's kingdom …"

A rifle barrel impacted the woman's skull. Hit like a ton of bricks, she slumped to the concrete. Her horrified husband immediately moved toward his wife but was held back by the same rifle, which was now pointed at his head. The soldier's demoniacal voice bellowed, "Another sound from any of you, and you'll all be shot!"

Lucja was guilt-ridden with blame. *Me and my big mouth!*

At the end of the day, a train whistled into the station. The passengers were counted and inspected as if they were a herd of cattle being crammed into freight cars. The *livestock* were being transported to unknown fates. Scattered on the platform were the dead bodies of the rabbi and his wife. The holy man had refused to leave his unconscious spouse, and he was summarily executed.

Lucja endured the torturous journey, jammed side by side with many others in vile unsanitary conditions. The rail spur ran directly to Auschwitz-Birkenau. For some, this was the end of the line. Many elderly and young children had already perished on this savage journey.

Three days later at midnight, the train transporting these victims of Hitlerism rumbled into Auschwitz-Birkenau, thirty-seven miles from Krakow. Having traveled without food or water while breathing only putrid air, they were physically and emotionally drained. Lucja felt she no longer belonged to this world, or to any other.

The train screeched to a halt. When the freight doors were

opened, the inmates saw SS men with machine guns at the ready, ferocious dogs barking at their sides. *"Raus! Schnell!"* (Get out, quick!)

Cudgel blows rained down on those too weak to obey. Assailed by beatings and snapping dogs, Lucja was tormented by memories of being head-whipped. The dehydrated and starving girl was herded onto a stadium-like platform with the others. Instantly, SS brutes began separating men from women. The men's line proceeded first. Standing in front of the women's line, Lucja was able to observe a slender man, wearing a dark-green uniform adorned with shiny medals, seated at a long table. While she couldn't hear what was being said, she saw this Nazi officer's white-gloved hand wave left and wave right. She didn't realize that a wave to the left sent you to an immediate death, an instant murder. Or that a wave to the right meant you were chosen to work—to slave to death. *Links* or *rechts* (left or right) carried the power to determine who lived or died.

Now it was Lucja's turn to face the embodiment of evil—SS Haupsturmführer, Dr. Josef Mengele, a cold-hearted killer who felt no empathy with humanity. He was aptly referred to as *The Angel of Death*.

This tawny-dark thirty-two-year-old—with a bent nose and eyes like coal—hardly fit the description of Hitler's dream of a pure Aryan race. "Come closer," Mengele ordered. Rising from his seat, he rounded the table and intensely examined a composed Lucja. When the doctor's probing eyes reached her deformed foot, he bared his pearl-white teeth. With a flick of his wrist, Mengele roared, *"Links!"*

Surrounded by those consigned to die, Lucja was shoved into a line of elderly men and women, mothers with babies, young children, and the disabled, blind, and deaf. These discarded humans were clueless to their fate, having been told that they were being taken to shower. The mass of people pressed onward. Then, out of the blue, a loud voice instructed someone. "Bring that one back," Mengele ordered, "the gypsy woman with the crippled foot."

Lucja screamed in pain as she was brutally dragged by her arms and hair back to the Mengele's examination table. The Angel of Death flashed a powerful torch beam in her face. "I don't know how I missed this, but, undeniably, you have a distinct eye color. Does this coloring run in your family?"

"No" was Lucja's blunt reply. She was irate. *Why is this beast so interested in my eye color? My parents had blue eyes. So what?*

The nefarious line of questions would soon reveal its purpose.

Mengele's deep-seated ambition was to achieve greatness in the medical sciences. He chose to dedicate himself to genetics, to unlock its secrets and discover the sources of human imperfections, especially those of eye color. Now, the doctor was accepting this new challenge. Lucja's cursed wolf eyes saved her from being sent to the gas chambers, but, in time, she would wish that the monster Mengele had not changed his barbaric mind.

Lucja's survivor spirit would be torn asunder by unimaginable crimes.

One hateful month turned into another. December 1943 arrived with temperatures hovering below zero. Prisoner number 25402, the number tattooed on the inside of Lucja's arm, was *selected*. Males were tattooed on the outside of the arm. (Tattoos are forbidden under Mosaic Law—Leviticus 19:28. Obviously, this sacred proclamation was scoffed at by the Hitlerian murderers!)

A deathly pale, head-shorn Lucja, a mere bag of bones with little muscle—wearing dirty, threadbare, striped pajamas—was singled out from the Block C (formerly an abandoned Polish army barracks), which she shared in appallingly cramped conditions with 200 other women. Lucja was now a shadow without an identity, but she was alive thanks to her tenacity. Totally blinded by Mengele's eye-drop experimentation, she was frogmarched with the latest arrival of Hungarian Jews, many of whom were dwarfs. The *selected* were taken to an underground facility designed to resemble a shower room. There, Zyklon B, a cyanide-based pesticide, ended the life of the beautiful, loving, and kind Lucja. The last thing she heard was music, the ghetto orchestra playing Wagner's *Bridal Chorus*. She did not see the bellowing flames flying from the chimneys of ovens that could not incinerate bodies quickly enough. This horrific manner of death would soon desiccate her gas-poisoned body and that of her unborn fetus to bone shards and ashes. Not only had she been a guinea pig in Auschwitz, but she had also endured paralyzing trauma, shame, and degradation at the hands of her jailors. The Nazi racial laws prohibited Germans from having sexual intercourse with Jews, but this had not applied to the eight drunken SS guards and two SS physicians who used her as a comfort woman, gangraping her for two hours.

Lucja had not menstruated since entering the killing center. She was unaware of her pregnancy when she was selected!

Hitler had decreed, "No future enemy should ever come into the world." Auschwitz actively carried out this policy of genocide, and Ruth, a camp prisoner, was an unwilling Jewish participant.

Ruth was a thriving Jewish gynecologist in Romania before WWII. In 1944 she was deported to Auschwitz and put to work in the infirmary, where she treated the prisoners without the benefit of anesthesia, antibiotics, bandages, or anything else that could lessen their pain. Under threat of death, Ruth assisted Mengele, who she knew ran experiments on pregnant women, twins, and the physically handicapped before delivering them to the gas chambers. When Ruth was *ordered* to report pregnant woman to the Angel of Death, she did just that, unaware that the mothers-to-be were not going to another camp for better nutrition and milk, as they had been told. It was all an unforgivable ploy. Desperate women who wanted to save their babies had been running to Mengele to inform him, "I'm pregnant. I wish to go to the camp you have promised will help me take better care of myself."

Instead of receiving improved care, these unsuspecting women were having their babies ripped from the wombs without anesthesia. Most died, but those who survived the surgery were gassed.

When Ruth finally learned of the fates of these pregnant women, she began to conduct surgeries that, before the war, she would have believed herself incapable of performing—abortions. Contrary to her professional and religious beliefs, Ruth undertook concealed abortions on dirty floors and bunks using only her unwashed hands.

After the war, it became known that Doctor Ruth had ended the lives of 3,000 fetuses in the hope that the mothers would survive and later be able to bear more children.

But this *Angel of Mercy* arrived too late for Lucja.

The moment Lucja's body and that of her fetus were being consumed by fire in the inferno, a young girl gawked. Circling the compound high above her was an enormous raven. The girl was puzzled. No feathered creature had been seen in this hell since the chimneys began to belch forth their death knells.

The girl darted inside Lucja's former barrack. "Quick, come outside," she appealed to a roommate. "You're not going to believe it!"

"It's a sign from God. He has not forgotten us," another barrack inmate remarked.

"This bird isn't God's messenger," another woman argued. "This bird is a *bad* omen. We are all going to die like Lucja, sooner or later."

Their debate about good and evil was immediately disrupted by truncheon blows from their barrack Kapo, a fellow Jewess who received special privileges (extra bread rations) for performing acts of cruelty on her own people.

"Return to your bunks!" she screamed.

Her time spent on Earth was over for the childless, sacrificial Lucja. Would *Yahweh* be appeased and finally absolve the *mother* sinners—Rebekah, Debowrah, Palomba, Fajcia, and Bronislawa—for bedding their kin? Or had the raven taken the spiritual essence of Lucja's unborn child on a repeat journey: *You will live and die and repeat.*

Lucja would never know that the Roma child she helped smuggle under a fence before the liquidation of the Gypsy camp was still *alive*. Her name was Maria. She was *Jewish* of Ashkenazi descent, and she was related to Palomba of Spain.

Was the heredity "curse" waiting for *her,* as well?

It was inevitable! Fate's wheel continued to rotate.

CHAPTER SEVENTEEN

- 1945 -

The British Commonwealth of South Africa

"The reincarnated souls lived ... but not happily ever after."
——ANONYMOUS

On Christmas morning a wild, painted hunting dog stealthily planted one paw after another on arid red soil, moving in a stalking posture. The animal was bone thin. Its hair was matted to its skin, and its sagging teats, the result of numerous pregnancies, hung low. With nostrils twitching hungrily, the bitch began to forage through a pile of corn husks searching for something tasty to eat, some prey she could tear apart to appease her ravenous stomach. But today was not her lucky day. A rock hit her on the back of the head. The startled bitch howled in pain but was not about to give up the possibility of food. She bared her fangs menacingly and stood her ground. Her attacker growled, "Go! Get gone! Shoo! Go away!"

As her heart pounded in her chest, Anele lifted another rock. The next projectile tore the animal's scalp. The yelping dog, with hungry yellow eyes, bolted into a thick brush nearby. She sat on back limbs and watched.

Nothing could have prepared Anele, a runaway, indentured servant, for what she saw lying helpless in the compost pit. Her brown eyes widened with disbelief as she dropped to her knees and scooped up a tiny newborn, cold to the touch. Anele stared at the abandoned infant, who, although dark-skinned, wasn't of the African race. On the baby girl's tiny, dirt-encrusted face was a dark, oval skin blemish. Her limbs were gangly, with one leg shorter than the other. Wisps of fair hair mingled with birthing blood clung to the child's scalp. A mystified Anele questioned, *Who does this white newborn belong to?*

Anele gasped when the infant's eyelids drew back exposing irises that were a pale shade of yellow topaz. "God of the Zulus, how could I have been so blind?"

A recent dialogue became crystal clear. "*I set you free.*" As the door to Anele's memory opened, she recalled some disturbing events.

Eight months earlier, freshly laundered clothing flapped in the breeze, held fast with wooden pegs. It was the start of autumn, which runs from April to May in South Africa. Anele, a domestic servant, observed some people advancing. As the foursome neared, Anele's inquisitive eyes examined them: a young girl flanked by an elderly man and a short woman of similar age, and, behind them, a young man who looked to be nineteen or so. But Anele's eyes focused on the slim girl. She was the most beautiful foreign-looking girl she had ever seen. Her black hair, as thick as a horse's mane, glistened like polished coal. And her dazzling topaz eyes! They were the color of the yellow gemstone plentiful in these parts. What the girl wore seemed strange in these modern times. Her full-length calico dress buttoned at the front—like the English clothing pioneers wore in America—was out of place in this time and age.

Anele's musings were disrupted when the elderly man spoke in broken English, "Signora, are you the proprietor of this plantation? We need work."

Anele didn't recognize the accent, but she sensed danger. *The master will devour this child faster than a fox in a henhouse.* She spoke her next thought out loud. "If you understand me at all, take your family and leave. The plantation owner isn't hiring now ..."

The clatter of fast-approaching hooves halted their conversation. All heads turned. The rider came to a halt. Lord Alan Hallworthy dismounted. Anele's heart skipped a beat. It was too late!

Alan removed his sunglasses and stared at the strangers. "Are you Spaniards?" he queried.

"No," the elderly man replied. "We are Sicilians."

"You're a long way from home," Alan remarked. "What brings you to these parts? Or shouldn't I ask?" he ended cynically.

"Bad times from the war," Cesare responded. "We needed a fresh start, and here we are. Can you give us work?"

Alan ignored him as he turned to face Maria. "You're a beauty. What's your name?"

Maria shrunk behind the elderly Cesare, who quickly commented, "She doesn't talk. She has … how you say?" The man tapped his head, "… brain sickness. No good in the head."

"What a shame," Alan uttered in a voice that could melt butter. "I'm sure I'll be able to find her something to do. You all can work for me, but for food and lodging only."

Anele cast aside her reflections to focus on a more pressing concern. She pulled out a length of horse grass from around the baby's intended gravesite and used it to tie off the bitten, mangled umbilical cord. Using the hem of her skirt, she wiped as much dirt as she could from the infant's ashen face. Then she nestled the newborn girl between her breasts. Supporting the baby's head, Anele ran back to her former hiding spot. She slipped into the cave, where a previous unexpected *visitor* had caused her to cry out, "Don't sneak up on me like that, Maria. You nearly frightened the life out of me!"

As the earlier encounter subsided, Anele felt a rush of adrenaline. "Come out, here *now!*" she hollered angrily. "How could you do such a terrible thing, Maria? Your baby is alive! She needs to be fed."

A deathly, empty silence greeted the angry servant. The cave was devoid of life. Maria had disappeared without a trace.

CHAPTER EIGHTEEN

- 1932-1942 -

The Island of Sicily

*"We shall draw from the heart of suffering itself the
means of inspiration and survival."*
—WINSTON CHURCHILL

M aria was privileged, pandered to by her wealthy, devout
Catholic parents. Nothing was too good for their only
child.

Her father, Alberto Genovese, a native-born Sicilian, and her
Spanish-born mother, Sofia Del la Llerena, were Ashkenazi Jewish
descendants. And they *were* second and third cousins! The couple
was blood related to Maimon and Palomba de Spinoza of medieval
Spain.

Today was Maria's tenth birthday. It was the day her childhood would crumble.

That evening, in a bedlam of celebratory spirit, the mansion filled with party guests. The birthday girl, above average height for her age, sidled down the staircase clothed finely and fashionably in a lilac silk dress with matching satin ballet shoes. Her long black hair, styled in curls, hung down her back. Her dark Gypsy complexion masked an oval facial blemish. Her long princess dress hid her deformity, one kneecap slightly larger than the other.

At the stroke of midnight, the exhausted birthday girl said her goodnights and headed upstairs to bed. Fast asleep, she didn't hear the sash window being pried open. Suddenly, a sweaty hand clamped her mouth shut. After being jolted terrifyingly from her dreams, she wanted to scream, but her larynx was paralyzed. The shadowy figure looming over her looked muscular. "Don't make a sound," the intruder whispered. "If you want to see your parents again, you'll do as I say. I'm going to take my hand from your mouth. Do not even think of screaming!"

There was no mistaking *that* voice. It was imprinted in the little girl's heart. Her puppy love for her cousin had no bounds. But his behavior this night was too much to rationalize. Speaking with ease, she was not quiet when she said, "My father is going to kill you if he catches you in my bedroom. Paolo, what you doing here? And why did you come through the window?" The bedroom drapes flapped ominously in the night breeze.

"Shut up," hissed her cousin. "I will kill you if you make a noise. I will not hurt you. I'm only here for the money. Get dressed. You're coming with me."

Paolo's words sent a jolt through the child. She no longer knew her cousin, a person she had, until now, adored.

Maria Genovese was kidnapped from her bedroom by her sixteen-year-old fourth cousin, Paolo Girdazello. He and his aging parents, Maria's impoverished relatives, had been given a home by the Genovese family, not out of compassion but for alternative motives. They slaved daily and were poorly paid by the controlling Alberto Genovese. He was in charge!

Paolo's mother, Raphaela, a tiny, birdlike woman in her sixties, was a cook. She worked long hours in the kitchen, usually to the point of physical exhaustion. As a youngster, Paolo had witnessed his mother's tears of exhaustion after standing on her feet from five in the morning until ten at night. Cesare, Paolo's father, was employed as a general dogsbody—Do this! Do that! Go fetch! He was called to work at any time of the day or night. At age seven, Paolo was put to work mucking out the stalls that housed Alberto's prized Andalusian "dancing" horses.

Paolo was disgruntled thinking his family had no control over their lives, couldn't stand up for themselves, had no rights, and were not viewed as *blood*. He felt they were treated with blatant disrespect for their feelings, opinions, and wants, and that their human dignity was being violated. Rage had festered within him beginning in his early teenage years. Envious of his wealthy relatives, especially the indulged Maria, he yearned to wear the same fine clothes, throw equally lavish parties, and own horses just as beautiful.

Now, his accumulated anger was telling him it was payback time!

Was this revengeful turncoat prepared to see Maria's family collapse into pieces? Oh, yes! But his get-rich-quick, rags-to-riches plan would backfire.

The old and wise Don Alberto refused to be a victim of blackmail. The note discovered in Maria's bedroom demanded a payment within a deadline of ten hours. Cash was to be left at an old monastery fifty kilometers from the mansion. The kidnapper did not realize that he had accidentally dropped a silver ring, jewelry given to him by his uncle. Alberto was incensed that a member of his family could stoop so low for greed. It was against all codes of decency and family ties.

"I will find the *bastard* and hang him by his balls!" vowed Alberto.

Alberto sent for Cesare. His cheeks flushed red with rage when he growled, "Your bastard son has taken my child. You better find him before I do. Have him return my Maria immediately. Tell him that I will kill you and your wife if this is not done!"

Cesare was dumbfounded. "Don Alberto, you are mistaken. My son is an honorable boy. He would never harm Maria. He loves her, as we all do."

Alberto shot him a contemptuous grimace. "Then tell me why …" He paused as he retrieved the ring from his pants pocket. "I found this in Maria's room. There is no good reason for it to be on her bed!"

Cesare's head hung limply. He couldn't believe it! Were his ears deceiving him? However, a niggling doubt came to his mind. "I hate my life," Paolo had previously told him. 'I'm tired of being the slave all the time. I'll find a better way to live."

The old man's musings were interrupted by Alberto's angry voice. "Round up the men and find your bastard son before I do!"

For a split second, Cesare felt immeasurable relief. He hadn't been executed on the spot. Cesare rushed to the downstairs kitchen. "Raphaela, something bad has happened. Pack your things. We have to leave *now!*"

His wife was perplexed. "Why? What have you done?"

"It's not what I have done. It's what our son has done!"

"And what is that?" she demanded.

"Our stupid son has kidnapped Maria to get money out of Alberto."

In disbelief, she retorted, "Are you crazy? Paolo wouldn't harm a hair on Maria's head."

Cesare seized her arm fiercely. "Do as I tell you, woman. Get our things. Let's get out of here before we all end up dead!"

Paolo's coconspirator, a local boy acting as lookout, rushed into the underground catacombs yelling, "You need to get out *now!* Maria's father, Don Alberto, and fifteen other riders are heading this way. It won't take long for this old building to be surrounded …" The boy inhaled a panicked breath, "… and you know what will happen to us. Hurry up. I have a cart nearby. Let's get out of here before we're slaughtered like pigs."

The bewildered Maria was hurriedly blindfolded and gagged.

Her urine-soaked nightgown was clinging to her legs. She was elated. Her father was coming to rescue her. She would soon go home to her mother and tell her about this awful ordeal.

To Paolo, his relative was nothing more than an object he could use to lift himself out of the impoverished conditions he had been raised in. He had hoped for a big payout, but now he grew depressed and panicked. He had risked it all for greed.

When all seemed lost and hopeless, Paolo hatched another audacious plan. There would be no room for errors this time!

Back at the mansion, Sofia knew her husband well, but nothing could have prepared her for his ultimate decision. "The bastard is not going to get one lira out of me, and he won't get far. I have men scouring the island and ferry landing," Alberto stated, incensed.

Sofia begged him, but no amount of pleading for their daughter's safety swayed her mule-headed Mafia boss husband. He was angry and vengeful.

On learning that the rescue mission had failed, the clock kept ticking with no word of her precious daughter. Sofia, in her late fifties, began to decline. She refused to get out of bed or eat or wash.

It was 5 A.M. Alberto observed Sofia's cat sitting outside the master suite meowing. He opened the door. The room was pitch-black. The dim hallway light barely illuminated the figure lying on her back with arms outstretched, appearing to be asleep. Alberto reached for a lamp. "Oh, Christ!" he cried. It was surreal. He checked for a pulse, but Sofia's cold neck provided the answer. Her life on Earth had ended.

Alberto noticed her Spanish eyes were half open and crusted with foam. Sofia was dead. Prescription sleeping pill bottles littered the carpet.

Screaming in anguish, Alberto cried like a baby, but the tears did not ease his guilt. He couldn't help thinking. *If only I hadn't been so stubborn!*

As time passed, Alberto would not sleep without having disturbing flashbacks of the moment he'd found his dead wife. Feeling strongly that his precious daughter was still alive, he continued searching for her.

By 1950 Alberto believed that his daughter was, indeed, dead. He ended his life with a single bullet to the head.

The night sky was ablaze with iridescent splendor, but not a glimmer shone in the sedated girl's wolf eyes. Her fate was now in her cousin's hands.

On the Messina boat dock, Germans and Italian military officials awaited the overnight ferry to the mainland. Paola, his cap pulled low, gripped Maria's hand. Disguised as a boy, hair cropped and wearing peasant pants and jacket, she was escorted onto the boat. Their fares were paid for by a wallet picked from the pocket of the owner of a local grocery store in Messina.

＊

At the stroke of midnight, the sailing vessel, escorted by a German attack boat, commenced its voyage through the narrow strait of the Mediterranean Sea to the Italian mainland. Later Paolo and Maria disembarked at Calabria and boarded a train heading for Rome.

Though the cobbled plaza was thronged with German soldiers in steel-toed boots, the Eternal City of Rome was something out of a storybook to Maria. The morning sun shone brightly on the ornamented facades of a magnificent cathedral surrounded by colorful flora. It would be the last memorable splendid scene she would see in her young life.

Paolo's dreams of obtaining more money than he could spend in a lifetime were shattered. Soured by reality and afraid for his life, Paolo hurriedly sold Maria to the highest bidder—a German brothel keeper—for a fraction of the money his ransom plans would have realized. This debauched sale would not have a fairytale ending. Maria's nightmare was just beginning. She was about to confront the worst of mankind's evils.

The two-story brothel, owned by a German woman with no heart and her Italian husband, a former priest, was situated next to a Catholic church.

＊

Abandoned to her fate, Maria beseeched her new owners, "I'm not a beggar on the street, as my cousin told you. He kidnapped me from my home in Sicily. My parents, Alberto and Sofia Genovese, will be worried sick. Please, contact them, and they will reward you. They are rich."

The heavens were not listening. Neither were her jailers.

Little Maria became, by force, a sex worker for depraved Nazis with sadistic predilections, a pedophilic desire for children. In time her self-image diminished, and she came to equate love with sexual exploitation. Eventually, Maria saw nothing wrong with the sexual abuse of her by others. Her privileged, happy childhood no longer existed; however, she was knowledgeable, and she had been gifted with an exceptional memory. Maria would store these traumatic events in her memory banks for the rest of her life, as she would her religious upbringing. Her recollections would inspire many poignant questions: *Where is the Creator? Why has He not come to the salvation of the modern-day Jews, as He had to the enslaved Hebrew people in Egypt? Why has he not sent hail, a flood, locusts, and frogs today, as he had for the Children of Israel in the past? Why has He not destroyed the Nazis and saved the hapless Jews, His people?*

Later in life, a mature Maria would turn away from religion and ponder, *Strike the sea with your stick? God parted the Red Sea?* Maria couldn't fathom how people could believe these stories. Her reason told her it was not possible to part such a vast expansion of seawater, also not likely that the Israelites arrived at a small estuary where freak underwater currents and hurricane winds had parted the seas.

Day in and day out Maria suffered at the hands of perverts, yet she somehow found the strength to hang on to some element of control over her own life. She rode out the evil by helping the other victims.

Maria purloined money from the wallets of her abusers and distributed it equally among the other fourteen needy girls and boys. Then she set in motion an escape plan for all of them: "When she brings our evening meal, I will bash her head in with this." Bending, she retrieved a brick from under her bed, one that she had dislodged from a wall. "Then we will rush upstairs, out the front door, and find our way back to our homes."

A soft voice was heard from the end of the row of cots. "I have no home to go to. The Germans killed my family. We are Jewish. My parents hid me in the attic, but the Nazis found me and brought me here."

Maria sighed. "Then you can travel with me. You will love my mother and father, his prized horses, and the pony he bought me for my birthday." Tears of recollection pooled in her eyes.

Maria's brave and kind intentions were thwarted when on May 1943, the German-operated brothels were closed down on Mussolini's orders.

Maria had been given the best education, starting at age four. Home-schooled by the most exceptional teachers, she spoke several languages. On the day they were ordered to dress for a journey, she overheard a female Italian guard say, "It's the end of the road for them." A German male guard heartlessly added, "The fewer dirty

Jews and Romani (gypsies) on Earth the better."

Maria imagined the scarfed fortune-tellers, faces as black as night, that she had seen at various fairs. The male guard had included her in his bigoted comment. His sentiment was to have a dire effect on her subsequent incarnation.

Maria's dark skin, facial blemish, and kneecap deformity had been discussed by her parents. "She's *different* from our blood, yet she is *our* blood, correct!" Alberto remarked with a look of doubt on his face.

"Someone in our ancestry must have been dark, like her," Sofia concluded simply.

"So tell me, Wife, who in *your* family had wolf eyes? I have brown eyes, and yours are green!"

"They are not animal eyes!" Sophia argued fiercely. "They are rare gems!"

One May morning, following the evacuation of the brothel, an ear-splitting train whistle shrieked. The transport cargo, 140 brothel children from across Italy, were tightly packed into a freight wagon. This would become the least of their discomforts. They traveled without food or water, breathing only stale air, for thirty-three hours.

It was 3 o' clock in the morning when the train rumbled through the arched, warehouse-style building and approached the railhead of the Auschwitz-Birkenau death camp.

Dr. Josef Mengele surveyed his prey with dead, gimlet eyes.

With a flick of his gloved hand, children who didn't interest him were sent to certain death. His attention peaked when the eleven-year-old Maria, head lowered, stood in front of him. He studied her carefully before commenting, "And what do we have here? A *Zigeuner* (gypsy), another subspecies as offensive as Jews."

A brazen Maria, with her head still lowered, declared in German, "I'm no damn Gypsy! I'm Sicilian, you idiot!"

Crunch! Blood gushed forth from Maria's nose.

"That will teach you to be insolent to Dr. Mengele," the female kapo said, lifting her cudgel to strike another blow. Mengele raised his arm, preventing the second punishment. "She's a lively one, for sure!" he said. "I like that. Come closer and show me your face." The doctor's eyes lit up. "I've seen this eye color only once before on a Polish Jew, and here you are, with the same remarkable coloring. I doubt that you and the Polish Jew are blood-related. This is fascinating," he added, rubbing gloved hands in delight. He turned to the kapo, who held Maria in a tight grip. "Take her to be deloused, shaved, and tattooed, then put her in the Roma Block until further notice."

The German guard who had accompanied the children from Italy spoke up. "Herr Doctor, I hope you don't mind my saying, but she was a brothel prisoner. Should she not be taken to the Pleasure House?"

Mengele glared at the guard with his evil Nazi eye, and Maria's heartless chaperone hurriedly left the examination area.

With tears cascading, a naked, shivering Maria was led to the showers. The cold water satisfied her thirst, but not her emotional numbness. Nor did it soothe the bleeding razor cuts that covered her shaved head. The chilly waters did, however, ease the discomfort of the needle punctures to her inner arm. Prisoner number 10888 Z (Roma identification letter) joined the 23,200 Gypsies in Auschwitz-Birkenau at a barracks known as the Gypsy Family Camp. Her fellow prisoners had come from Germany and territories annexed to the Reich, including Bohemia, Moravia, Poland, Hungary, Yugoslavia, France, Belgium, the Netherlands, and Norway.

Like the Jews, Gypsies were classified as non-Aryan by the Nuremberg laws of 1935. They were singled out by the Nazis to share the Jewish fate of racial persecution and annihilation.

Maria was taken to Mengele's hospital. There, the doctor began his examination. A day later he performed surgery on her distorted knee without anesthesia. Medically unknown at the time, Maria had, in fact, hereditary morphological chondromalacia: softened hyaline cartilage of the knee cap. Her inhumane surgery resulted in debilitating agony. Maria was no longer able to place any weight on her left leg or to see correctly out of her left eye because of eye drops that had been previously applied.

As 1943 was coming to an end, Maria learned that SS guards were planning to invade the gypsy quarters and forcibly lead the residents to their deaths. She hatched an escape plan. Earlier she had spotted a breach in a fence that separated the Roma camp from the Jewish compound. Was it big enough for her to crawl through?

That night, while her fellow inmates were sleeping deeply, Maria snuck out of the barracks. Using every muscle she could, she stomach-crawled in the mud to the fence, which, fortunately, was not electrified. Maria eluded the powerful spotlights blazing from a soaring guard tower operated by machine-gun-toting guards. Digging a trench with her hands, she wiggled through the breach in the fence. As she was making her way to the darkened barracks area, she froze. A solitary figure emerged from the latrines. "God above, you nearly frightened me to death," Lucja cried. "Who are you?"

While Maria related her tragic story, Lucja's head spun. "Hide behind the latrines, and I'll come for you in the morning," she instructed.

At daybreak, Lucja skipped the breakfast lineup to smuggle Maria into the infirmary. There, Jewish doctors concealed her under the floorboards during the SS doctors' inspections and during *Appell* (roll call).

Each morning and evening prisoners were marched to an assembly point, an extensive area that held 40 to 50,000 people, to be counted. From her hiding place, Maria heard a resonating, roaring voice. It didn't sound like the voice of a human but, rather, that of a raging animal. She cringed in fear and stiffened on the soil beneath the infirmary.

One day Lucja stopped coming to see her. Sadly, Maria learned that her guardian angel was dead. Lucja had been gassed, her remains incinerated. To Maria, Lucja Mandelbaum was her heroine, risking her own life for a person she didn't even know.

⟡

On an icy winter's morning in January 1945, the infirmary floorboards were removed. Maria heard a voice calling down into the dank darkness. "You're free. Come out! The bastard Germans have fled, abandoned the camp! The war is over!"

On January 27, the 32nd rifle division of the Soviet Red Army entered the main camp. Maria was one of 7,000 starving survivors who had been left behind by the camp overlords. She had not been discovered by the Germans, and if she had, she would have been considered too feeble to undergo the death march orchestrated by them to erase evidence of their evil activities. However, the bodies of those who had been left behind were emaciated, and they were not immune to death.

Having spent most of the war in her squalid, underground space, Maria, her body crawling with lice, was in the throes of a slow and agonizing death. Her wasted body, weighing only forty pounds, had little strength to fight typhus, an epidemic killer in the camp.

Fading in and out of her delirious state, Maria welcomed death. Was her fate in her own hands?

Could her genetic heritage have already mapped out her fate?

CHAPTER NINETEEN

- END OF WORLD WAR II -

Displaced Person Camp, Italy

"Out of suffering have emerged the most stalwart souls; the most massive characters are seared with scars."
—KHALIL GIBRAN

I t was touch and go for the critically ill, unconscious patient lying dormant in the displacement camp's hospital. Maria had been in a coma ever since she had been removed to Italy by the International Red Cross. Though the typhus infection was now under control, it was baffling why she still hadn't regained consciousness. Luckily, someone had the answers.

Well on his way to recovery from typhus, fifty-three-year-old Stanislaw Vogel, prisoner number 65312, had also survived the death camp. Before the war, he had practiced as a forensic neuropathologist in Warsaw. He was born to an Italian Christian mother and a Polish Jewish father, and after he was arrested, he was sent to Gross-Rosen, a labor camp in occupied Poland. There, Stanislaw was assigned to brutal labor, repairing roads seven days a week. After witnessing the barbarism of both German and Polish doctors in the prison camp, he never revealed he was medically trained.

Now, he came forward and identified his former occupation to the displacement camp's medical team. He asked if the hospital had an X-ray machine. "No," was the reply. Two days later, a U.S. Army field unit delivered this life-saving device.

Ironically, a *German* physicist, Wilhelm Conrad Rontgen, first produced and detected Röntgen rays (X-rays) in 1895 while working at the University of Würzburg. His phenomenal invention was able to penetrate certain solids and other opaque materials.

Dr. Stanislaw Vogel relayed his diagnosis to the displacement camp's medical team: "In my professional opinion, she has *concutere* (Latin for 'to shake violently). At some time she has received a traumatic brain injury. However, I see minimal damage to blood vessels from her concussion."

As were other critically ill patients, Maria was monitored around the clock. Stanislaw suspected her post-concussion syndrome would eventually manifest itself in depression, anxiety, and cognitive memory problems.

Time paused for Maria, who had once, at age six, vowed to her parents that she was going to be a doctor when she grew up.

At the end of February 1945, Maria opened her eyes. She didn't know who or where she was. Had she lost some normal brain function? Alas, yes!

Still, in the recovery ward, Maria did not recognize the person who stood at the foot of her bed, his mouth gaping with astonishment. If her brain had been functioning correctly, he was the last person she would have wished to see.

The tall young man broke out in a cold sweat and clasped his hands to his mouth, trying to prevent crying out in shock. He didn't think she had survived the Pleasure House in Rome, let alone the notorious death camp of Auschwitz!

His muscular legs pumped with speed as if his life depended on them.

"She's *here!*" Paolo exclaimed frantically.

"What are you babbling about, son," Paolo's father, Cesare, asked. "Whose is here?"

"*Maria Genovese!*"

Paolo's doubtful mother responded. "Your eyes are deceiving you. I was there when the officials came and informed Alberto that Maria was dead, had died in Rome."

Paolo uttered profanities. "*Fanculo, fanculo.* I'm screwed!"

Lost in another world, the dazed and confused Maria spent most of her recovery time in silence walking the hospital corridors and smiling at other patients. Stanislaw visited her every day. One day his visits ended.

The Red Cross had located his wife and mother. Both had survived the gas chambers. Reunited, they immigrated to the U.S., where Stanislaw continued practicing neurophysiology until his death at age seventy-five. But the gypsy-looking girl was never far from his mind. All attempts to find her toward the end of his life were in vain. Nor was the critically ill teenager forgotten by her treacherous, conspiratorial kidnapper.

This once privileged Sicilian girl, believed by most to be dead, was about to enter another portal of Hades. It would open its fire-breathing mouth and swallow her up.

Would cosmic powers prevent this darkness and shield her from evil human forces?

It seemed unlikely, but … perhaps?

CHAPTER TWENTY

- AUTUMN, 1945 -

The Valley of a Thousand Hills, South Africa

"Hell is—other people."
—JEAN-PAUL SARTRE

The day after Paolo had discovered Maria alive, he feared for his life should Don Alberto ever learn of her survival. So he spawned an audacious plot and put it in action.

That day his parents listened in astonishment to his proposition. Blinded by love for her only child, Paolo's mother was easily persuaded. She would have done anything to save her son from being shot by Don Alberto in Italy.

The trio walked into the International Red Cross Emigration Processing Unit where Paolo's mother, with flushed cheeks, staged an Oscar-winning performance: "Oh, you have no idea how happy I am to have found my niece here, and alive! All her family perished in Auschwitz! My husband, my son, and I are all she has left in the world. We are her guardians now, but she has no identification papers. She will need a new passport to sail with us to South Africa. I can give you her birth date and other supporting verbal documentation."

The ocean liner, crammed with refugees, set sail for South Africa in late February of 1945. Unashamedly, Paolo rejoiced. He had gotten away with kidnapping and escaped being murdered by a mafia boss. Was luck still on his side?

On the last night of their long voyage, Maria was further victimized. "You made me do this to you!" her twisted abuser yelled.

The same shame she'd experienced in the brothel, a twisted truth now lost to her impaired memory, triggered Maria's dysfunctional bond with her abuser. She followed Paolo around the ship like a faithful puppy. But he was hardly a caring angel looking after a brainsick girl with enduring mental scars.

Maria and her self-proclaimed escorts arrived at the Port of Durban in autumn. Suffering from memory loss, Maria was oblivious to the logistics of boarding the ocean liner and landing in South Africa. Nor was she aware of her own identity.

Later, entangled in the Hallworthy estate in a web of lies, Maria, an unwilling victim of deception, sheltered behind her uncle. While the phony family gathered and conversed in their native tongue, Alan Hallworthy took hold his slave's, Anele's, arm. "Take the girl to

…" he hesitated briefly before adding, "… *the-you-know-where*." Put Maria to work. Give her cleaning cloths. Make sure that the place is spotless from top to bottom," he ordered. I will take her family to the stables. They can stay there."

Alan's chilling orders were as clear as a spring thaw. The "you-know-where" was the place that murdered a child's innocence. To Anele and the others before her, the old gamekeeper's abode was a house of horrors, where heinous acts laying bare the darkest of human behavior were carried out.

Anele's brown eyes filled with tears. Past depravity had stabbed and cut and sullied her soul, leaving a permanent traumatic scar. But she knew if she did not obey her master's bidding, she would not live to see another day.

Later, locked in the gamekeeper's cottage with no protector in her corner, Maria joined previous Hallworthy plantation victims and was brutally sexually assaulted.

In the months that followed, Anele attended to Alan's now pregnant prisoner's needs. One day Anele could barely look into the mother-to-be's mournful eyes. "Maria, my heart bleeds for you, and I'm going to help you. I will leave the door unlocked tonight. Run, girl, as fast as you can. Find the nearest house and tell the people inside everything he has done to you." Anele sighed in resignation. "You don't speak any English!" Anele reached into her apron pocket, pulled out a charcoal pencil, and wrote "HELP" on Maria's hand. It was the only English the servant knew how to write.

Anele's mind screamed, *"Run, girl. I'm setting you free! And I will soon follow you."*

Because of Maria's baby, Anele's own flight for freedom was now fraught with additional fear and complication. What should she do with the Caucasian baby Maria had earlier buried, whose life now depended on her? Anele tilted her head skyward: "*Unkulunkula*, god of the Zulus, this *intandane* (foundling) is not of my race. I can't return her to the white people, especially to her father! Please tell me what must be done?"

Anele did not know that the baby she strapped to her chest was Paolo's flesh and blood!

"… Any other than kin …"

CHAPTER TWENTY-ONE

- 1950 -
Tswanas Kraal, Zululand

"If you have been brutally broken but still have the courage to be gentle to others, then you deserve a love deeper than the ocean itself."
—NIKITA GILL

She had no playthings. Nevertheless, Shiya (the Forsaken One in Zulu), the foundling, was a happy five-year-old living an idyllic life in the African bush. There were, of course, hard times, such as when food was scarce. From sunup to sundown, the tribe's lives were centered on finding food either by fishing, snaring creatures, or illegally poaching game animals. The little girl's intense love of animals brought on many a tear when she witnessed wild animals being skinned in preparation for the cooking cauldron.

But there was one creature that would be saved from the boiling water.

One evening, on their way back to the village, the men carrying the meal of the day—four dead vervet monkeys—were followed by a group of children. At the rear of the group, a small boy who knew no better was dragging a baby vervet by its tail. Shiya had no problem keeping up with other children, despite her uneven legs. She ran up to the boy, slapped him in the face, snatched the howling monkey from his grip, and rushed into the mud hut she shared with Anele.

Anele's jaw dropped in horror. "Take it out of here, immediately!"

"No!" came Shiya's impudent reply. "I love this baby monkey, and she's *not* going in the cooking pot," Shiya concluded with a defiant look that Anele knew well. When Shiya's mind was made up, nothing would sway her stubbornness.

"Okay. I give up," Anele said, laughingly. "But *it* stays outside, tied up."

The little girl's amber-copper eyes glistened with mischief. "No, *Umama* (Mother). She'll sleep with me. I'll tie you up, and *you* can sleep outside." Anele's laughter was overheard by the many eavesdroppers outside her hut. Shiya sported an impish grin that lit up her face like a gaslight. Guess where the rescued baby monkey slept!

Anele adored her child. She recalled the earlier days when Shiya had not yet been *accepted* by the other tribe members. They were deeply suspicious when Anele had returned home with a *white* baby.

On the day of her arrival, Naboto, her father and the Tswanas chieftain, was stunned. "Daughter, you have been lost to us for twenty-nine summers, and now you return with a child obviously not of your blood! Explain!"

With apprehension, Anele related what had happened to her all those years ago, when she and her twin sisters had sneaked out of the kraal in search of work in the white townships. At the time of their flight, swarms of locusts had descended on the village's food crops, and the people were starving. Anele continued her story with details of how the twins were shot and killed by the plantation owner, Lord Hallworthy, and how she'd been captured and spent her time as a slave in this man's house. She described how she'd escaped, starting with how she met the foreign girl, found Maria's abandoned baby, and was driven by compassion to give the orphan a chance in life.

Anele's honesty failed to appease these primitive people, steeped in ancient superstitious beliefs. The chief called upon the one entity he believed could verify Anele's incredible revelation—Twazli.

Over seven feet tall, the witchdoctor's gangly limbs were gnarled like the boughs of an ancient tree. A white, powdery substance adorned Twazli's wrinkled face, accentuating his sunken red eyes that glowed like embers. Creepy, dried bird feet dangled from enlarged lobes. Twazli spoke. "Before I was summoned, the sacred messenger told me of this white-born child among us. I cast the ancient stones. They do not lie. This incarnated child is of an ancient spirit from Judean times. She has had many rebirths, and through no fault of her own carries ancestral suffering."

Silence filled the air. Then the ancient witch doctor continued. "At the beginning, Shiya's first foremother, named Rebekah, broke the laws of Yahweh, their supreme being. Angered by this, the Judean woman's God placed a punishment of suffering on all future rebirth entities carrying her blood. Tragically, baby Shiya has not been spared. She will have little choice but to suffer for many, many summers. And this child will not break the *curse*. She will pass it on to three daughters born in later times."

Anele was so touched by the witch doctor's incomprehensible revelations that she blurted, "So, do I have *your* permission to keep my child?"

"Anele, daughter of Naboto, I feel the love strongly in your heart for this unfortunate child, but prepare yourself for this *intandane* (orphan) to be taken from your heart forever. Because of your decision to save her, you will not see the African sun for many, many years."

Eventually, as foretold by the witchdoctor, Shiya's life would be a difficult one. Horrendous, cursed suffering was lurking in the distance. For this ancient reincarnated soul, making every day count was a thing of the past.

Nonetheless, the love Shiya had for her foster mother, Anele, who had hugely affected her young life, would never be forgotten. Anele would remain in Shiya's memory banks, stored for all time.

CHAPTER TWENTY-TWO

- 1950 -

The Hallworthy Estate

*"For every tear of sorrow sown by the
righteous springs up a pearl."*
—Matthew Henry

Two days after her fifth birthday, Shiya was forcibly removed from the only home she'd known by Alan Hallworthy, the plantation owner who had abused her mother, Maria. After a trip home to Tswanas Kraal to see his family, a sugar cane worker at the Hallworthy plantation had divulged to a fellow worker that he had seen a white child in his village in the care of Anele, who had run away from that very plantation.

When Alan heard the news of the white child, his innate diabolical character surfaced. He and his band of trackers and horsemen set out for Zululand. Alan was convinced that this was Maria's child and, therefore, *his* child. He could never have conceived differently!

Shiya, clinging to a piece of material she had ripped from Anele's skirt during their forced separation, was brought to the manor and secured in the infamous gamekeeper's cottage. There, she suffered the same fate as so many before her, including her mother.

The heavens were not listening to her pleas, and the border of hell loomed ahead.

When Shiya was nine, Alan Hallworthy, the newly appointed Mayor of Durban, devised a devious and deplorable scheme to ensure Shiya would never breathe a word to anyone about what happened in the gatekeeper's cottage. Alan had Shiya taken to a convent for orphaned *colored* children. The Caucasian Mother Superior conspired with him in this scurrilous arrangement. After all, this aristocrat was their most significant and wealthy benefactor, and he was unpunishable in the eyes of the law, and in the eyes of the *needy* Catholic Church.

"If you want to keep this convent afloat," Hallworthy threatened, "fake the records, hide the truth, and do whatever else is necessary. I don't *ever* want my name associated with that *thing!*" To Hallworthy, Shiya wasn't human. She was merely a discarded and embarrassing object!

"Rest assured, it will be done, Lord Hallworthy," Mother Superior agreed.

The nun registered the forlorn child as deaf and dumb. She then racially identified her as *colored*. Now Shiya was merely a number without a face. No compassion was offered to her. From that day on, Shiya blocked out her trauma by living as an *elective* mute. She withdrew from the outside world and existed in self-imposed silence. She had not uttered a word since the day of her capture from the kraal.

Shiya continued to suffer horrific abuse at the hands of these servants of a Christian God. Shortly after her arrival at the remote convent, Alan arranged for Shiya to undergo a forced sterilization, leaving her unable to ever bring *her kind* onto this earth.

This was the tip of the iceberg. Was Shiya a victim of circumstances, or was she a cursed human being?

Though Shiya dwelled in a silent world, she committed to memory every detail of her miserable existence: mental, physical, and sexual torture at the hands of Alan Hallworthy, Mother Superior, and, later, nursing aids in an adult mental institution for the criminally insane. Alan guaranteed Shiya would never be released and able to enter his private world.

With incredible resilience, the abandoned Shiya survived. She locked away the horrors she suffered in her episodic memory, deep in the hippocampus of her brain. There, her emotional pain would be held for over six decades. Shiya would spend her life on Earth outwitting the depravity of others by storing memories of the wickedness visited upon her. It became her mission to one day expose these criminal deeds.

And that she finally did!

But will Shiya's persecutors ever be brought to justice?

Yes, partly by her actions but also by the invisible force of Karma. If you mistreat other people, you also will ultimately suffer at the hands of others. All evil actions and behavior will finally have inevitable and inescapable consequences.

"What goes around comes around!"

❦

Lord Alan Hallworthy was arrested in 1980 and charged with the murder of a young African sex-worker. He was sentenced to life without parole. In acute infection stage, he died three years later of AIDS in a sanitarium for the criminally insane.

❦

The Good Shepherd Convent for children burned down in 1958, the year that South Africa gained its independence from Britain. Arson was suspected. Mother Superior and several of the nuns died in the fire, taking the *dark* secrets of this orphanage with them to their graves.

❦

The black surgeon who had *botched* Shiya's forced sterilization at age nine was finally arrested and sentenced to death, under Nelson Mandela's rule.

❦

In 1992, after many years of suffering from Alzheimer's disease, Anele, baby Shiya's savior, died peacefully in her sleep.

❦

At age fifteen, Shiya finally escaped from the mental institution she was wrongfully condemned to, with the aid of a most unlikely person. The new resident psychiatrist had sat in utter disbelief listening to the astonishing story told her by this young girl, the only teenager in the adult institution. Cecelia and her brother, Roland, a British Consular official, arranged her breakout. Roland smuggled Shiya out of South Africa, the country that had robbed her of her humanity.

She vowed that the people involved in her illicit incarceration would be punished, it it was the last thing she did.

Shiya had been discarded like a rotten fruit; however, the years following her exit from South Africa were no fairy tale, either.

Shiya still carried a hereditary *debt* that had not yet been satisfied.

CHAPTER TWENTY-THREE

- 2018 -

British Columbia, Canada

"The boundaries which divide Life from Death are at best vague. Who shall say where one ends, and the other begins?"
—Edgar Allan Poe

Shiya, now known as Maddeline Clark, withheld her hoard of shocking secrets for decades until she began to unveil her brokenness in the pages of her books. Her first novel, *Rented Silence*, opened doors to the unimaginable atrocities suffered by her and others during a brutal period of British Colonel history in South Africa.

Maddie's writings continue through her fifth book, *Addicted to Hate,* which continues to chronical her life into the twenty-first century. Here she reveals the abuse she suffered at the hands of a former husband, and the shocking physical and emotional damage inflicted on her by her offspring, three daughters. Maddie opens an expansive window that exposes the human spirit, its resilience, and stubborn ability to survive against the odds. Giving hope to similar victims, she states, *"You're not alone, and you are not to blame."*

✦

When Maddie was in her late forties, an astounding twist of fate reunited Lala, the flower of the Judean desert, with her long-lost love, the Fellahin Hassam el-Din, now known as Hernando. They formed an unbreakable bond. They loved each other immensely, and their love story, dating back thousands of years, was timeless.

"Until death do you part" had been omitted from their wedding vows.

✦

Twenty-five years before writing her books, Maddie had seen a dark-eyed, dark-skinned young man staring in her direction in a nightclub. He did not appear to her to be Italian or Jewish. He sauntered over to her and said, "Hi, there." with a glorious smile. "Haven't we met before?"

Maddie snickered. *How pathetic! That dumb pickup line isn't going to sway me or move me from soup to dessert!*

"I don't think so," she returned. "I have an *excellent* memory!"

"Sorry, but you seem so familiar," the twenty-eight-year-old said. Casually, the man sat down next to Maddie and introduced himself. "My name is Hernando Esteban. I'm a Cuban of Arabic descent. What's your name? And where are you from?"

"Madeline Clark …"

A distinct sense of deja vu hit Maddie. *I do know him! But how is this possible?*

Now a skilled conversationalist, Maddie came across as friendly, but she was guarded as to how much personal information she should disclose to a stranger. Nevertheless, she wanted an explanation for the strange nostalgic sensation tingling through her.

Hernando smiled. "We have a lot in common. You are going to laugh at this, but we must have known each other in a past life …" He paused to touch her hand.

Maddie felt an electric pulse that transported her to another time and place. Her head screamed the long-forgotten declaration of love: *"I'm going to marry you, Lala!"*

In times to come, Hernando would suffer a fatal heart attack. At his deathbed, Maddie vowed to join him, for she never wished to be parted from the only love she had known. But before she set about ending her life, she cried out, "Yahweh, God of the Jews, my name is Lala, the Desert Flower. Please now release these tormented souls from damnation: Rebekah, Debowrah, Leandra, Palomba, Laurencia, Ester, Fajcia, Lyveva, Gabija, Lidiya, Bronislawa, Lucja, Sofia, and Maria, for all eternity. I beseech the debt for past wrongdoings now be duly paid and that the punishment you cruelly bestowed on the rebirths is over! I have broken the curse because *I* did not lie down with *any kin* like my ancestors did!"

Little did she know!

Maddie was blood related to the Scottish father of her last-born child, Mara.

Holding Hernando's hand, Maddie inhaled deeply, as if a tremendous weight had been lifted from her shoulders. Reaching into the bedside drawer, she retrieved a syringe and murmured, "We will soon be *free* and all together, my persecuted ancestors and my beloved Hassam el-Din!"

The Arabic boy's name had been spiritually etched on all of Maddie's reincarnated lives since Lala's first imprint of life on earth.

As the lethal injection surged through Maddie's body toward a ticket to a debt-free life, she thought. "My darling, Hassam, I'm coming, never to be parted from you again."

Better to suffer harm than to do it, was Maddie's (Lala's) final silent message to the mortal world she was leaving behind.

Will the generational curse finally die, stemming from the suicide of the first incarnation, the Desert Flower of Judea? Was the series of rebirths resulting from the sins committed in previous existences over?

This demanded a response from a higher power.

Had Yahweh finally forgiven the sinners?

Things That Go Bump in the Night

"I have the wisdom of the ancients. I am timeless."
—LALA, FLOWER OF THE DESERT

n the early hours of that morning, a four-year-old girl, her lower lip trembling, bolted upright, eyes wide open. Her shaky voice cried out, "Where are you? Come out now! I am scared!"

The temperature in the room fell to a chill.

A pale misty cloud formed in the wan light of the girl's bedroom. It materialized an ethereal figure clad a long white robe, who was accompanied by a pleasant floral fragrance. The presence glided in silently across the space to the child's bedside. "Hush, dearest," the unworldly voice comforted. "Don't be afraid. You have had a bad dream. I will lie beside you and protect you."

Fear departed from the child, who heaved a long sigh of relief as her eyelids closed over dazzling amber-copper eyes. A tiny, muffled voice could be heard beneath the cotton comforter. "Sing me a song."

The spectral figure softly sang a classic tune, not in an earthly manner, but in a celestial tone:

"Twinkle, twinkle, little star, how I wonder what you are,
Up above the world so high, like a diamond in the sky,
Twinkle, twinkle little star, how I wonder what you are,
When the blazing sun is gone,
When nothing ever shines upon,
Then, you show your little light.
Twinkle, twinkle, all the night ..."

The little girl sighed contentedly.

Sometime later the child's bedroom door opened. Now wide awake, words gushed from the girl's mouth: "Mummy, I had bad dreams last night, and Maddie came and sang a lovely song to comfort me. You know, Mummy, she has the same pretty color eyes as me and the same beauty mark," she said, touching the dark, oval pigmentation on her cheek.

After a period of silence, something unbelievable dawned on Mara, Madeline Clark's last-born daughter. *Oh, my God! How could she know this? There are no photos, and my mother's name has never been mentioned in this house.*

Mara's whole body stiffened in fright as a book gently moved off the bookcase and sailed across the room, falling onto her daughter's bed: "*Grimm's Fairy Tales,* a book Mara had kept since childhood, now her child's favorite read.

Suddenly an overpowering scent of lilacs, Madeline's favorite flower, filled the room.

"The little girl looked into her mother's stricken face and said, "Don't be scared, Mummy, it is only Grandma Maddie letting you know that she is here with us."

Mara cast a speculative gaze towards her child. So it continues, she thought. "*Grimm's Fairy Tales.*"

⟿

Immortal souls that love us never leave us, but they are the captains of their own destined ships, or so we are led to believe.

However, Shamanic teachings state that when human beings overcome the evil in their spiritual pathway before death, they become the embodiment of love; then they are *perfect* and will incarnate no more on Earth.

Has the wheel of human fate—you live and die and repeat—now turned full circle?

Only time had the answer for the otherworldly Grandma, Madeleine Clark.

"*... Other than kin ...*"

The End

ABOUT THE AUTHOR

Lucia Mann, humanitarian and activist, was born in British colonial South Africa in the wake of World War II. She now resides in British Columbia, Canada. After retiring from freelance journalism in 1998, she wrote a four-book African series to give voice to those who have suffered and are suffering brutalities and captivity.

Visit www.LuciaMann.com and
www.ReportModernDaySlavery.org
for more information on how you can help
alleviate the scourge of modern-day slavery.

BOOKS BY LUCIA MANN

BOOKS IN LUCIA MANN'S AFRICAN SERIES

(In sequential order)

Rented Silence

CBC BOOK AWARD WINNER

The Sicilian Veil of Shame

Africa's Unfinished Symphony,

INDIE EXCELLENCE AWARD WINNER

A Veil of Blood Hangs Over Africa

ALSO BY LUCIA MANN

Addicted to Hate,

LITERARY TITAN AWARD WINNER, WISHING WELL BOOK
AWARD WINNER, BOOK EXCELLENCE AWARD WINNER,
IPPY BOOK AWARD WINNER, INDEPENDENT PRESS AWARD
WINNER

Made in the USA
Columbia, SC
22 November 2019

83575600R00176